The Herbalist

Heather Morrison-Tapley

ISBN 978-0-578-37401-7

CONTENTS

Dedication

To Ian and Charlie, my inspirations every day.

Always follow your "knowing."

And to Amanda, the most magical person I know.

Chapter 1

Her night started in high heels and cocktails. It ended in heartbreak and death. And twenty-four hours later, she would find herself three thousand miles away, her whole world turned upside down.

In the small English village of Barton Heath, summer was coming to an end. The evenings were cooler, the fog lay thickly on the fields in the morning, and the invigorating smell of wood smoke filled the air. Mabel Harrison spent the evening with her close friend, Peg, tending to Peg's beloved horse, who had come down with colic. They called the vet and then walked the horse for an hour in the paddock, waiting for him to arrive.

In the end, the mare had an injection and was recovering in her snug stall in the barn. Peg and Mabel went to the pub and recovered themselves in a snug booth by the fire.

It was later that night, as she was going to bed, that Mabel began to feel sick. *Too much wine at the pub*, she thought. She must be more careful at her age. At ninety-one, she shouldn't walk a horse in the rain for an hour and then have three drinks before bed. Of course, she felt unwell. This ache in her back, the nausea, they would be gone after a good night's sleep. She pulled the thick quilt up to her chin and sighed a contented sigh as she drifted off to sleep.

A few hours later, in a small apartment on the Upper West Side of Manhattan, a young woman was trying, unsuccessfully, to squeeze into a dress that didn't fit. Or was it a life? She tugged at the fabric until she realized it couldn't be forced, then changed into a looser-fitting dress, stepped into black heels, and headed out to her Uber.

Eden Martin was a professor of medieval history at Washington University in New York City. Her specialty was the history of medicine. Herbalists and apothecaries populated her mental world, and it was in her imagination that she lived a large part of her life. She was most comfortable in a pair of jeans, deep inside a thick book in the university library, not in a designer dress, sipping pink cocktails with banking executives. But that's exactly where she found herself surprisingly often. Eden looked out the window of the car as the streets of New York City flew by. Lights, cars, people, activity…it was an exciting place to live.

Funny, Eden thought, *I feel like I should be looking at something and loving it, but I'm not. I know objectively I live in the greatest city on Earth, but I kind of hate it too. And I'm headed to the hottest restaurant in New York, but I want to go home. God I'm a mess,* she thought, and she decided it was time to stop thinking for the evening.

Twenty minutes later, she arrived at the chic eatery and gave her name at the door. Robert's bank was always hosting these events, thanking someone for something, or hoping to entice someone into something else.

"May I take your coat, madam?" the man at the entrance said as Eden walked in.

"Thank you, yes," she said and handed him her wrap.

She entered the packed party and looked for Robert. Eden was engaged to Robert Nagle, an investment banker at a top Wall Street firm. They had been together since meeting at graduate school, and when he had proposed to her two years ago, she wondered if it was more out of a sense of obligation than out of passion. They had grown so different over the years. But if he had proposed out of obligation, she had accepted out of fear. She was thirty-eight years old and thought it was about time she married. Wasn't that what she was supposed to do?

All her friends kept telling her it was. So, there she was, downtown, at yet another cocktail party at a restaurant people waited months to get into, wishing she was at home with a good book. Still, she was here for his sake.

Smiling and trying to look nonchalant, Eden scanned the faces in the restaurant, looking for Robert. Not seeing him right away, she decided she needed reinforcement in the form of alcohol.

"A red wine, please," she told the bartender.

"We have several. What do you prefer?" he asked.

"Malbec, please," she replied, and then turned back around to look at the crowd while he got her drink.

Everyone was smiling. Everyone was having a ball. Everyone was wealthy and satisfied with themselves. *I wonder if these people ever think they should've worn a different dress or that they may have made all the wrong life choices. Probably not,* she thought with a frown. *These people probably never doubt themselves. They spend their time planning sailing trips and deciding between shiplap and wainscoting for their Nantucket beach houses. Not questioning everything they do and say all day long.* Her pep talk had definitely taken a wrong turn.

"Here you go, ma'am," the bartender said.

When did I go from "miss" to "ma'am"? she wondered. *Depressing.* She took a large gulp of wine and let the feeling of tingling warmth spread through her body.

"Hi there," a voice said from behind her.

Eden turned and saw Simon, a balding, middle-aged man from the bank, just slightly senior to Robert. He had probably been awkward as a youth, but was now emboldened by his substantial wealth.

"You're looking delicious tonight," he said with a leer.

"Thanks, Simon," Eden replied, "You ass," going unspoken. "How are you these days? How was summer in the Hamptons?" she asked, knowing nothing about this man except that he owned a multi-million-dollar home in the Hamptons. The reason she knew this was because he made sure everyone knew it within a few minutes of meeting him, and then he talked of little else.

"Perfect. It was truly perfect," he said. "Diana had this exquisite designer come out, and we told him all our dreams, aspirations, and fears, and he totally redesigned the interior of the home to match our vision." He continued, "Cost a fortune, of course, but totally worth it. We were so over that white and blue beach thing. That furniture and that look are so overdone. Now we are a sort of hip midcentury mod meets Scandinavian plastic and very streamlined. It's fabulous."

Eden thought to herself how much she would prefer soft, comfy, white and blue sofas in a house to midcentury Scandinavian plastic. But, of course, no one was asking her.

"Well, it sounds perfect for you," she said, trying to be supportive, but honest. *God, I hate this,* she thought as she kissed Simon on the cheek with a sugary smile and walked away, waiting for the next round of insincere chitchat to start.

She didn't have to wait long.

"Eden, darling, you look amaaaazing!" said a voice from somewhere in the crowd.

From behind a man in a suit came Laura: blonde, thin, gorgeous, dressed to kill, and the queen of the art of small talk.

"Darling, look at you. That dress really accentuates your strengths," she said, air kissing either side of Eden's face.

Accentuates my strengths? Eden thought, and she had to stifle a smile. *What the hell kind of backhanded compliment is that?*

"Hi, Laura. You look nice. How are you?" Eden asked.

"I'm fantastic. Utterly fantastic. I, just this morning, had my contractor pack all his messy, loud equipment up and leave the apartment. It was driving Jonathan and me crazy. Two months just to redo a bathroom! That said, the Moroccan tile is divine, and the whole renovation was worth the strain, but I'm celebrating the fact that my home is my own again!" She raised her glass and toasted herself in triumph at having had someone replace her bathroom tile. "Now tell me all about your summer. Was it unbelievable?" Laura cooed.

Man, people use a lot of superlatives here, Eden thought with another inner smile. *Isn't anyone ever just* fine*?* Eden had spent her summer researching medieval remedies for serious childhood illness. But this hardly seemed a topic that would fit in.

So, in an impulsive moment of utterly adolescent rebellion, she answered, "Actually, my summer got a little slowed down because I had to have my hemorrhoids surgically repaired."

Eden found herself simultaneously stifling an almost hysterical desire to burst into laughter, with a feeling of self-loathing for being so petty and judgmental of the cocktail crowd. They were perfectly nice, and she was ridiculous to be so petulant. *Still*, she thought, *it was funny.*

"Oh…Oh my," Laura replied with wide eyes, clearly desperately flipping through her mental note cards to see what response might possibly fit this situation. "Well, these things do happen. I hope you're feeling much better," she said with a smile, and then she waved into the crowd as if she had just seen someone very important, excused herself, and walked away.

And then Eden finally saw Robert. He was in what looked like the middle of a story. He was surrounded by a group of people and had them all riveted.

"And then," he added with a long pause for effect, as Eden neared the group, "the man picked up his pants and shoes, apologized, and left!" He delivered the punch line to the story he had been telling, and the circle of guests burst into laughter.

And then one very young, very attractive woman leaned in and whispered something to him.

A loud alarm went off in Eden in that split second, and she felt a chill rush over her. It was as if she knew she had seen something much more serious than a little whisper. A glimpse into something much more dangerous.

She walked closer, and Robert smiled as he saw her approach.

The young woman took an almost imperceptibly small step back, and Robert slid his arm around Eden's waist. "Everyone, this is Eden. Eden, this is…everyone."

By nine p.m., Eden's head was pounding. All she wanted to do was peel off the designer outfit and slip into some yoga pants. She found Robert, who had wandered off, leaving her to fend for herself.

"I'm going to get a cab home, Robert. My head is killing me," she said.

"I'm sorry, sweetheart," he replied. There was a pause and then he asked, "Do you want me to come with you?"

She was sure he was hoping she'd say no. Which she did.

"No, thanks. I just want to go home, take some Tylenol, and go to bed. I'll call you in the morning."

"Okay, let me get your coat," Robert said, and he disappeared back into the crowd.

A minute later, he walked her out into the cold drizzle and hailed her a cab. A brief kiss good night and she was on her way back uptown.

Halfway there, her cell phone rang.

"Eden, it's Mom." It was hard to understand what her mother was saying, partly because she was sobbing and partly because Eden's head hurt so much she was flinching and holding the phone away from her ear.

Then the words started to sink in.

"Eden, Gran had a heart attack. She died, Eden. She's gone!"

Eden sat bolt upright. "Mom, slow down. What happened? Oh

my God. What happened? When?" Eden asked, her heart pounding wildly in her chest while her mind screamed *No! No! I won't believe it, it isn't true!*

Eden's grandmother was one of the most important people in the world to her. She had spent every summer of her life in her granny's four-hundred-year-old thatched cottage in the small English village of Barton Heath. Her gran was brash and outspoken and hilariously funny, and Eden had always looked up to her, always gone to her for advice, and always counted on her to lift her spirits and set her straight. And now, in an instant, she was gone.

"Eden, will you fly over with me?" her mother asked between sobs. "I don't think I can face all this on my own."

"Of course, I will, Mom. Of course, I'll fly over." The conversation seemed to be moving so fast. They were already talking about the practical matters of funerals and notifications. "I'll tie up a few things at the university and fly over right away. Oh, Mom, I'm so sorry," she said, realizing that, no matter how much this hurt her own heart, this was her mother's *mother*. Eden shivered just imagining how shattering it would be to lose your mother. "I love you, Mom. Call me back if you want to. Anytime tonight, even if it's late. I'll call you tomorrow and let you know when I'm getting there. I'm so sorry,

Mom. I love you."

After she got off the phone, the tears poured silently down Eden's face as the reality of the news sank in. As crowds of anonymous faces whizzed by in the New York night, Eden felt very small and very lonely.

She was nearing her apartment when she realized she couldn't face being on her own that night.

She leaned forward toward the cab driver and said, "Can you turn around please? I've changed my mind. I want to go to 214 Franklin Street instead. Thanks."

So, the cab headed back downtown. To Tribeca, to Robert's apartment. She would wait there for him to get home. She needed to sleep next to a warm body that night, needed to know she wasn't alone.

It was still raining half an hour later when, after battling some midtown traffic, the taxi finally pulled up outside Robert's building. Eden got drenched in the few seconds it took her to run into the lobby.

Look at me, she thought as she caught sight of herself in the hallway mirror: hair soggy, eyeliner running down her tear-stained cheeks as she fumbled in her bag for her keys and unlocked the door to Robert's loft.

As she was kicking off her shoes in the foyer, she heard a

noise.

That's weird. He must have left the TV on, Eden thought. She took a step into the room and listened again. *No, those are voices...they're muffled, but definitely voices.*

She felt a jolt of fear. This was how people ended up on the local news—walking in on intruders in New York City. But the door had been locked. *It must be the TV*, she said to herself, trying to calm her nerves, *or Robert must have left just after I did and be home already and on the phone.*

No suspicion entered her mind as she opened the door to the bedroom, which made the shock even more powerful. Eden pushed open the bedroom door as she had hundreds of times, and there he was. In bed. With her, the young woman from the party. Tangled in the bedsheets.

Bizarrely, her first thought was, *Those are the eight hundred thread-count Egyptian sheets I gave you for Christmas! They cost me a fortune!* The sheets on which Robert and she had made love, watched TV, and slept for almost a year.

Eden's eyes grew wide, and her mouth fell open as she watched for a split second before Robert noticed she was there.

"Oh my God, Eden!" is all she heard, and then she was off,

running out the door and down the stairs, tripping and almost falling as she raced to get out of there before he caught up.

She burst out the front door and ran almost two blocks in her bare feet before she saw a cab with his light on and waved him down.

Later, Eden walked to her apartment door, unlocked it, stepped inside, and slumped down the wall till she was sitting on the floor inside. She was in shock. Her mind raced back and forth between her grandmother's death and the image of Robert on top of that woman.

This can't be real, she thought. *Maybe this is an awful dream, this whole night.* She wished it was. She knew it wasn't.

"Hot bath and then tea. Hot bath and then tea," she said aloud.

This was a mantra she had learned early in life for what to do in any crisis. Most things look a lot better after a hot bath and a cup of tea, her gran would always say.

Eden drew a steaming hot bath, took off her designer dress, and lowered herself into the tub. And then she broke down. At first, racked by sobs, but eventually, not able to cry anymore. She felt numb. She sat there until the water had gone cold. And slowly she came up with a plan.

At midnight she started packing her largest suitcase. By the next evening, Eden was on a plane to England.

"Bob, I'm quitting my job." Eden had said matter-of-factly the night before, on a late-night phone call to Bob Ryan, her friend and the head of the history department at the university where she worked. "I'm listing my apartment for rent, and I'm leaving New York. I'm moving to England."

"What are you talking about, Eden?" Bob asked clearly shocked.

"My grandmother just died. My engagement is off, and I'm sick of New York City. I've lived here all these years, and I still feel lonely walking around here. I can't take it anymore. I'm moving to England and I'm quitting my job."

"I'm coming over," he said. And half an hour later, her boss and friend was sitting in her apartment, having a glass of wine with her.

"Eden, you can't quit your job. You have a tenure-track position at one of the best universities in America. You've worked all your life for this. What happened? Start at the beginning," he said.

"I walked in on them. Just now, earlier tonight. In bed. Robert and some skinny young woman he met at a party," she said. Then the awful thought occurred to her that maybe they hadn't just met at that party. Maybe this had been going on for a long time.

"Oh my God, Eden. I'm so sorry. That pig. God, I never did

like him," Bob said under his breath.

"You didn't?" Eden asked, surprised.

"Sorry, I shouldn't have said that. He's fine. I just never thought he treated you as well as you deserved. But who cares what I think. Ignore what I said. Okay, so you walked in on that pig cheating on you. Good riddance. But why are you quitting your job? People would kill for the job you have!"

"I know. It's just...something happened tonight. When I found out my grandmother died, and then walked in on Robert, something sort of snapped. I know it sounds insane to make decisions on a night like this, but in another way, I just feel absolutely a hundred percent sure this is right. I know I have an amazing job. I know others would kill for a tenure-track position. But I've never felt like myself doing it. The research part I love. But standing in front of huge classes, lecturing, forcing myself to be ultra-competitive and publish or perish every year. All the parties and receptions. I hate all of that. I'm sorry. I know I'm so lucky, and I sound like a horrible ingrate, but I hate it. I like to be alone with a book. Or with one or two people. I should be a researcher or a writer. But I don't like teaching, I never have. I guess, mostly, for me, it pays the bills so I can do research. I get a nervous knot in my stomach every single day that I have to teach. I dread it. I have told myself all this time to suck it up, just as you said, I'm so lucky to have this job. But I don't know, tonight it all just seems clear. What am I doing? I'm engaged to a man who doesn't love me, doing work I don't love, in a place I don't love. It's crazy. And I'm done."

"Okay. I hear what you're saying. And I know you," Bob said. "I know you don't like the crowds of students, the pressure, all of that. I also know it's midnight, you're exhausted, you just had two major life traumas, basically simultaneously, and I am not allowing you to quit your job right now. Go, be with your mom, take care of things in England, the funeral, the estate. I'm sure there's a lot that you and your mom will need to sort out. I'll appoint a sub to cover your classes while you're gone. One of the grad students can take over in a pinch. And if you still feel this way in a couple of weeks, I'll do my very best to get you this year as a sabbatical year. That way, you can have a moment to catch your breath, separate this from what just happened with Robert, and make a sound decision that you won't regret. How does that sound?"

"Well," Eden said, thinking. "I guess that sounds reasonable. And mature. Neither of which is how I'm feeling right now, so it's kind of stealing my moment here, being so levelheaded." She smiled. "But you're right. I'm tired. I'm upset. I'm angry. I'll go to England and call you in a week or two. But all that said, I think I'm done, Bob. I know it's sudden. But I feel it in my gut. It's crazy, it's impulsive, but it's also right." And as she said it, she knew it was true.

By three p.m. the next day, Eden had cleaned her apartment, put her personal items in a locked closet, listed her apartment for rent online, and was bumping two suitcases down the sidewalk to the corner to her Uber. By seven p.m., she was sipping the first of several terrible glasses of airplane wine.

"Ladies and gentlemen, your flight attendants will be coming around with your choice of tea or coffee. A light breakfast will be served," a voice with a lilting English accent said in a soothing tone.

Suddenly lights were flickering overhead, and the stewardesses were leaning over sleeping passengers to open the shades. It was one a.m. in New York, but this was the moment that marked the shift when everyone was expected to jump to English time. Early morning light streamed through the windows, and Eden squinted and rubbed her temples. Her mouth was dry and sticky and her head pounding. Five glasses of airline chardonnay had not been a good idea. But she was excited.

She sipped her coffee, thinking of what she had just done, of how crazy it was to have just left her job, her relationship, and her home in a single day to move to a cottage in an English village. But timid as she often was, she had no fear now. She knew, on some deep level, this was right. Her eyes stung with tears, and she thought how much her gran would have approved of the bold, impulsive move. Then she smiled, feeling somehow sure that Gran was there with her.

Chapter 2

"Eden, what on earth are you going to do in Barton Heath all by yourself after I've gone?" Eden's mother, Susan, asked. She was standing in the kitchen in her bathrobe, holding a steaming mug of tea, looking at her daughter with concern.

It had been a week since the burial. A week of lawyers and papers and going through closets, all of which had been very depressing and draining. Eden and her mother were going to Newmarket, the nearest big town, later that morning to have lunch. A treat after two weeks of that strange mix of grief and business that death creates. Susan was also on her own. Eden's father had walked out on them when Eden was just six months old. Eden had never known him, and he had never made an attempt to get in touch with her. Susan had lived alone all this time, dating now and then, but never seeming to find someone she thought was worth risking her heart for again. Eden worried about her, but her mother insisted she was fine. She worked as head nurse at a local hospital, had a group of good friends she saw often, and had a small but pretty house she'd lived in for forty years. She was organized, efficient, and reliable. Not the flaky, emotional woman that Eden was herself, Eden thought. Susan had spent so many years taking care of the two of them, and then herself alone. Eden wasn't sure if her mother was actually happy, but she was certainly doing fine. Maybe that was enough.

Still, Eden had been trying to convince her mother to throw caution to the wind and move into the cottage with her for the year. So far, she wasn't biting.

"Did you hear me, Eden?" Susan called out. "You seem a hundred miles away."

"Sorry. Yes, I did. Well, I've been thinking about that, and I think I'm going to write. I have always wanted to put together a book on herbal cures and lore, and what better time or place than this? I have a year's sabbatical...well, either that or I'm unemployed, and I will be living less than an hour from Cambridge University and one of the best collections of medieval documents on earth. That's what I have..." she trailed off and a look of surprise appeared on her face.

Her mother came to stand beside her at the window. There, crossing the front garden, was a man in the English country gentleman's uniform of checked shirt and battered tweed jacket. But he also had on a cowboy hat with some large feathers sticking out of the side, cowboy boots, and a pair of large sunglasses. The man had a spring in his step that made him appear younger than he probably was, and he was singing loudly and completely out of tune as he approached the house. The women were both giggling as they heard him ring the bell.

Eden answered the door as her mother dashed upstairs to get dressed before meeting the eccentric local.

"Hello. Please come in." She gestured, and the man ducked his head through the low doorway and walked through into the living room. "I am Eden Martin," she said, holding out her hand.

"Yes, yes, wonderful. I know who you are," he said gripping her hand tightly and shaking it enthusiastically for longer than was normal, till Eden wondered if he'd ever stop. "Very good to meet you, yes. Of course, I have heard all about you. I knew your grandmother. She was very close with my father, you see. Yes, yes."

"Oh, I'm sorry I don't seem to remember…"

"No, no, we haven't met. No, I have been living in the States for many years, in Florida in fact. Lovely and warm, lovely climate, but a bit of a cultural wasteland, isn't it? Yes, so we never met. My father passed away last year, and I moved back as the only son and heir, that sort of thing, don't you know. Took over the family money pit. I'm Peter Penley-Smith. I live just outside the village."

Well, that's an understated way of saying who you are, Eden thought.

The Penley-Smith family had lived in an enormous country mansion on the edge of the village for hundreds of years. In fact, she was fairly sure this eccentric man was *Lord* Penley-Smith, though he didn't seem eager to flaunt it. The estate still owned a large amount of land, but at one point, the entire village had belonged to it, with much of the revenue of the people living and working there being paid to the lord and masters in the big house. Times had changed. But the villagers still thought of the Penley-Smiths as a sort of royalty. Eden's grandmother had been great friends with Peter's father for many years, and Eden herself had been to lunch at the manor house many times.

"Please, come in. My mother is just upstairs. She'll be right down. Can I offer you a cup of tea?"

"Oh lovely," Peter said.

She walked into the kitchen, wondering how living in Florida had led to a cowboy look. He was certainly not what one expected of a country lord. She liked him; she knew that already.

Eden was handing Peter a cup of tea when her mother came down the stairs. She saw Peter glance up, then do a quick double-take.

"Hello. You must be Susan," Peter said as he stood and held out a hand.

Her mother shook it and said that yes, she was. Eden then sat, totally ignored, for about thirty minutes, watching in awe as the pair, both in their sixties, talked and laughed without pause, completely oblivious to Eden's presence, looking more and more engaged with every minute that passed. They were interested, very interested in each other.

Eden didn't know if she'd ever seen her mother look like that—so focused on a man, yet so relaxed and talkative. S*he's glowing*, Eden thought, looking warmly at her mother. Her short, bobbed hair was fading, still, mostly light brown, but gently turning to steel gray. Her face was softly lined, but her skin was clear, and her blue eyes sparkled as she laughed.

Eden excused herself and went upstairs. She wasn't even sure they noticed. *Interesting development*, she thought as she began arranging her room.

There had been so much grief, and so much to do in those first two weeks, that Eden had barely unpacked. But now it was time to get ready to write. Putting her computer on a small table, along with books, pens, journals, and her enormous *Materia Medica* of herbal medicine, which was like a Bible to her, she paused and stuck her head out the small window and looked around.

The straw thatch of the roof lay thickly on either side of the window. She could hear chickens and smell a bonfire. She felt completely happy and at peace in a way she had only ever known in England. It was the opposite of New York in so many ways and suited her so well it was no wonder she had left Manhattan. Things here were old. They weren't always being torn down and "improved." Life was slower, it was okay to have rugs worn thin and holes in your sweater. People stopped and talked at the village shops.

From her perch, she could see the tops of several old stone houses in the village, and beyond them, rolling green hills separated by low stone walls and dotted with white sheep. To the right, at the edge of her view, was the thick grey Norman church, square and comforting, watching over the ancient graveyard, as it had since it was built in the twelfth century. The village was human, rich, real, and Eden breathed in deeply, shut her eyes, and smiled.

A few minutes later, Eden stared at her blank computer screen. She took a deep breath and then she typed, "The History of Herbal Medicine in Medieval England." She knew she'd have to get more specific, but she always found starting to be the hardest part of any project, so she wrote the title, and then dove in.

Her fingers flew as she wrote without stopping for almost an hour. She was surprised to find how much she knew off the top of her head from her years at the university. But she also realized that her book was going to be a cure for insomnia if she didn't add something more than dry information from centuries-old texts.

I need to find some stories of real people, stories readers can relate to. But how?

Stumped by that question, she stopped for the day and went downstairs to make a cup of tea.

*

This would become a soothing and productive routine in the coming days and weeks, hours spent writing, punctuated by cups of tea, and occasional walks around the village. And if she did those things in quick enough succession all day long, she stayed one step ahead of the pain of the life she had just abandoned, and more importantly, the deeper pain that echoed somewhere far back in her being. A pain that felt overwhelming and nameless, a pain that longed for her attention. One that she couldn't quite name. But she was genuinely happy when she wrote and walked and rested, so surely that meant there was no point in poking around in the dark for problems.

"This is heaven, Mom," Eden said one evening, sitting in front of the fire. "I don't remember when I've felt this relaxed." She let out a contented sigh and took a swig of wine.

"I have to agree. I don't know when *you've* been this relaxed either," her mother said jokingly. "But, yes, I feel it too. Of course, it's a strange sort of holiday, a death-induced holiday. But still, a nice, long holiday, so no wonder we are relaxed. England has always made me feel that way too." She lifted her own wine glass in cheers.

"Okay, so if that is the case," Eden started, "I think you should stay. If not for the whole year, then at least a little longer."

Susan didn't reply at first. She looked into the fire and was silent for a few minutes. Eden had expected an instant "No" from her sensible, cautious mother, so the hesitation was a good sign, she thought.

"I don't know, Eden," Susan said. "On one hand, I told the hospital I would be back after two weeks. And you know I believe in keeping one's word. But, that said…" She trailed off and looked again into the fire, as if the answer lay in the dancing flames. Maybe it did. "I guess losing my mother has made it all so real, that life is finite. It ends. I mean, that sounds silly, because of course we all know it does. And I'm a nurse. I've seen lots of people die. But it's funny, when it's your own mother, it's different. For me it is anyway," she said. "I'm not going to suddenly have a late midlife crisis or anything, but it has made me think about things. So, that is a very long way of saying, I think I will stay a bit longer. Not a year!" she quickly added as she saw Eden jump up off the sofa and come towards her for a hug. "But for a little while longer." She smiled and hugged her daughter tightly to her.

In the end, Eden's mother extended her ticket and stayed another three weeks. This was unheard of for the reliable, predictable Susan, but it seemed she had thrown common sense to the wind after both losing her mother and meeting Peter Penley-Smith, and Eden was all for it.

She loved watching her mother spend day after day with the hilarious and nutty Lord Penley-Smith. He seemed to be made of one-third chivalrous knight (opening doors, sending flowers, and ordering drinks for her mother), one-third intelligent, serious man (he had a law degree from Cambridge, seemed to know all current events and world politics in amazing detail, and was a generous philanthropist), and one-third total nut case. He was often found wandering his extensive gardens in nothing but a bathrobe and cowboy boots, surrounded by a pack of dogs of all different shapes and sizes, or giving lectures at the local pub on how it was a distinct possibility that aliens had infiltrated the human race, or breaking into song at the drop of the hat, seemingly unaware that he was completely and painfully tone-deaf.

The combination was absolutely charming, and Eden's mother seemed to agree. Susan seemed almost surprised by her own feelings toward him. He was everything she was not. And in that way, they fit together perfectly.

It had been a wonderful three weeks. They had gone to the horse races in Newmarket, watched cricket in a cold drizzle on the village green, and had daily pints in the local pub, sitting by the crackling fire as September turned into October. All the while, the pair smiled and laughed and talked with a twinkle in their eyes that Eden didn't know was possible at sixty-five. It made her absolutely certain she had done the right thing in leaving Robert.

But finally, Susan did have to go. She had a job and a home and a life, and she wasn't about to give it all up, even for Peter. Not after three weeks anyway.

As Susan was packing to leave, Eden sitting on the bed, helping her fold clothes, she asked, "Have you spoken to Robert at all? You haven't even mentioned him in all the time I've been here. I haven't brought it up before, because I don't like to pry, but have you spoken with him? Is it definitely over?"

"God. Robert…" Eden said, trailing off and looking out the window. "That whole life seems a million miles away already. No. I haven't spoken to him. He's been calling my cell phone the whole time I've been here, leaving messages, begging my forgiveness and promising that his heart is mine, all that kind of thing. Sort of hard to believe when you've actually watched your fiancé screwing another woman!" she said, anger flaring. "I know I eventually have to deal with him. I mean, we are engaged, after all. Or we were, and there are things to unwind, things to give back, things to undo. But it's all so depressing and, at the same time, infuriating. I guess I'm just not ready to deal with it yet. And another part of me doesn't want to deal with it *ever*, to be honest. What is there to know? It's over."

What Eden didn't say out loud was that, when she saw her mother's and Peter's faces slowly melting into expressions of love, Eden knew she didn't feel anything like that for Robert, and she knew that, if she ever did marry, it would be to someone who made her look as silly, sappy, and giddy as her mother had looked for the past month.

The next day was sunny and windy. Peter loaded Susan's things into the trunk of the car, and Peter and Eden drove her mother to the train station and waited for the train to London so she could catch her flight home.

Eden hugged her mother. "I'm going to miss you so much, Mom. I love you, and I'm *so* glad you're going to come back for

Christmas. That isn't that far off, is it, Peter?" Eden asked, turning to look at her mother's beau.

Peter's eyes look extra bright, as if he might cry, but in typical British fashion, he said simply, "Not at all. It will be here before we know it. And it will be wonderful. We'll have a real knees-up when you get back."

Eden went into the station to give her mother and Peter some privacy on the platform, or at least the illusion of privacy, as she couldn't stop herself from peeking out the window and watching as her mother and Peter locked in a passionate embrace. This was not a small thing, Eden knew, after having watched her mother date other men, sometimes for months, without showing anything like that kind of emotion.

Peter waved until the train was out of sight. Then the sad pair drove back into the village.

"Pint, my dear?" Peter asked as they rounded the village green and passed the long white building with the thatched roof and the sign of The Horse and Cart swinging slightly in the wind.

"Definitely," Eden agreed, not ready to face going back to the cottage, where she would now be alone.

Pints in hand, seated in a wooden booth, Eden looked around.

She had already begun to recognize many of the faces: Mr. Park from the shop. Mr. and Mrs. Chapman from the house full of children down the road, out for a quiet dinner. Tom Harper, the local handyman. Mr. Pringle, without his dreary wife, Deidre.

"I love her, you know." Peter's voice brought Eden's attention back to the table.

Surprised, she lifted her eyebrows and smiled.

"I do," he said. "I'm sure it seems ridiculous to someone like you. I mean, I must seem ancient. And I've only known her for a few weeks. But I do."

"I believe that," Eden replied after a pause with a look of sweet affection on her face. "And I think it is very possibly mutual," she added.

"Do you think so?" he said excitedly, pouncing on the possibility.

"I do. I have never seen my mother so smitten. She's a very practical woman. Smitten isn't a word I've ever used before describing her. But she lights up around you. It makes me so happy to see."

Peter said nothing, but sat with an enormous smile that made him look about five years old. *I get it*, Eden thought. *I get what my mother loves in him.* And with that, they clinked glasses and drained their pints.

That night, as she got back to the cottage, it started to rain. Eden closed the door behind her, and there was total silence except for the sound of raindrops against the windows. It was the first time since she had arrived that she'd been alone.

She was alone. It suddenly hit her like a punch to the stomach, and she leaned her back against the closed door and shut her eyes. Tears poured down her face, and she felt a panic rising in her, tightening her stomach into a knot, making her chest hurt. What was she doing with her life? She was shocked to find that, suddenly, she felt she might drown in sadness. It felt like a wave that had come out of nowhere and overtaken her, washed her overboard, and she could not get a hold of anything to pull herself out. She cried and cried, grieving it all—Robert, her grandmother, the life she had abandoned until slowly, the wave receded and left her there, like a survivor of a shipwreck washed ashore.

And as suddenly as the wave had come, it had gone. She straightened up and wiped her eyes. She hadn't expected the meltdown, and she felt shocked by the intensity of her own sadness. But as she walked to the living room and lit the fire, she thought, yes, she was alone, but there was a peace to the solitude, too, and room to think, room to breathe.

Chapter 3

The next morning, Eden moved her writing things downstairs now that she knew she wouldn't be getting in anyone's way. She made herself a pot of tea and sat at the table in front of the big living room window overlooking the front garden. It was a large, flat, private garden, shielded from the lane and neighboring cottages by a very tall hedge.

The cottage itself was some sort of plaster. She would have to find out what it was made of...some kind of English, sixteenth-century adobe. Best of all, Eden thought, whatever these ancient plaster walls were made of, they were painted pink. As a little girl, she thought this was unbelievably wonderful. A pink cottage. She'd begged her mother to paint their tiny white house in Rhode Island the same dusky shade of pink, but, sadly, the answer was always no. Eden now knew this color was traditional to the area, especially for old and historic homes like this one. Suffolk Pink it was called. It still made the house seem just a little more like it was out of a fairy tale, rather than a real-life house with plumbing and a fridge and a dodgy furnace.

"Yoo-hoo!"

A thin old man in a flat cap waved at Eden from the path leading to the front garden. Eden stepped outside.

"Hello, love. I'm Tony Miller. Gardener. So sorry to hear about your gran." He held out a bony hand.

"Hello, Eden Martin, Mabel's granddaughter. Thank you. We miss her terribly" Eden shook his hand.

"No doubt. No doubt. So, would you like me to do the usual fall tidy of the garden, love? Your gran liked to have things tidied up, burlap round the evergreen, that sort of thing," he said.

"Oh, yes. I hadn't thought of that. That would be lovely, thank you. Would you like a cup of tea before you start?" she asked.

"No, thank you, my dear. Lots to do today. I'll just get my bits and pieces from the car and get to work."

"Thank you, Tony, and nice to meet you," Eden said.

As she watched Tony gather rake and clippers and burlap and twine, she cupped her steaming mug of tea in both hands and wandered over to the large flower garden out front. The air was still warm, but the threat of colder weather was there, the little chill when the wind blew, and Eden smiled. This was her favorite time of year. The garden was mostly dead now, but Eden remembered it from her summers there, a riot of perennial flowers in all heights and colors. There was a pear tree and an apple tree, so old that their branches were covered in patches of lichen, and knotty, like twisted, arthritic hands. They may have been there for a hundred years or more, Eden thought. They still produced fruit though, abundantly, she knew that. She smiled at what was all so familiar, yet, in some ways, being seen for the first time now that she was here not as a visitor, but to live. At least for now.

Returning to the house, Eden decided it was time to make a call.

"Eden, it's so good to hear from you!" Bob declared. "How are you?"

"I'm great, actually. Thanks. How are things in New York?"

"Fine, fine. The semester is getting underway. No major crises. Yet," he added, and she heard the smile in his voice. "We miss you."

She knew he was really asking her plans.

When there was no answer, he asked, "So what is it like over there? What are you doing with yourself day after day in the middle of the English countryside?"

"Well...let's see," Eden answered. "I wake up and make a pot of tea and write every morning. Then I usually head down the road to Park's, the only store in the village, to shop for my evening's meal. Then I might go for a walk along the lanes. Or, some days, I just build a fire and watch awful local TV. Oh my God, the TV here is so bad it's good. I watched a show about the man who invented cat's eyes reflective lights for the highway, and once a documentary on cheddar cheese. It's totally bizarre, but even these things seem interesting to me here!" she said, laughing as she said it.

"Sounds like the entertainment options there are just ever-so-slightly less exciting than New York," he said with a laugh.

"You can say that again. Someone is coming next week to install a satellite dish so I can get internet access, and that happens to come with ninety-eight television stations. I'm almost sad to know I will, no doubt, lose my innocent interest in things like hedge management and the history of coal, but I need to get online, to start researching my book, and the stations came with the internet, like it or not. Anyway, I'm not here to watch television. So, basically, really exciting stuff happening here in Barton Heath. Definitely a culture shock, after twenty years in New York. But I'm loving it."

"Okay," Bob replied. "So, it sounds like you're not on your way home tomorrow. So, what does this mean? Would you like the year as a sabbatical? Because I think that will work, if you want it. We will hold your position for you for a year. I really hoped you were going to say it was quaint but boring and you were on your way back, Eden. But if you need a year, then take it. The university isn't going anywhere."

"You're amazing. Yes, if you can get the year sabbatical approved, I'll take it. I just don't know what the heck I'm doing with my life. And to be honest, I don't feel like worrying about it right now. I'm having too much fun."

"Okay, I'll let the department know, and I'll fill you in on details when it's all finalized. Do you think you'll be able to research anything there that can be published? That's the expectation with a year's sabbatical, especially if you're not teaching over there."

Eden thought for a minute. "Well, I definitely will do some writing. Whether or not it will end up being academically acceptable, let alone publishable, is still in question. I'm not entirely sure what I'm writing. But I will keep you posted. And thank you, Bob. Truly, thank you," she said with tenderness in her voice.

"You're welcome," he replied. "You're lucky you're my favorite history nerd, my friend."

*

The next day there was a definite chill in the air. After a morning spent writing, Eden donned a thick sweater and her wellington boots, know the country over as "wellies," and headed out for a walk along the ridge above the village where she could look across two different valleys at once, walking a thin path across the hills that had been worn down by feet for centuries. She loved to walk the old paths and breathe deeply of the English countryside, replacing years of New York smog with pure, damp English air. She always returned home feeling clean and calm and happy.

Today, the wind whipped her hair around her face, and she was just starting to feel rainfall when she heard a whimper. At first, she thought it was the wind, but when she heard it again, she turned to listen and followed the sound to a small group of trees down a slight hill.

Lying there, beneath a bush, was a wet, filthy dog. He looked up at her with pleading eyes and whimpered again.

"Hey there, little one," Eden said, cautiously approaching. She held out a hand and the dog licked it eagerly. "Oh, you're sweet. Can you get up? Come on...up, up."

Eden stood up and patted her knees to encourage the dog. He slowly rose to his feet, tried to walk toward her, and crumbled to the ground again, yelping in pain.

"Oh, my goodness, you're hurt." She looked around in distress, hoping to see someone else on the ridge. The rain was falling heavily now and there was no one else to be seen.

She thought for a minute. *Should I go back to the village and get help? It would take a long time and the poor dog is shaking with cold. Who knows how long he's been lying there. He isn't that big.*

She slowly approached, stroked the damp head, and, having been greeted with a thumping tail, decided to just carry him home herself. She slid her arms under the dog, lifted him with a grunt, and started the long, slow walk back to the cottage.

Back home, she quickly started a fire and put a blanket in an old cardboard box. She laid the dog carefully on the blanket and got a towel to dry him off. He was all black except for one long, white leg. *Like a white boot*, Eden thought.

"I'll call you Wellie," she said, and the responding thumping tail seemed to mean that he was in agreement.

She brought over a bowl of water and some leftover beef stew, both of which disappeared in a flash. Wellie let out a long, satisfied sigh and fell asleep beside the crackling fire. Eden felt a rush of well-being watching the little creature lie there, sleeping, with a stomach full of stew. She wondered whose dog he was. And she wondered if Barton Heath had a vet. First thing in the morning she'd have to find out. But, for now, she was soaked and cold and dirty, and there was a terrible storm raging outside, and she was starting to feel unwell. It was a hot bath and an early night for her.

*

Eden awoke the next morning with an ache all over and a bad cough. Wellie jumped up, whimpered as he lifted his paw, then went about wildly wagging his tail as Eden came down the stairs and into the living room. She smiled and went over to pat his head. *What a nice way to start the day*, she thought, being greeted that warmly for no reason at all.

"And how are you, Wellie belly?" she asked, rubbing his head and neck, as he wagged his tail with such enthusiasm he almost fell over.

She carried him out to the soggy garden so he could take care of business. She felt miserable. She was sure she had a fever, and everything ached. After his trip out front, Eden put Wellie back in his box, stoked the fire and added a log, and went back upstairs to bed.

Later that morning, she repeated the process with Wellie, gave him some bread and cheese to eat, and headed to Park's in search of cold medicine and dog food.

"Oh, you should see Mrs. Welsh for that, love," Mrs. Park said with affection, hearing Eden cough as she searched the medicine shelf.

Mrs. Park was a big, round, rosy-cheeked woman, who had

known Eden since she was tiny, coming into the shop in the summers to buy little bags of penny candy. Mr. Park looked just like his wife, and the two had taken Eden under their wings since her mother left, checking in on her now and then to see if she was all right and helping out when needed.

"Who is Mrs. Welsh?" Eden asked.

"Who is Mrs. Welsh?!" Mrs. Park repeated in shock. "How can you have been coming here all these years and not know Mrs. Welsh? Hazel Welsh, she's the village healer. She has the herbs and such for anything that ails you. You go to her, and she'll set you right. She'll have your cough gone in no time. We all rely on her completely. And with the nearest doctor fifteen miles away, she gets a lot of business, let me tell you! You should go see her, love. You could use it, and she always loves the visits."

Eden was fascinated. A local herbalist, right here in Barton Heath! She would, indeed, go and see her, for her cough and out of plain curiosity too.

"Wonderful," she said to Mrs. Park. "Do you have her number? I'll call and make an appointment."

Mrs. Park laughed heartily. "Oh, you don't make an appointment, dear. This isn't New York, remember. She doesn't even have a phone. Says all that ringing would drive her to distraction. No, you just go knock on her door. She's usually there. Third cottage down the lane to the church, with the blue door. Just go on over, and she'll set you right. She knew your gran, of course. They were much the same age, I'd say. I'm sure she'll be glad to meet you."

"Great," Eden said. She paid for her things and left, determined to go see Mrs. Welsh that very day.

She had also found out the name of the village vet, and Mrs. Park had gone so far as to call and make Eden an appointment for later that day.

With business at the village HQ tied up, Eden headed home.

By the afternoon, she needed to visit Mrs. Welsh, indeed. Eden coughed and blew her sore, red nose, feeling miserable. She pulled on a thick sweater and jacket and hunched forward, a posture that seemed to help the ache that ran through her body, and she headed for the road to the church. She felt the bite of the cold, damp October air, and she pulled her jacket closer around her and looked down to avoid the sharp wind.

Eden was half-asleep, and her mind was conjuring images of the old herbalist, when she looked to the left, stepped off the curb, and heard a terrible screech as a car slammed its brakes on and swerved wildly to avoid hitting her.

Her heart pounded, and her eyes were wide as the car pulled over, and the driver jumped out, visibly shaken.

"What the hell are you doing?" Eden yelled. "You almost killed me!"

She felt a jolt as she noticed the man walking toward her was tall and gorgeous, with messy brown hair and a disheveled blazer over a tucked, but rumpled, shirt. She cleared her head and returned to being furious at his recklessness.

"Are you all right?" he asked, looking at her with real concern in his eyes. "You just stepped right off in front of my car. I barely had time to swerve."

"Well, maybe if you looked before driving so recklessly," Eden snapped…but as the words came out of her mouth, she realized what she had done.

"I'm sorry, but I did see you. I just didn't expect you to step out in front of me. I hear you're American. I think, perhaps, you were expecting cars from the other direction?"

It was true. It had been her fault, in her fog of sickness, she had forgotten where she was, and that cars drive on the other side of the street there. She had looked left and stepped out, not realizing that he was driving down the road to her right, just feet from her. It was her fault, and he was the one being gracious and polite.

"Oh my gosh. I'm so sorry. Yes, it was me. I'm sorry, I looked left. I was thinking about something, and I just stepped off. I'm really sorry," she apologized, feeling like a jerk.

"Well, thank God you're all right. Listen, if you're sure you're okay, I'd better go. My daughter is in the car," he said. "I think I scared her when I slammed on my brakes."

Ah, his daughter. Figured. The good ones were always taken. She felt surprisingly disappointed, considering she didn't even know his name.

"Yes, I'm fine. I'm really sorry. Thanks. Bye." And with that, she looked both ways and carefully crossed the street toward the little cottage with the blue door.

Chapter 4

Mrs. Welsh's cottage was right out of a storybook. Eden stood with her hand on the gate of the low white picket fence, which seemed to be barely holding back the explosion of herbs and flowers that filled the little front garden. She saw that most of the plants were dry and withered by this time of year, but Eden imagined it would be glorious in the summer. *Echinacea, lavender, foxglove, mint, mugwort.* She ticked off a mental list of flowers and herbs she recognized as she opened the gate and walked up the short path to the front door. She'd raised her hand to knock when, to her surprise, the door opened.

"I'm so glad to see you," said the small, white-haired woman in the doorway.

Eden stood on the step, not sure what to say. How did she know Eden was coming?

"Well, thank you. I am Eden Martin, Mabel's granddaughter. I've got a cold and I was told—"

Mrs. Welsh gently interrupted her. "Yes, dear, I know who you are. I've been expecting you for a long time."

And with that, she turned and walked into the cottage, leaving the door open for Eden to follow her in.

"Have a seat by the fire, my dear, and I'll bring in the tea tray," the sweet old woman said.

Eden sat in a soft armchair next to a cheerfully crackling fire, and a few minutes later, Mrs. Welsh was seated in the chair on the other side of the hearth. They each had cups of tea in hand, and there was a plate of biscuits on the tiny wooden table between them.

Mrs. Welsh was about five foot two, with snow-white hair pulled up into a bun. She was wearing a dress with a shawl pulled round her shoulders. She had creamy white skin with pink cheeks and her eyes crinkled as she smiled.

Eden looked around the room. It was small and furnished with floral-patterned chairs and a side table with a lace cloth draped over it. A worn rug lay on the floor, with a big cat sleeping happily beside Mrs. Welsh's chair. It was cozy, comfortable, and strangely familiar. Eden felt sure she had been there before, but she knew she hadn't.

Mrs. Welsh watched Eden's face. "Seem familiar, does it?" she asked softly.

"What!?" Eden said. How did she know that's what she was thinking?

"Oh, I'm sorry. I'm rushing you. Let's start with your cold. How are you, dear?"

Eden brushed off the unsettling comment and told the old woman about her symptoms: cough, runny nose, sneezing, body aches. The usual. Mrs. Welsh asked her a few more questions and then told her not to worry. After their tea, she would mix her up a brew that would have her better right away.

"Thank you," Eden said. "I'm fascinated to find you here. I never heard of you in all my summers here."

"Well, I guess it just wasn't our time until now," Hazel responded with a small smile. "I'm sorry about your grandmother, dear. She and I were good friends, and she will be missed."

Eden thanked her for her kindness and the two sat in silence for a minute.

Finally, Mrs. Welsh spoke. "So, dear. What else can I do for you? Surely you aren't here just about your cold."

Again, Eden was disconcerted by what seemed like her ability to read minds. "Well, as you mention it, I would love to know a bit about what you do," Eden said. "You see, I am a professor of history, and I study the history of medicine. Particularly in Medieval Europe. I would love to know if some of the things you're using today are similar to those I've read about. It's actually something I'm planning on writing a book about, so I'm thrilled to find an herbalist right here in Barton Heath.

Perhaps I could come by some time, and you could tell me about yourself."

"Well, isn't that fascinating? A professor. Interesting way for you to find yourself here. I do love how these things work. I would like that. I use many of the recipes that have been handed down by my family for hundreds of years, so I'm sure there will be a few things you recognize from your books. Yes, that sounds lovely. Why don't you come by next week sometime, and we'll have a nice little chat?"

Eden thanked her warmly and said that sounded wonderful and then rose from her seat.

"Let me get you that tea for your cold, dear," Mrs. Welsh said, and she disappeared into the kitchen for several minutes. Eden heard some light clinking and banging as jars and pots were opened and used.

While she was waiting, Eden noticed a wall full of small, painted portraits. They were fascinating. Some looked very, very old. Near the end of the wall was a small cameo painting of Mrs. Welsh. And next to it was a picture of—

Eden gasped. She almost fell over, struck suddenly with fear and confusion. Her instinct was to run. It was a picture of *her*. Or at least someone who looked just like her.

She whirled round as Mrs. Welsh appeared in the kitchen

doorway holding a jar of herbal tea. Eden's eyes were wide.

Mrs. Welsh gave her a gentle smile. "Oh dear. You saw the picture already. Well, dear, we will certainly have a lot to talk about next week, won't we? Bit of a shock, I expect. But don't you worry yourself. All is well. I was expecting your visit, that's all. Nothing more."

"But that's crazy. Why do you have a picture of me? It is me, isn't it? I mean, it looks just like me"

"Well, I don't know, dear," Mrs. Welsh said. "I painted it myself some years back. It certainly does bear a great resemblance to you. Isn't that something? The world is a mysterious place. That's what I always say. Now you go home and get to bed with that cold, my dear. And I will see you next week."

And with that, she walked Eden briskly to the front of the house, gave her a pat on the back, and closed the door behind her.

Two hours later, Eden, head still reeling from her visit with Mrs. Welsh, loaded Wellie into her car and drove to the far end of the village to see the vet. She sat in a waiting room with an old man with a cat lying peacefully in his lap and a little boy holding a birdcage with a pale blue parakeet in it. After a few minutes, the door to the surgery opened and Eden heard her name called.

She looked up to receive the second jolt of her day. It was the man who had almost run her over just a few hours before. He looked as surprised as she was.

She lifted Wellie and squeezed past him into the examining room as he held the door open. Her stomach was suddenly in a knot. But this time it wasn't fear. It was butterflies.

"I didn't expect to see you again so soon," he said as he lifted Wellie onto the table with a smile. "I'm James Beck." He offered his hand. "I'm sorry again about this morning. My hands were shaking for an hour, I can tell you that."

"I'm Eden Martin, Mabel Harrison's granddaughter," Eden said, shaking his hand. "No, I'm the one who is sorry. I was very rude, and it was all my fault. I wasn't feeling well and just wasn't paying attention."

He smiled at her, and the butterflies flew furiously around her stomach. Of course, she was there in an old sweatshirt, with greasy hair in a messy ponytail, and a bright red nose from her roaring cold. Typical Eden, she thought to herself.

James had soft green eyes, and had a gentle but very definitely masculine air about him, she noticed. *This won't do*, she thought to herself. He was a married man with a child. The last thing she needed was a scandal in this small village.

She gave herself an invisible shake and straightened up. "I found this dog, and he seems to have hurt his paw. I hope you can help him, and then maybe help me find his owners," Eden explained.

"Well, let's take a look," James said.

He examined Wellie with great tenderness. He had large, strong hands, but his fingers touched and felt the animal with great sensitivity. He checked the dog from head to foot, ending with the painful paw. He suspected it was broken. An x-ray confirmed it.

"Fractured, I'm afraid," James said, walking back into the examining room from the back of the office where the x-ray machine was. "If it's all right with you, I'd like to keep him here tonight. I'll sedate him to set the bone and put on a cast and give him some pain medication. If you're willing to come to collect him in the morning, maybe we can find his owners." He gave her a sort of lopsided smile that made Eden's head swirl so that she had to focus to be able to speak.

"That sounds good. I'll take him back to my place tomorrow. Hopefully, we can find his owners, but I don't mind taking care of him till we do. He's so sweet," she said, and she ruffled his head, which caused Wellie's tail to thump on the examining table.

"You're awfully nice to do that," James said with that same intoxicating half-smile. "Lots of people wouldn't. So, thank you. You're doing me a favor, as otherwise, I'd have to figure out what to do with him tomorrow and start searching for a foster home for him. It's sad, but a lot of dogs end up abandoned. Of course, he might belong to someone. I hope he does. But, examining him, I can see he's quite skinny, and dirty. A lot of times someone will move to a new place that doesn't allow pets, or get a girlfriend who is allergic, or any number of reasons. And instead of taking the dog to a shelter, they just kick it out on the side of the road. I've never understood how someone could do that and then go home and have dinner and go to bed," he said, looking off as if he were trying to imagine doing those things.

"That's awful," declared Eden. "I can't imagine that either. How could anyone do that? No," she said resolutely, "Wellie will stay with me till we find him a good home."

"Wellie?" James asked, cocking his head and smiling in a way that she was sure was half laughing at her.

"Oh. Yeah. That's what I named him. Looks like he has a white boot on. And I was out in my wellies when I found him so..." She trailed off.

"It's the perfect name," he said. "And he's a very lucky dog to be going home with you."

There was an uncomfortable pause as they both seemed to notice the double meaning of the statement.

Eden felt herself blush. *Pull yourself together, you idiot*, she thought. *This guy is married with a child.*

She thanked him and said she'd be round in the morning to collect Wellie. James shook her hand and seemed to hold it an instant too long, looking at her as he did so. Then he turned quickly and went back to work. Or maybe she had imagined it. It had been a lonely few weeks, after all, and her heart wasn't fully healed from the catastrophe with Robert. Surely, she was seeing things that weren't there.

*

As arranged, Eden went back to Mrs. Welsh's cottage the following week. She felt nervous and a bit angry, though she wasn't sure why. She felt as if she were being tricked into something. Why did this old woman have a picture of her on the wall? Maybe she'd seen pictures of Eden at her grandmother's place, and she'd painted her without realizing it. Who knows? But Eden wanted to find out.

Plus, there was the practical side. Eden needed to earn a living now that she wasn't teaching, and her year off from the university was already going by fast. She hoped that her writing could support her, if she could figure out exactly what she was writing. She'd been doing a lot of research online, and had even gone to Cambridge once earlier that week, to the magnificent library there, but she needed real-life, hands-on stories and lore.

So she knocked on the little blue door, a frosted teacake in hand as an offering, and waited.

Mrs. Welsh opened the door with the same gentle smile and greeting as before. "Come in, my dear. So glad to see you again. Come in and sit by the fire. I'll be right in with the tea tray."

Eden sat in the living room, in the plush chair by the fireplace again. Mrs. Welsh brought in the tea tray and the sliced cake Eden had brought. She served the tea.

"So, my dear. You are writing a book. That is wonderful. I'm sure there are things you could teach even me about cures, with all that studying you've done," Mrs. Welsh began.

Eden smiled and sipped the sweet, milky tea. "Yes, I just love it—the history, the pictures in my mind of these women, hundreds of years ago, with mortar and pestle, healing just from nature. And of course, the constant threat that, if they became too powerful as healers, or if there was any kind of scandal at all, they'd be accused of witchcraft, or some other thing, and likely be killed. Quite a job hazard,

I think."

Mrs. Welsh laughed out loud. "Goodness, yes! Aren't we lucky to be here in this day and age? There were some women in my line that were burned as witches. Just two, I believe," she said, looking off into space for a moment, as if running through a mental list of her ancestors. "But, still...oooh, awful to imagine." She shuddered and reached for her tea cake.

"In your own family line!? Women burned for witchcraft?" Eden asked.

"That's right. There was Gwyneth in the 1200s. Well, actually, I think she may have been hanged, not burned. Or was it drowned? And then, a century later, her great-great-great-niece, Nesta. Tragedies. Cake, dear?" she asked, offering up a slice of the cake Eden had brought with her.

"Yes, thank you," Eden said. "But you can't stop there. Tell me what happened to your ancestors!"

"Well, let's see," Mrs. Welsh said, looking up to the ceiling for a moment. "The story is that Gwyneth was having an affair with the Prior of the nearby cathedral, and so, of course, when the first whispers of that came out, she suddenly was accused of witchcraft and killed. Easy enough back then for a high-ranking member of the church to convince terrified villagers that someone making herbal concoctions was, in fact, making potions and conjuring spells, and from there…well, poor woman never stood a chance. The story of Nesta is even more tragic. She was very young and innocent, and beautiful, and very good with the herbs. Soon, more people in the village were going to her cottage for cures than to the university-trained monks at the infirmary. Of course, it seemed that the devil must be involved in keeping folks away from the cathedral hospital. I suspect it was more the loss of money than the loss of souls that inspired it. But she, too, met an awful end. Burned on the pyre. I suppose, with all the herbal healers in all the centuries, my family has been fairly lucky to have only lost two to witchcraft!"

Eden listened, wide-eyed, to the story. She was so engrossed she'd forgotten to take notes. When Mrs. Welsh finished, Eden remembered where she was and why, and jotted a few things down. These were the stories she needed, not the dry tomes from the libraries.

"How incredible!" she said when Mrs. Welsh went back to her tea. "I can't imagine the stories you must know, just from your family alone. Are they all written down somewhere?"

"Well, no, dear. They are just in my head. I never thought to write them down. I guess none of us did. We pass them on." There was a long silence as, clearly, Mrs. Welsh thought deeply. "But, my dear, I do believe that's one of the reasons you are here. To write them all down. Yes. That's right. That's one of the reasons."

This was enough of an opening, Eden felt, to bring up that disturbing painting of herself on the wall, and to ask what statements like this one meant. "Mrs. Welsh, why do you have a picture of me on your wall? And why do you make it seem like I'm here for a reason? I'm just randomly here due to all sorts of events in my personal life that came together unexpectedly. This wasn't planned."

"Oh no, of course, it wasn't planned…by you. But we silly little people don't have that much to do with the plans. Maybe you don't know that yet. You were meant to come here, and you did. It's simple. Nothing to worry about. So, about the painting, let me explain—"

Just then, there was a loud bang on the door, and Mrs. Welsh excused herself to answer it. It was Mr. Henway, an older man from down the lane, whose wife had been very ill lately.

"Mrs. Welsh, it's Sally. please can you help her? She's got that thing again. She's being sick over and over, and she's so frail. The doctor sent her home yesterday with medicine, but it's not helping. She's sweating and pale, and I'm very worried."

"Of course, David," Mrs. Welsh replied calmly, cutting the tension with her serenity. "I just saw Sally this morning, so I know all about it. I'll mix something up and be right over. You go home now, and I'll be along shortly."

Mr. Henway thanked her profusely and hurried back down the lane.

"Come on, dear. I'll tell you about the painting later. Life is calling. You can start learning in earnest now." And with that, she tottered off to the kitchen and Eden followed.

Mrs. Welsh's kitchen was magical. Dried herbs hung from the ceiling, a small fire crackled in a tiny white and blue-tiled fireplace, and glass jar after glass jar lined shelves all along the walls. Some contained dried flowers, others roots, others shells, and some looked suspiciously like they contained dead bugs. There was a big scrubbed wooden farmer's table in the middle of the room, and an AGA cook stove in the corner. It was cozy, welcoming, and mysterious all at once.

Mrs. Welsh wasted no time, climbing a tiny step stool to deftly grab several different jars. She put the kettle on the stove to boil, then added various ingredients to a big bowl.

A few seeds needed grinding, so she poured those into a large mortar and pushed it, and the pestle, toward Eden, saying, "Here you are, dear. If you don't mind grinding those to a fine powder, I'd be so grateful."

Eden grabbed the large, cool, stone pestle and began leaning in with her shoulder, grinding the hard seed pods. As she did so, she suddenly felt a strange tingle all through her body, like tiny icicles or sparkles of sunlight flittering through her entire being. It was so pronounced, she stopped her work and looked around.

Mrs. Welsh gave her a very quick look out of the corner of her eye.

It was a strange cottage for certain, but there was something so right about it all, so much more real and earthy and alive than all the dusty books she'd had her nose in for the past twenty years. She couldn't help but smile, too, as she got back to her work.

A few minutes later, she and Mrs. Welsh were knocking on the Henway's door with a large jar of hot herbal tea. The door opened, and they were shown up to the bedroom, where Sally lay, looking frail and thin.

"I'd like to introduce Eden Martin. She's Mabel Harrison's granddaughter from America. Here for a while. She's an herbalist, too, and is helping me," Mrs. Welsh said.

"Hello, Eden. Lovely to meet you," the old woman said,

polite, even when ill.

"Oh dear, Sally, you're having a hard time of it, aren't you, dear?" Mrs. Welsh said.

"Well, not feeling my best today, Hazel," she said in the usual understated English way.

"Now you keep taking that medicine the doctor gave you, but I think there's a missing piece that the medicine isn't treating. We need to mend it to get you to stop being sick and getting any weaker. I want you to drink a cup of this three times a day for two days. After that, nothing but beef broth for a day, and then you will be better, and we'll just work on building your strength back up, dear. All right?"

"Oh, thank you, Hazel," Sally said with great relief, sure now that her friend had attended to her that she would finally get better.

Mr. Henway thanked her profusely, too, then handed her a small fold of bills, and saw them to the front door.

That night, Eden was buzzing with excitement. The stories, the witches being burned, the emergency run with an actual herbal formula taken to a villager, as had been done for hundreds of years...and that strange tingling in Mrs. Welsh's kitchen. She felt more alive and excited than she had in years. She couldn't wait to go back in a few days to record Mrs. Welsh's stories and formulas, and to finally hear about that painting on the wall.

Chapter 5

In Rhode Island, Susan Harrison was just getting home from work. She had done a twelve-hour shift at the hospital and was arriving home with groceries for the weekend.

It was a beautiful sunny day, and she always thought there was nowhere on earth like New England in the fall. Her small white house was towered over by enormous oak and maple trees, leaves ablaze in orange and yellow in the deep blue November sky. Her home was cozy and neat, and she found great comfort in simply having lived there for so many years. The house, the street, the town were all so familiar to her, they kept her company in times when she felt lonely living by herself.

She took a deep breath of the crisp air, filled with the scent of dry leaves, and turned up the path to her front door. She looked up and stopped in her tracks.

There was Peter Penley-Smith, sitting on her front doorstep, with a handful of flowers and a boyish grin. He leaped up as he saw her.

There was a moment of awkwardness. Had he come all this way just to see her? Their time together had been weeks before, and there was some hesitation in both of them, as if they were each a bit embarrassed by the abandon with which they had both dived into their relationship back in England. But those thoughts and many others like them raced through both their minds and flew right out again in the space of a few seconds. Simultaneously, they put down the flowers and the groceries and embraced.

"I couldn't wait until Christmas, you see. Not knowing you were just a quick plane ride away," Peter explained while he hugged her to him.

"I'm so glad you came. I can't believe you're here. But I'm so glad. I've missed you so much!" Susan said, hugging him back.

They gathered up the strewn flowers and food from the front path and hurried into the house together, both with wide grins and butterflies.

*

The Horse and Cart pub, with its stout white building, glossy black front door, and thick thatch on the roof, had stood in Barton Heath on the road to Cambridge, serving food and drink to travelers, for four hundred years. It was still the center of village life, though some teetotalers would argue it was the church that held that position. But most people ended up in the cozy pub at least once a week, some people more often, and a few people daily. Gossip was spread, information was shared, and a sense of community was enjoyed.

There was no real equivalent in the US, Eden realized. She had gone into a nice bar in her neighborhood in New York once, just wanting to be among people, to read and have a glass of wine. But a single woman alone in a bar in the US apparently sends out one message and one message only: "Please come hit on me." She hadn't been there half an hour and three different guys had sidled up to the bar and started small talk, trying to buy her a drink, trying to pick her up.

Dejected, she had paid for her wine and gone home to read in her living room.

She loved that a pub had a very different role. Lots of people went there alone, to see other villagers and chat, or just to sit and read, or grab a bite to eat. It wasn't considered sad to be there alone, and it wasn't an invitation to be picked up. It was normal. So, Eden was thrilled to have her seat near the fire, dinner on its way, and a glass of wine in front of her as she sat reading about herbalists in the thirteenth century.

"Hello. Evening," she said, nodding to the bar and then the room in general, as she had learned was the general custom of locals.

She had shared a few smiles and greetings as she'd walked in, and then she had been left alone. And because this was the norm in a British pub, Eden let down her guard.

When a man suddenly appeared at her little table, she assumed he just needed a place to sit. She glanced up from her book with a quick smile, then returned to reading.

"Wotcha reading?" the man slurred, and his head bobbed slightly as he leaned forward, leering at her.

Oh God, she thought. *Even here?!*

Eden looked around. No one else was paying any attention to the man, so she thought he must be a harmless local.

"A book on history. I'm reading it for work, so if you don't mind…" She trailed off and returned to her book, turning a bit away from the table as she did so.

"You're a pretty lass. American?" he asked, obviously noticing her accent.

"That's right," she said without looking up, hoping he'd get the hint without her having to be outright rude.

"I hated history in school. Boring as shit, it was, I thought." His hand was unsteady as he went to put down his half-empty beer, clearly not his first, and he spilled it all over the table. Some ran into Eden's lap before she could get out of the way.

She jumped up, brushing at her wet jeans with a napkin. Now she was angry.

"Oh, sorry, love. But good thing is, I get to see the 'hole of ya now. You are a sexy lass, aren't ya?" he asked, leaning on the table.

Jim, the barman, came over with Eden's dinner and laid a hand on the man's shoulder. "All right, Kevin, that's enough now. Leave our nice American guest alone. You've had enough. Time to go home." He said it in a friendly tone, but he stood there, all six feet and three inches of him, not taking his hand off the man's shoulder.

There was a tense moment as the man stood there, not moving. Then the door opened, and James Beck walked in. He smiled and said a general hello and instantly noticed that everyone's attention was on something in the corner of the room.

He walked to the bar, taking in the scene of Jim with his hand on Kevin's shoulder, and Eden looking irritated and slightly nervous. James started to sit on a stool, but changed his mind and remained standing.

Kevin swung his arm up and swatted Jim's hand from his shoulder. The sudden movement made the drunken man stagger, and he had to grab the back of a chair to keep from falling over.

"Get your bloody hands off me, you shit!" he yelled at the

amiable Jim.

"All right," the pub owner replied, no friendliness left in his tone. "That's it. Get out, Kevin. Come back another night when you aren't pissed drunk before even getting here." He grabbed the man by the collar of his jacket and pulled him, effortlessly, to the door, opened it, and pushed him out, closing the door behind him.

The door instantly opened again, and Kevin stood in the doorway. Now the whole pub was riveted. This was good stuff. Much better than the usual Thursday night gossip.

"You're a flirt!" he yelled into the bar, looking right at Eden. "Think you're too good for a local worker, do you? Bastard Americans always thinking they're better than everyone…"

He would have continued, but James strode over to the door. He and Jim now filled the doorway together looking at him with furious expressions.

"Get out you drunken idiot!" James said loudly. "And you can apologize to Ms. Martin when you've got your senses back."

And with that, Jim shoved Kevin more forcefully this time, and the man fell backward, landing hard on his rear end on the pavement. Jim closed the door and stood in front of it, waiting to see if Kevin would be stupid enough to try and come back in again. He didn't.

Jim walked over to Eden's table. She sat in stunned silence.

"I'm so sorry," Jim said. "He's a bloody idiot. Kevin Spencer. Lives in the village. He lost his job a few months back and has been a drunken fool ever since. Not all the time. He's actually a nice guy when he isn't pissed out of his head. But I'm so sorry. Dinner's on the house tonight. And don't even think twice about him or what he said. He talks total nonsense when he's drunk. He won't remember a word of it tomorrow, so just pretend like it never happened."

"Um, okay," Eden replied. "Just a bit of a shock in a village pub. I'd expect it in New York, but not here."

James joined them at the table. "There's not a village in the world that doesn't have its angry drunk. Just too bad you had to meet him right after getting here. I hope he doesn't give you the wrong impression of the place," he said with a hint of a grin. "We're a bad lot in general, I'll admit, but not that bad."

"Well, I'm glad to hear it," Eden replied, smiling back at him.

Jim looked from one to the other, and he raised his eyebrows slightly. "Well, I'd better get back to it," he said, and he walked back behind the bar to get drinks.

"Are you staying?" James asked. "If so, I'll buy you another glass of wine."

Eden would have loved to stay and have wine with the handsome vet, but the encounter with Kevin had given her a pounding headache, and she was starting to feel a bit nauseous.

"I'd love to, but can I take a rain check? I've got a terrible headache suddenly," she said, wincing slightly and instinctively rubbing her temples.

"Of course. No wonder after that shock. Would you like me to walk you home?" he asked.

Gorgeous *and* chivalrous, Eden thought with a sudden jolt of something in her belly that felt like desire.

"No thanks," she said. "I'm fine, and the cottage is so close. But thanks. And hope to see you again soon." She smiled. Then, frowning as her head began to pound in earnest, she walked out into the dark evening.

Eden's cottage was around the corner from the pub. She cut through the small parking lot to shorten the walk and get home to a bottle of ibuprofen and bed as soon as possible.

Suddenly, out of the corner of her eye, she saw a figure lurch at her. Before she had time to react, she was pinned up against a car, a man's strong hands holding her arms down and his body pressing against her with such force she was unable to move.

It was Kevin.

"Not good enough for you, eh?" he said, his face just inches from hers, his breath a sour mix of stale beer and cigarettes.

"Get off me, you ass!" Eden yelled, as she struggled to get her hands free. His grip was too strong, and she remained pinned to the car.

"It's all right, love, I'm a good guy, you see. I think what you need is a little fun. Lighten up a little," he said with a disturbing grin. He leaned in and tried to kiss her mouth.

Disgusted, she turned her head to the side, and he ended up kissing her jaw.

He tried again, getting closer this time.

"Get off me or I'll scream!" Eden yelled, and then, deciding that she wouldn't, in fact, wait to do this, she let out a scream at the top of her lungs. "Get off me! Get off me, you bastard!"

Inside the pub, James was sitting near the window. He heard the scream, and before he could even think, he had bolted out the door. He heard Eden's voice again, this time not quite as loudly.

"You ass!" she said, as she brought her knee up, full force, into Kevin's groin.

Good girl, James thought, impressed.

Kevin bent forward and let out a loud groan of pain.

"Cow," he sneered at her, but he let go of her and lifted his hand as if to strike her.

Before he even saw it coming, James was on him. He grabbed Kevin, spun him around, and punched him so hard in the face that Eden thought she heard bones crunch. Blood trickled from the side of Kevin's face, and he roared in pain.

He swung back at James, but he was drunk and unbalanced, and James easily stepped out of the way. James hit him again, and this time Kevin fell to the ground like a limp doll. He was out cold.

James shook his hand and sucked in his breath. "Damn, that hurt," he said with a laugh. "I haven't done that since I was a schoolboy. I forgot it really hurts!" He turned to Eden, "Are you all right?"

Eden looked behind James and saw Jim and several other men had gathered, ready to spring to her defense if needed. She felt touched. In the window, other villagers had their faces pressed to the glass, staring wide-eyed at the drama.

"I'm fine," Eden said. "My God, who is that guy? He should be locked up."

"Yes, he should. Do you want me to call the police? I'd be

happy to," James said, getting his phone out of his back pocket.

"No, he's just drunk. Though if it ever happens again, I'll drag him down to the police station myself!" she said.

"You had a good knee in there. I was impressed." James smiled. "I think the tide would have turned in that scuffle, even if I hadn't shown up. I'm so sorry this happened. It's inexcusable. And it has gone too far. I think Jim and I will pay him a visit tomorrow. He needs to get some help. Alcoholics Anonymous or anger management or something. Probably both. Since he lost his job, he's been getting worse and worse. Clearly, he's not handling it on his own."

He picked Eden's jacket up that had fallen to the ground, and he turned to face Jim and the others. "She's all right," he called toward the pub.

"Thank God," Jim responded from the doorway. "So sorry, Eden. This kind of thing never happens here!"

"Thanks Jim," Eden turned back to James. "If the offer still stands, I'll take you up on that walk home now."

James put his arm through hers and walked her to the cottage.

*

Two days later, the village green had been taken over. It was the annual village fete, put on to raise money for various local causes, like the pre-school and the new roof needed on the church. There was a tent for tea and cakes, another for beer and wine, another where jams and cakes and pickled vegetables were neatly displayed and would later be judged, each participating cook hoping for a blue ribbon in their category.

There was lawn bowling, a game to try and hit a coconut off a cone to win a stuffed animal, and even a dunking game, where a ball was thrown at a target. If you hit it hard enough, a hapless volunteer, perched on a lever, would instantly fall into a huge tank of water. One of the schoolteachers was currently the sitting duck, and the village boys lined up with all their money trying to win that one.

Eden wandered through the stalls with a warm feeling in her heart. Village children raced around in excitement, eating candies and looking for the next game to play. Elderly women stood with their little handbags over their forearms, sipping tea and talking. Men, and some younger women, sat around tables in the pub tent, laughing and chatting. The vicar wandered in and out of all of it, looking pleased.

"Hello there," Eden heard from behind her.

She turned and saw James, standing close.

"How are you?" he asked. "I haven't seen you in the past few days. I hope you weren't too shaken up by that idiot, Kevin. He's agreed to sober up and join AA. He felt horrible when we told him the next day what he'd done. No memory of it at all! Scary really. Jim and I told him, if he didn't get help, we were going to report the incident at the pub to the police."

Eden was impressed he had followed through on talking to the man. "That's good. He needs some help, clearly. I'm okay. Was a bit shaken up for a day. But I'm fine. Thanks."

"And how's my patient?" James asked, bending down to pet Wellie's head. His daughter had already dropped to her knees and was petting the happy dog that Eden had on a leash beside her.

"Oh, he's wonderful, thank you! Healing very well. Almost as good as new. Still no word from any of the shelters about anyone who has lost a dog. And no calls from the posters I put up. So, for now, I guess he's mine," Eden said with a happy smile.

The little girl stood up and smiled at Eden.

"This is my daughter, Beatrice," James said, looking warmly down at his daughter. "Bea, this is Ms. Martin."

"How do you do?" the little girl asked in the formal English tradition.

"How do you do?" Eden replied with a chuckle.

It had taken her a while to learn that the question was never actually answered. When asked, "How do you do?", it was very bad manners to say, "Fine thanks." It was always meant to be replied to with the same question back, "How do you do?" She'd never understood it as a child, or an adult, but she liked the quirky English traditions, so she had taught herself to do it.

Beatrice was a pretty child, with big brown eyes and dark blond hair cut in a bob with bangs straight across her forehead. She had a ready smile and pink cheeks and looked the picture of health. She bent back down to pet the dog again, already bored with the adults.

Eden wondered where Mrs. Beck was. She had yet to meet her. "I'm sorry I haven't had a chance to meet your wife yet, James," she said politely.

James's expression changed just slightly. His eyes grew a bit sad as he replied, "My wife died three years ago, I'm afraid."

Oh my God, I've totally put my foot in it! Eden thought. *As always! How did I not hear that from anyone in the village in all this time?* Maybe because the news was old enough that people weren't talking about it much anymore.

Beatrice seemed to either not have heard her father, or not to be upset by it, as she continued to ruffle Wellie's head and receive his happy licks to her face with squeals of laughter. Eden realized the child must have been so young, maybe a year old or so, when it happened. She probably didn't even remember her.

"I'm so sorry," Eden offered, looking with kindness into James's eyes.

His eyes warmed and he looked into hers intensely.

Eden finally pulled her gaze away, feeling flushed. "I didn't know. I'm sorry I didn't know," she added, looking at the ground.

"It's all right. How would you know? It was some time ago now. I couldn't talk about it easily at the time. But I'm able to more and more. It was cancer. She was very young. But I suppose there are no guarantees in life, are there?" He looked straight at her with a mix of wistfulness and resignation.

"No, there certainly aren't," Eden replied. "But even so, I am very sorry for your loss."

James laid his hand on her arm and said quietly, "Thank you. I do appreciate the kindness."

Eden's arm tingled, and her heart raced as she felt his hand through her sweater. Their eyes were locked together, and they stood that way for several long seconds.

The spell was broken only by Bea standing up suddenly and declaring she needed cake immediately! The two laughed, and James asked if Eden would like to join them in the tea tent. She said she most certainly would, and the three of them walked off toward refreshment, with a large part of the village watching every step of this interesting development.

James and Eden enjoyed tea and slices of Victoria sponge as Bea ate a huge slice of chocolate cake and told them all about the play that was being rehearsed at the village school, in which she played a tree, but, according to her, the most important tree in the forest, for she had the only speaking tree part.

"This way, my dearie," she would say to a traveling Little Red Riding Hood.

James and Eden listened attentively, occasionally striking up short conversations while Bea concentrated on her cake for a few moments.

"Have you always lived here?" Eden asked. He was clearly local, yet he had an air of someone who had seen more of the world than Barton Heath.

"I'm from here, yes," he answered. "Then I went to university in London, then veterinary school in Edinburgh. After that, I moved to Boston, just to see a bit of the world." He paused and took a bite of cake. Then he continued, "I liked Boston a lot. But after a year of waiting tables, I was ready to move on, so I spent the next year traveling, cheaply, round the world, spending every penny I'd saved. My mate, Colin, and I went to Asia, America, South America, and a lot of Europe before running out of money and coming home. It was fantastic."

"That sounds amazing!" Eden said. "What an adventure."

"It was perfect because we saw a bit of the world and then I knew I was ready to come home to Barton Health and open a practice. I'd wanted to do that since I was a small child," he said with a smile. "My late wife, Jane," he went on with that same wistful look in his eyes, talking to Eden, but looking lovingly at Beatrice, "was a schoolteacher in nearby Newmarket. We met at a party. We were very happy, but just four years after we got married, shortly after Bea was born, she was diagnosed with cancer."

Eden did the math and realized that she'd been right, Beatrice had only been about one when she lost her mother.

James looked up, as if waking from a trance. "I'm sorry. I've gotten all heavy and morbid on you. I'm sure you don't need to know the sad details of my life," he said, looking almost embarrassed.

"Please don't apologize. I'm just so very sorry for your loss. And I'm glad you feel you can talk about it now. I am absolutely useless at chitchat, so I'm actually much more comfortable if you tell me heartfelt morbid stories than talk about the weather. I'm strange that way," Eden said, feeling embarrassed herself now.

James smiled. "And what about you? Where are you from originally?"

"Well, I grew up in Rhode Island. I don't know if you know it, but it's just a couple of hours south of Boston. Oh, right, if you lived in Boston, you definitely know it. My father wasn't ever around, but my mother still lives in the house I grew up in. I went to college and graduate school in New York City and that's where I live now. Or *lived*. I'm a professor of history at a big college there. I am here now for…" She trailed off. Vacation wasn't the right word. Forever didn't seem right either, not yet anyway. She really didn't know what she was doing in Barton Heath. She just knew it was exactly where she wanted to be. "I guess I'm here for the time being. A year. Maybe more. Not really sure," she said. "I was in a relationship that didn't really work out, and when my gran died, I decided to spend some time here."

She didn't mention that she had been engaged, or that she had caught her fiancé in bed with another woman. That was hardly chitchat for the tea tent, even if they were being honest. They both offered sympathies at relationships mourned and gone. But after that, they got to general topics like the village and work and what they liked and disliked, and they could have gone on for hours, except that Bea got fidgety and wanted to go outside and run around.

"Well, what did I expect after an enormous slice of cake? Better let the girl run it off," James said with a laugh as they all got up.

Eden didn't want to seem like she was clinging, so she said, "I'm going to head home now, but thank you. It was so nice to sit with both of you." She looked at Beatrice with a smile. She untied Wellie from the leg of the chair, next to which he lay fast asleep, and said goodbye.

She had started back toward her cottage when she felt her elbow get lightly grabbed. James had run up behind her.

"Just a quick question. Don't suppose you like to get dinner this weekend? I mean you probably don't know a lot of people here yet and... well, no, really it's just that I'd like to have dinner with you," he said, with an embarrassed smile that made him look more like a schoolboy than a forty-year-old man.

"I'd love to!" Eden replied almost before he had even finished his sentence, instantly wishing she hadn't sounded quite so eager. She was never good at playing it cool.

"Wonderful!" he said with equal enthusiasm, then started to

jog back toward Beatrice, turning to yell, "I'll call you!" over his shoulder as he did.

Eden's elbow felt hot from his touch, she could still feel the spot where he had very gently held her arm for just a moment. She watched him lope effortlessly across the green, his body carrying him with ease.

He scooped Beatrice up in his arms and twirled her around as his dirty blond hair fell into his eyes.

Her breath grew shallow, and her heart started beating a bit faster again.

"Oh my gosh," she thought to herself. "What am I doing?"

Chapter 6

That night Eden had a dream. She was dressed in a rustic dress with a
linen apron and a cap, and she had the feeling it was a long time ago.
She was standing in a room full of women singing. And somehow, she
knew all the words. The women sang together as they worked, mending
and dying clothes:

> I have a yong suster
>
> Fer biyonde the seae;
>
> Manye be the druries
>
> That she sente me.

> She sente me the cherye
>
> Withouten any stoon,
>
> And so she dide the dove
>
> Withouten any boon.

> Whan the cherye was a flowr,
>
> Thanne hadde it no stoon;
>
> Whan the dove was an ey,
>
> Thanne hadde it no boon.

When she woke, Eden felt totally disoriented. Where was she? She had to sit up and turn on the light to remember she was in England. But also to remember she was in England with a laptop on the desk and an electric light next to the bed. It wasn't the 1400s. It was the twenty-first century.

She had no idea what the words in the song meant, or where they came from. Though she had a feeling, in her sleep, she had understood them. The dream had been one of those dreams that feel like more than just a mash-up of random thoughts in one's mind. In her mind, she looked through the crowd of women in her dream, stoking a fire, dying wool in a vat, sewing a stitch, and some of the faces were familiar. One was young and Eden couldn't quite place her. One was old and Eden knew her in an instant. It was Mrs. Welsh.

Eden got a cold shiver down her spine, and she turned off the light, huddled deeper under the down comforter, and tried to go back to sleep.

The next day, Eden was due at Mrs. Welsh's to listen and observe and record. She still felt like she was in that half-light of her dream, half here and now and half in some distant time and place. It was unsettling. But then, most of her time with Mrs. Welsh was a little unsettling. But it was also exciting. Like coming home after a long journey. Today she wanted an answer about that portrait of her on the wall. Mrs. Welsh had never actually told her why a picture of her was hanging there.

"Good morning, Mrs. Welsh," Eden said as the door opened, before Eden had even knocked, an event Eden was already starting to get used to.

"Good morning, my dear. So good to see you. Do come in," the old woman said before tottering off to the living room.

It was November, and Eden happily warmed the sting of cold from her fingers in front of the fire that burned cheerfully, even at ten in the morning.

When the two were seated in their chairs by the fire, Mrs. Welsh said, "What would you like to know today, dear?"

Eden thought for a moment she would start by asking for some recipes or stories. But, instead, she heard herself say, "I want to know why I'm hanging on your entryway wall."

Mrs. Welsh laughed aloud. "Oh that. You are still wondering about that old thing. I can see you like clear answers and explanations for things. I'm not like that. General information, or even a bit of mystery, is fine for me, but you are a researcher, after all, and a professor! So, I will tell you."

Eden involuntarily leaned toward the old woman. She had a feeling this story might actually affect her life.

"I saw you in a dream, my dear. And I knew you were next. You see, healers come all different ways to this line. Many are born to it. Many are the daughters of healers before them. But others aren't. I never had children, so I knew, one day, I would be shown who was to come after me. It might be the girl down the lane, or it might be someone I've never met. Which was the case with you, my dear. Some dreams are dreams. But some dreams are tellings. Are *knowings*. And you know the difference when they happen."

Eden thought about just the night before and wondered if those women coming to her, singing with her, had been a *knowing*, though she wasn't sure exactly what that meant.

Mrs. Welsh continued, "So, you see, you came to me clearly in a dream. And I painted you. You are here for a reason, my dear. I don't want to rush you or scare you. But you are. Things aren't random, even when they seem it. I know you feel you're here because of a waterfall of quick events and choices. But that waterfall was meant to be. And the events leading to the waterfall were meant to be. And so on. In both directions through time. And you being here is meant to be.

I saw you in my dream several years ago, and I painted you. And a few months ago, I saw you again in the flames of the fire, and I knew you were coming soon. That's all, dear. Nothing to be shocked by, I promise."

"Nothing to be shocked by?" Eden exclaimed. "I have no idea what you're talking about. I'm not an herbalist. I'm not a witch. I'm a university professor from Manhattan, here on a whim after a bad breakup. How could my coming be part of some master plan?" she asked, railing against the thought that even this bold brave move to England was not fully her own. That she was still, somehow, a puppet in someone else's plan. "What if I don't want to be a healer?" she asked angrily.

There was a long pause as Mrs. Welsh looked at the fire, smiling. Then she asked, "Do you not want to be a healer, then?"

The question was so simple it caught Eden by surprise.

"I might. Or I might not," she said, realizing she sounded like a petulant teenager, not a well-educated adult. "That's not the point. The point is that I don't want to be told what to do. This is my year. My...breaking free, a year to be impulsive and do whatever the hell I want. Now, suddenly, you're telling me I had no choice, that this was all set up for me, like I've fallen into some trap set a hundred years ago."

"Go have a walk in the garden, dear," was Mrs. Welsh's simple reply. "You'll feel better with some fresh air."

So Eden went to the French doors at the back of the living room, opened them, and stepped out into the cold sunshine. The back garden was magnificent. An enormous area, fenced in with an old wooden picket fence, divided into three large rectangles on each side, with an uneven brick path down the middle.

Wow, Eden thought, I *would love to see this in springtime. I wonder what she has in here.*

She was so intrigued by the healing garden that her anger immediately started to fade. She recognized some things, as she had out front, even in their withered winter forms: chrysanthemum for coughs, garlic for infections and fever, mint for headaches and irritability, purslane for stomachache. *She has a whole pharmacy out here*, Eden thought in wonder, looking at several other plants that she didn't recognize at all.

She wandered slowly down the path, with her hands outstretched, touching the tips of the taller stalks. She felt the tingle again, like a tickling in her hands that moved up her arms.

Then she saw flashes of images, like someone was playing just one or two seconds of a movie, then turning it off. An old man lying sick and a hand offering a steaming bowl…then that was gone. A very young child coughing fitfully, dressed in clothes from another century, then a mortar and pestle grinding licorice root and coltsfoot. *Licorice and coltsfoot: Strengthens the lungs*, she thought. Then that image was gone. It was as if the plants themselves held their stories and were showing them to her.

She stood still in the center of the garden, closed her eyes, and breathed in deeply, smelling the dry, dusty smell of a winter garden. And a smile spread across her face. A peaceful but excited smile.

She turned and walked back to Mrs. Welsh, who was standing at the foot of the garden.

"Yes. I do. I do want to be a healer," Eden said. "I don't know what that means exactly. I mean, I may not be staying here permanently or anything. But I don't want to study herbal medicine anymore, I want to *do* herbal medicine. And the weirdest part is, I'm not sure why I'm even saying this, but it's not even a question really. It feels just so true that it can't be any other way," she said. "I'm sorry I was so rude just now. This just all comes as a bit of a surprise, this story you have about my coming here. But it also feels right. I can't deny it does sort of feel meant to be, do you know what I mean?"

"I know exactly what you mean, dear. That is the *knowing*. It doesn't show up with bells and trumpets. You just know it deep down, suddenly, and fully. That's the *knowing*," she repeated with a smile.

"The *knowing*?" Eden asked.

"Yes, dear. There is a difference between being an herbalist and being a healer. Anyone can make a tea. And that's very useful too. An herbal tea maker puts herbs together and offers a remedy. But a healer has the *knowing*. It is something extra. It is touching your patient and knowing what they need, that one extra herb, that one different seed. It is touching the herbs and having them talk to you."

"Yes, that's what just happened to me!" Eden interrupted.

"I know it is, dear. Because you aren't just an herbalist; you are a healer. Practice it, my dear. If you think back, you've always had the knowing. But most of us are told as children that we are bonkers when we talk about it, and so we pack it away and ignore it. But you've always had it. And whoever is the next herbalist after you already has it too. That's what drew you here, that's why you want to stay. Your knowing knows you are meant to be here. And the plans made for us are hard to fight. If you do fight them, you're not likely to have a happy life, I'm afraid. You'll spend your life paddling upstream the whole way if you fight it." Mrs. Welsh paused and let that information sink in, then she said, "Let's get in out of this cold, and I'll show you a few of my favorite remedies for November illnesses."

Eden smiled and followed the old woman in.

Mrs. Welsh had several jars and bunches of dried herbs already laid out on the big wooden table in the kitchen.

"I make a big batch of remedies for the coming months on each turning of the seasons day: Imbolc remedies for spring when people get worked up and irritable, Beltane for summer when heavy hot colds can set in, Lughnasa for dry fall ailments, and Samhain now, heading into winter, when all sorts of coughs and fevers appear."

She showed Eden some recipes, which Eden eagerly wrote down.

Then she turned to Eden and said, "And now you finish them off." She pushed one large bowl full of herbs and leaves toward Eden. "This one," Mrs. Welsh said, "is for a little girl with a bad cough. Lots of yellow phlegm. But also, she is quite afraid of her father, who is, by all accounts, a large man with a nasty temper, and her constant worry is bad for her health. What would you add to her formula?" She stood back and watched her apprentice's face.

Eden looked up at the jars lining the shelf. Three of them had the faintest glow about them. Like a very slight light pulsing from the jars.

Eden reached up and took down the jars, her hands tingling as she touched them. She knew the plants on sight.

"Thyme to fight lung infection," Eden said. "And lemon balm and lavender to calm her fears, which she will need if she's to heal," she added.

"Absolutely correct, my dear," the old woman said with a big smile. "And now you know, you feel, the difference between mixing ingredients from a recipe, and healing. Well done, my dear. Now, perhaps, just a little bit of sherry by the fire. It's been a long morning for an old woman."

And with that, the two retired to the living room to rest and sip their wine.

Chapter 7

The thoughts in Eden's head bounced back and forth constantly between Mrs. Welsh and James. The first, a wholesome fascination with a sweet old woman. The second, thoughts and images that were not wholesome at all.

It had only been two days since the village fete, but she was already wishing she'd run into him, or that he would call about that dinner invitation he'd made. Eden didn't have to wait long to see James again though.

She was walking Wellie the next day when she turned the corner to see the village green had once again been quickly and totally transformed, this time into a playing field, upon which a rugby match, with a sizable crowd watching and cheering, was in full swing. As an American, Eden knew little of rugby.

She saw a woman her age, Tara, whom she had met here and there, and she walked over and stood next to her.

"Hi, Tara. Nice to see you," she said.

"Hi, Eden, lovely to see you again. Haven't seen you around much. How are things?" Tara asked.

"Good, thanks. Been busy helping Mrs. Welsh out, and

working on some projects," she said, not yet confident enough in her writing to tell someone she didn't really know about it. "How are you?"

"Great, thanks. Busy myself working at the nursing home. And seeing Martin when I can." Tara turned to Eden and probably saw from her expression that Eden didn't know who Martin was. "Martin's my boyfriend. Emergency room doctor in Newmarket," she said with a big smile. "You're here for the match, I see." Tara turned to watch the action on the green.

"What match is it? I actually was just walking Wellie. I had no idea this was going on," Eden said.

"It's a rugby match. Barton Heath vs. Upper Barrow. Tied at the moment," she said.

Just then, a great catch was made, and a cheer erupted.

The two teams were covered head to toe in mud because, as Tara explained with a laugh, "If they canceled a game every time it rained, there would be no sports in England at all!"

"What on earth are the rules? They aren't even wearing helmets!" Eden was shocked at the brutality of the tackles when none of the men had any protective gear on at all.

"Right now, that's called a scrum," Tara explained.

Eden saw men locked, heads down, arms interlaced, moving

together in this odd position. Then the ball was high in the air.

"There don't seem to be any rules at all that I can figure out," Eden said, laughing. "One man picks the ball up and runs, then he throws it, and the next guy kicks it. What is going on?"

"It is a bit of a free-for-all, actually. Your aim is to get it across the goal line. How you get it there doesn't seem to matter much. I'm sure there are all sorts of complicated rules, but I have to admit, I don't know them either!" Tara said, and they both laughed.

It was fast-paced and very fun to watch. In another play, the ball was caught by a very muscular, very muddy man, who Eden realized, with a quickening of her heart, was James. He ran toward the goal, his thighs muscular and thick as tree trunks. His hair was soaked with the rain, and there was mud on the shirt that clung to his back. An opponent ran straight into him and tackled him forcefully, but James pushed him off and kept going, finally tossing the ball to a teammate, as several opponents began to descend on him.

It looked painful and harrowing, but James had a huge grin on his face as he tossed his head to flick the wet hair out of his eyes.

Just then, his glance fell on Eden, and after a split second to recognize her, he smiled even more broadly, mud caked on his cheek, then he gave her a wink and ran off after the ball.

Eden's heart raced at the wink, and she saw Tara subtly look over at her, having seen it too. Tara's eyebrows were raised, and she had a questioning smile on her face. Eden couldn't help smiling back.

Finally, cold and wet, Eden took Wellie home, glowing from the wink and the thought of having dinner with this handsome man.

Later that evening, the phone rang. "Eden, it's me, Tara."

"What?" Eden said loudly into the phone. There was so much noise in the background she couldn't hear the caller at all.

"It's me, Tara!" Tara shouted.

"Oh, hi!" Eden shouted back.

"I'm at the pub with a few friends. We hoped you'd join us for a drink!"

"I'd love to!" Eden replied. "Thanks! I'll be there in a few minutes!"

She hung up the phone, threw on a jacket, and walked down to The Horse and Cart. It was dark and cold outside. There was only the sound of the rain falling and the occasional hissing of tires on the wet road as a car passed. All else was quiet and almost sacred feeling, to Eden.

But the moment she opened the door to the pub she was hit by a wave of noise and light and heat. It was packed.

She turned sideways to fit between the people and finally found Tara and her friends at a table in the corner. She made her way back to the bar and bought the table a round of drinks, then settled in and sipped her beer.

"So glad you could come!" Tara shouted over the noise.

"Me too! Thanks for asking me!" Eden replied.

"These lovely ladies are Mary, Suzanne, and Nicola." Tara yelled into Eden's ear.

"Hi there. Nice to meet you all!" Eden yelled back to the table in general. The women all nodded or smiled or raised their glasses in response, knowing it was too noisy for real conversation and not even attempting any. Then they heard singing.

"Why is it so packed in here tonight?" Eden asked Tara.

"It's the two rugby teams, and all their fans, here tonight. That's why it's such a madhouse!" Tara yelled. " We are all seeking shelter after having stood in the cold rain all afternoon." She smiled. "Barton Heath won, and all players have been in here celebrating for a couple of hours already."

Suddenly, one large man, with a slight belly, climbed up onto a table and started singing. Eden laughed out loud.

"Men don't really sing in public in America!" Eden said.

"This is great: Large, rough, athletic men, linking arms in drunken solidarity and singing at the top of their lungs!"

Suddenly James was on the table, too, arm around his friend, the two swaying with their pints, singing their hearts out, clearly drunk as skunks. Then the words to the song became so shockingly raunchy Eden looked around to see if the other patrons were offended. But it was the opposite, the crowd was cheering and raising glasses, and at the cleverly rhymed, and very sexual refrain, all the men joined in, and a few bolder women.

"You English have always been a mystery to me," Eden said into Tara's ear. "Brits are so proper, and yet you all love lewd songs and raunchy jokes!" She chuckled. "Americans would be shocked and offended, or at least pretend to be, at these lyrics. You could never sing them at a bar. Someone would get upset and write a letter or sue for emotional damages," Eden chuckled.

James looked so handsome and so happy singing with his friend, "If I were the marrying kind, which, thank the Lord, I'm not, sir," that she beamed up at him. The words that followed had her staring, literally jaw open, in shock, but Tara just laughed and slapped her lightly on the back.

Eden snapped out of it, had a good laugh herself, and downed the rest of her beer. She had a feeling that beer played a significant role in enjoying this incredibly bawdy entertainment.

Two hours later, Eden, Tara, and her friends poured out of the hot, bright room, and felt the blessed cool of the evening on their flushed cheeks.

"I'm so glad you came, Eden," Tara said, their ears ringing slightly in the sudden quiet.

"Yes, me too," the other friends chimed in.

"It was so much fun. Thank you for asking me," Eden said. "Hope to see you again soon."

"Definitely. See you soon!" they all said, and the friends parted ways, each walking back to their house or cottage.

Eden ambled, smiling and swaying just slightly, singing to herself as she went, "I've played the wild rover for many a year. And spent all me money on whiskey and beer…"

*

Eden awoke the next morning as she did every morning, listening to the sound of the rooster in the garden of the cottage next door. Then the sounds of the excited little songbirds in the hedge. She had a terrible headache and an awful taste in her mouth. "Like the bottom of a birdcage," as she had heard someone describe one's mouth after a night of drinking. The English always had the best expressions.

Despite the headache, Eden smiled this morning as she lay under the down comforter, replaying the events of the evening in the pub, and then back to the fete, ending with the feel of James's hand on her arm, and the thrilling prospect of dinner with him soon.

She went to the window and turned the metal handle, pushing both panes outward and letting in the chilly air. There was the smell of a bonfire somewhere, dampness mixed with wood smoke, which always reminded her of England.

Downstairs she sat at the window with a steaming cup of tea, looking out at the gray day, as she started to write.

The book was not at all what she had planned. It had turned from a dry reference on herbal medicine into a fictional novel, to her great surprise. A historically accurate fictional novel involving a thirteenth-century herbal healer in a small village. There was the conniving, ambitious Prior at the cathedral, aspiring to become a bishop and willing to stop at nothing to get there. The village healer, trying to help the poor and the women of the village, but well aware she was always one accusation away from the noose or pyre. The handsome merchant, good-hearted and good-humored, hoping to win the heart of the young herbalist. Peppered throughout the book were actual herbal remedies for the illnesses various characters had in the story: cloves for pain and toothache, coriander for fever, sage to build strength.

It was part romantic page-turner and part herbal recipe book. She had no idea where it was even coming from, but every time she sat down to write, more of this story of church and medicine and lust and betrayal poured out of her and onto the screen of her laptop. It was only when the alarm went off on her phone that she realized it was time to head to Mrs. Welsh's house.

Eden walked the lane to Mrs. Welsh's, as she now did almost daily, helping Mrs. Welsh make tinctures and teas, or hanging and drying herbs, or sometimes helping with more mundane things that were challenging to an old woman—changing a lightbulb from atop a little ladder, or moving armfuls of firewood from the garden into the basket by the fireplace. Mrs. Welsh shared stories from her life in the village, life during World War II, or even earlier than that, and then stories that had been passed down for generations.

Eden had asked if she could record their meetings, and Mrs. Welsh had no objection, so Eden was able to enjoy the afternoons and not worry about remembering details because her little digital recorder was making a copy of everything said, as the two enjoyed their tasks together.

That day, Eden wanted to know more about Mrs. Welsh herself. Not as an herbalist, but as a woman.

"Can I ask you something?" Eden started, feeling uncomfortable switching her line of questioning from the herbal to the personal for the first time.

"Anything, dear," Mrs. Welsh replied.

"When did you lose your husband?"

There was a pause and then Mrs. Welsh replied, "Ah yes. Frank." She looked into the distance with a wistful smile. "It was a very long time ago now that I lost him. I had just one love in my life. But he gave me a lifetime of love in the short time we were together. His name was Frank Welsh. We fell in love at school here, and we married very young, at just eighteen. And just one week after our wedding, he was sent to fight in France. It was during World War II, you see. And he was killed. Just two weeks into his service, he and most of his battalion were killed trying to hold a trench line somewhere in France." Her face looked so sad that Eden regretted having asked.

The old woman walked slowly over to the mantelpiece and took down an old, framed photo of a handsome young man in uniform. She wiped away some invisible dust and smiled at it. "This is my Frank," she said, offering the photo to Eden.

Eden looked into the young, innocent face with sadness, knowing, as the subject didn't when the picture was taken, how short a time he had left in his life.

"He's very handsome," Eden said, meaning it. "And he has kind eyes."

"Yes, he was both of those things. The most handsome man I ever met. And the kindest. A very rare combination, that," she said. "I never did meet anyone I cared for half as much after he died. I only wish we'd had more time together. But, as we all know, nothing is promised. I'm just so glad we didn't wait to marry as many told us to, since we were so young. We loved each other strongly, we did." She looked adoringly at the photo. "We didn't have children. I am sorry for that, but we hardly had a chance to try before he received his orders. That's how I knew someone else would be coming to me to continue my work," she said with a sad smile.

"I'm so sorry, Mrs. Welsh," Eden said with sympathy in her eyes. "That is very sad."

"Yes, it most certainly was at the time, but there is a plan for all of us. And I'm happy now, because I know I will see him again soon, when my time here is done."

And with that, she gave the photo an extra polish with her

apron, and carefully replaced it on the mantel.

"And tell me about your family, your mother. Was she an herbalist?" Eden asked.

Mrs. Welsh's face brightened up. "She was indeed. She was one of the finest healers this village has ever seen. Mathilda was her name. Everyone called her Tilda. She was a lovely woman. Tall and slender and beautiful. I have no idea how she had a little round daughter like me." She laughed. "She and my father were very happy. He was a civil servant, worked for the town of Newmarket for forty-five years. Can't have been the most interesting job, but he never complained. He loved my mother with such joy. He lit up when she walked in the room, even after sixty years. Married sixty-three years, they were. Until he died.

"I was their only child. They were sad about that. They would have loved more children, but my mother became very ill with an infection after my birth, and she was unable to have more children. Some said that was because her real work was healing, and if she'd had a dozen children, as she and my father would have liked, then there would never have been time for healing." Mrs. Welsh looked out the window for a moment and then added, "They were probably right too. She had the gift. The knowing. She could know what was causing a child's fever just by touch—whether it was an infection in the lung, or white throat fever, or a blocked bowel. She knew. People came from miles around to be treated by her. She was a local celebrity, I guess you'd say. She was an incredible woman. Died at ninety-seven, and sharp as a tack until the day she died."

Just then there was a knock at the door, and Mrs. Welsh ran her hands down her dress, as if to smooth out both it and her emotions, before answering.

"Muriel! Wonderful, come in, come in," Mrs. Welsh said. "Muriel, this is our new villager, Eden. She's Mabel's granddaughter and is staying at the cottage now," she informed her friend.

Muriel, an equally old, but not at all frail-looking, woman stuck out a hand and gave Eden a firm handshake. "Very pleased to meet you, my dear. And welcome to our little corner of heaven," she said, smiling.

"Thank you very much. I'm very happy to be here," Eden returned.

"Muriel and I have plans to go to dinner tonight, Eden. Just at the pub. Would you care to join us?" Mrs. Welsh asked.

Eden seriously considered saying yes, thinking of the empty cottage waiting for her, but, clearly, the friends had plans to catch up, and she knew she would just be in the way.

"Very kind of you to ask, but no thank you. I really must go home and take care of Wellie," she said, using her dog as an excuse.

"Well, very nice to meet you," Muriel said in her loud, confident tone. "Perhaps another time."

Eden agreed that would be nice, and she took her recording device and her handbag, thanked Mrs. Welsh, and walked home.

She let herself into the cottage just as the sun was setting and felt pathetic at how glad she was that Wellie was there and that he made a big fuss over her coming home. She loved this village, but the evenings did get lonely. And nights like tonight she felt ridiculous. All these people lived here. They had lives here. They had jobs and kids and went to parents' day at school and to birthday parties for aunts and uncles, and all the business that makes a life full and makes one feel a part of something.

Eden realized then that she'd always looked in the windows of homes and wished she'd been invited in. She'd never felt at home in her own life. She also realized she needed to change that, or she would never feel at home anywhere, never find where she fit. That kind of loneliness was inside, and it would follow you to the ends of the earth, she thought.

Maybe Barton Heath would be the place she'd finally feel she'd come home.

Chapter 8

The next day was the busiest yet at Mrs. Welsh's. She and Eden were just having a cup of tea before heading into the garden for a lesson on what was growing when there was a knock at the door.

"Sorry to bother you so early, Mrs. Welsh, Eden," the man said, looking at Eden and nodding. "But Karen had the baby the other day," he said with a mixture of pride and nervousness.

"Oh, how wonderful!" Mrs. Welsh exclaimed, clapping her hands together. "Congratulations to both of you."

"Yes, congratulations," Eden added.

"Thank you. He's a fine strapping boy. Big and healthy, the midwife said. Nicholas, we've named him," he went on. "But Karen lost a lot of blood. They kept her at the hospital an extra day and sent her home yesterday. They said she was fine, but she's ever so exhausted and pale as a sheet. I thought maybe you could come take a look. They've given us some iron tablets, but they bind her up something awful. She's very uncomfortable."

"Absolutely, we will be over in just a few minutes. Let us brew a tea to build energy and blood, and a little something to unbind her, though we don't want to do too much forceful work on her. Right now is about building her up. As for you, you can have beef and chicken broth ready for her for the next several days, in addition to anything else she eats. Now, you run along home, and we'll be there soon," Mrs. Welsh said, with that reassuring and slightly authoritative tone that made everyone relax and feel like someone was finally in control.

Before the two had time to leave with the tea for the new mother, old Agatha Foxworthy, a widow in a large house on the edge of town, who was not particularly friendly or well-liked in the village, but always pleased to see Mrs. Welsh, arrived at the cottage.

"Yoo-hoo!" she called from just inside the front door, having knocked and then stepped right in, as some of the older clients, who had known Mrs. Welsh for decades, tended to do. "It's me, Agatha!"

Mrs. Welsh stepped out of the kitchen, wiping her hands on her apron, and the two old acquaintances gave each other brief kisses on the cheek.

"Is it the stomach, dear?" Mrs. Welsh asked straight off.

"Exactly," Agatha confirmed. "Burning. Just awful. Kept me up last night it was so bad." She pressed on her abdomen, as if to emphasize the point. "I'm on something the doctor gave me, Permacid or Paracalm, or something like that. Antacid. But your tea helps so much, and it helps right away, which is what I need at three in the morning when my acid stomach flares up."

"Of course, dear. Eden can just mix you up a bag of herbs and you can make the tea any time your stomach is sour. Do you mind if Eden takes care of that, while I finish what I was doing?" Mrs. Welsh asked, intentionally drawing Eden into the hands-on aspect of the visit.

"Um, yes, that would be all right," the woman said with slight reserve, making it clear that she would have preferred her old friend, but was willing to take the formula from the newcomer.

"Wonderful," Mrs. Welsh said with a smile. "I will see you soon, Agatha. We will drop the herbs at your house in a bit. Do drop by anytime!" she called back over her shoulder as she tottered into the kitchen.

There was another visit by a young man with an infected cut, and finally a fourth from a mother with a headache, and the two herbalists fell into their chairs by the fire and decided they would skip the lesson in the garden and do it another day. Word had spread that there was a new young woman out with Mrs. Welsh, and an American no less! But, as the villagers got to know her, and they saw the trust which Mrs. Welsh placed in her, Eden was accepted as an apprentice, and the village was glad to know there was someone there to help their dear old friend, who couldn't do everything on her own the way she once could.

Eden was daydreaming about James when she arrived at Mrs. Welsh's the next afternoon. When the door opened, she saw that Mrs. Welsh was in her dressing gown. Eden was quite shocked.

"It's all right, my dear," the old woman explained. "I'm just a bit under the weather today. I've made myself a tea, and I'll be right as rain in a day or two. Just a cold, I'm sure. But I'm so glad you're here."

"I'm so sorry you're sick. What can I get you? Can I make you a pot of tea? Or something to eat?" Eden asked.

"No, thank you, dear. I've had some tea and biscuits and now think I'll have a little rest. But there is something you can do. Little Timmy Bradley is ill. His mother is quite concerned. The doctor has him on an antibiotic, but he isn't getting better. He has a fever of 38 and a terrible cough. She asked if we'd bring a remedy for him. But, of course, I can't go. I'm not up to it, I'm afraid, and also, I wouldn't want to give him whatever I've got. So, I need you to make up a formula and take it to their house. Would you do that, dear?" the old woman asked kindly. "And when you're done with that, little Tommy Carter was round just now. He said his dad isn't feeling well, was being sick. I'm fairly sure I know the cause of that. The man drinks heavily, poor

Tommy. His mother died last year, and now he's stuck with a father who drinks himself half to death. He's called on me before, and I take round a tea of willow bark and milk thistle. It helps with the headache he'll have tomorrow, and with cleansing the liver. Not sure how much good we can do, but for Tommy's sake, I think we should try to help. Will you be all right handling both of those, my dear?" she asked with a weak smile.

"Yes, of course, I will," Eden replied. "Will they be all right with it just being me?"

"When Timmy's mother stopped by this morning, I told her I was ill, and I'd be sending you. They have total faith in you, my dear, because I do. Now I'd like you to choose a formula to make up. Cold gone to heat in his chest. You know what to do," she said with confidence. "And now, I think I'll take a little rest. Come see me when you're heading over, dear." And with that, she slowly mounted the little stairs and went into her bedroom and closed the door.

In the kitchen, Eden stood in a panic. Her first formula for an actual person. It was one thing to feel like an expert standing in a classroom in Manhattan, talking to a bunch of nineteen-year-olds. It was quite another to be mixing actual herbs for a very ill seven-year-old!

But then Eden took a deep breath and said to herself, "You know what you're doing. You've read all about this kind of thing, and you've learned from Mrs. Welsh. Now get to work."

Her little pep talk worked, and she deftly chose several jars of herbs and weighed out bits of each. Then, at the end, she stood and thought of each of her two little patients. A little sparkle came over the jar of oregano for Timmy, and the same light showed up on the jar of St. John's Wort for Tommy Carter's dad. She combined each formula into its own pot and then covered them with boiling water.

After the tea had steeped, she strained the liquids into two large jars and left them to cool for a moment while she went upstairs to check on Mrs. Welsh.

She opened the door quietly after a soft knock and found her mentor sitting in bed, reading.

"Come in, dear. And tell me what you made up," Mrs. Welsh said.

Eden recounted the herbs in each formula and told her she had made up the willow bark and milk thistle, with St. John's Wort added in, for Mr. Carter.

Mrs. Welsh grinned widely. "Absolutely spot on. Just the things I would have chosen myself. Very good, my dear. Now Timmy's family lives in the council housing estate, just past the church, at number twenty-three. Tommy's is number six. Off you go."

Eden went to the kitchen, put the large jars in a basket, and headed out to find little Timmy and Tommy.

Timmy's mother answered the door. The first thing Eden noticed was the noise. Several children were racing around, tackling each other or yelling. One was crying, strapped in a highchair. Mrs. Bradley looked harried, in a dirty apron and with her hair sticking out from under several bobby pins.

"Tanya, you hush that baby right now, and Jason and Anthony, stop it this instant!" she screamed into the background. She turned back to Eden. "So sorry, my dear. Bit of a madhouse on rainy days when I can't send them outside. Come in, come in."

Eden stepped into the cluttered house and was immediately shown upstairs. There was a bedroom with three beds crammed in it and atop one sat Timmy. He was pale, with dark circles under his eyes, and as if on cue, as soon as Eden stepped in, he launched into a racking cough that rattled and shook the poor boy.

When he finally stopped, Eden could see he was very sick, indeed, and his poor mother looked sick herself with worry.

"Doc has him on antibiotics, which should have worked by

now, but he's still ever so sick, you see. He has another appointment tomorrow, but I'm worried half to death."

Eden was secretly worried herself and glad that the boy had been to see a doctor. But she also had faith in the powerful remedies Mrs. Welsh had taught her, and though she couldn't always explain why, she knew that they worked.

"Well, Mrs. Bradley, Timmy is to have half a cup of this tea every two hours until it runs out. That will be in about two days. At that time, Mrs. Welsh or I will come back and see how he is and make him a new formula based on how his symptoms have changed by then. All right?" Eden asked calmly.

"Oh, thank you ever so much. I'm so grateful. Tell Mrs. Welsh I hope she's all better herself very soon. And, um, I can pay you on Monday, if that's all right. Reg gets paid on Mondays," she added, looking at the floor in embarrassment.

"Oh goodness, don't you worry about that. I'll be back in a few days anyway to check on the patient. We'll talk about it then. Don't give it a second thought," Eden said. Then she added, "Timmy, your mum has some tea for you to take. You're lucky. This mixture actually doesn't taste bad! Some of them taste like mud warmed up. But yours has honey and mint, as well as lots of other things, so it's quite good. Be sure to drink it all up!" She smiled.

"I will, miss. Thank…" Timmy tried to reply, but the effort of talking sent him into another coughing fit and Mrs. Bradley quickly showed Eden out.

As she walked down the road Eden was on cloud nine. She was worried about Timmy, but felt confident the herbs and medicine would make him better. She left the little house feeling elated. She had treated her first patient on her own, got it right, and been totally welcomed and accepted by the family. She was using what she had spent years learning, using it to do good. Using it for real. And she was dizzy with delight.

It wouldn't last.

Her next call was to Tommy Carter's house, also in the block of council houses. She knocked, and the door swung open.

Inside, a little boy who looked about five years old sat on the floor watching television. It was very dark inside. All the blinds were drawn, even though it was the middle of the day. The room was a total mess, with microwave dinner boxes, newspapers, and beer cans all over the floor.

The little boy looked up and, seeing Eden, leaped to his feet. The look of worry on his face made Eden want to cry. He should have been outside, racing around on a bike or playing games, not sitting, waiting for someone to come help his drunken lump of a father.

"Hello, miss. Thank you ever so much for coming. I'm that worried about me dad. He's been being sick all afternoon."

The two looked over to the sofa and saw Tommy's father, sound asleep, his mouth hanging open, food, and what was very likely vomit, on his t-shirt. It was unacceptable.

Eden turned back to the little boy and knelt down. "I'm Eden Martin," she said kindly. "I'm Mrs. Welsh's helper. I have some tea that will help your dad feel better when he wakes up. But I don't think I should leave you here like this. Who is looking after you?"

"I'm all right," Tommy said. "He's always been like this. Me mum used to look after me, but she died. So now, when me dad gets like this, I just eat some crisps and watch TV. He'll be better tomorrow. For a while."

The fact that this was clearly normal to this beautiful little boy made Eden's blood boil. How could the father be this selfish!

Just then the form on the sofa stirred and opened his eyes.

"Who the 'ell are you?" he shouted as he stood up quickly, staggered and almost fell, then steadied himself.

Eden felt a mixture of fear and outrage. "I'm Eden Martin. I am helping Mrs. Welsh, and Tommy here was kind enough to come around and ask us to bring you something to make you feel better." She wanted to add "You drunken ass!" to the end of her sentence, but she restrained herself.

"You did *what*?" the man bellowed at the boy.

Tommy shrank back and stood behind a chair. The drunken man walked over and slapped Tommy hard on the face. The boy fell to the ground crying.

"How dare you share me personal business with 'ole village! You're nothing but trouble, you are!" he screamed at the boy, who had tears silently streaming down his cheeks.

Now her fear was gone, and Eden felt only outrage. "You stop it right now, you idiot! You're drunk. How could you hit a child!? He's done nothing but try to help. I am going to report you to the authorities. Look at this place. It's not fit for a dog, let alone a little boy." She stopped as the large man began striding across the little room right at her.

He put two hands on her and shoved her so hard that Eden fell backward out the door. The door instantly shut, and she heard the lock turn.

She stood up in complete shock. She had never been treated

like this in her life, and she couldn't believe that it had just happened.

She started banging on the door and yelling, "You open this door instantly. I am going to call the police!" But to no avail. There were no neighbors around, and she wasn't sure what to do.

She got out her cell phone and did call the police. She was told a constable would be around within the hour. They had to come from Newmarket, as Barton Heath had no police force of its own.

She waited, sitting on the curb outside the home. Half an hour later, a police car pulled up, and two constables got out.

"Hello. Are you the person who called the police?" one of them asked as Eden stood from the curb.

"Yes. I was called to this house by a little boy inside, who was worried about his father. When the father woke up, he was drunk as a skunk and, as I said, was angry that the child had asked for help. He hit the boy, hard, right across the face! It's also a pig pen in there, filthy and unhealthy for a child. You have to do something!" She ended her passionate speech slightly out of breath.

"All right, ma'am. Thank you for your statement. It will be put in the record, and we'll go have a chat with Mr. Carter," the officer said.

"Good, I'm coming with you. That boy needs proper care,"

Eden said, striding toward the door.

The police officer put a hand on her arm. "I know you just want to help," he said with a soft tone. "But you can't come in, ma'am. We need to defuse the situation and sort out what's going on in there. You can't legally come in, I'm afraid. We will make sure the boy is all right. Thank you, ma'am. You can go now."

Eden realized that the brush-off wasn't a suggestion; it was an order. And the deep satisfaction she had felt just an hour before, leaving Timmy's house, was shattered.

The policemen knocked on the door, and Eden saw little Tommy over the shoulders of the policemen, again looking worried and frightened.

She winked at him and blew him a kiss. "I'll come see you soon Tommy, all right?" she called out.

He nodded back once, then the policemen stepped inside, and the door closed.

Eden turned and walked away. From elation to despair. *I suppose that's what happens when you get your nose out of a book and into real lives*, she thought, as she walked slowly away.

Back at Mrs. Welsh's cottage, she brought up some juice and tea and toast for Mrs. Welsh and told her about both encounters.

Mrs. Welsh was pleased with the report on Timmy, and then said with a sad shake of her head, "Poor Tommy. Mr. Carter is a drunken fool and a violent man. I wish so much I could do more for the boy. But even just going around with the tea is something. It helps Tommy know there are grownups in the village who care. And maybe this time something will happen, now that someone actually saw the wee child be hit and the police were called. Good for you for calling them and getting that all down on paper," her old friend said. "I wondered where you were all this time."

Soon Mrs. Welsh looked tired again, so Eden added some coal to the tiny fire in her friend's bedroom fireplace and let herself out. When she got home, there was a message on her machine. James had called.

"Hi, Eden, it's James. James Beck...the vet. I just wondered if you were still interested in grabbing dinner. If you are, my number is 01223 48790. Cheers!"

Eden replayed the message on her machine three times, smiling as she did so. Then she poured herself a glass of wine and called him back.

"Hello?"

"James?" she asked.

"Yes?"

"Oh, hi. It's Eden," she said, then waited, unsure what to say next. "I got your message. You are funny 'James. James Beck, the vet.'" She laughed. "I knew who you were at just James." She smiled and thought, *I've been waiting on tenterhooks for you to call. Of course, I knew who it was!*

"Oh. Okay. Great. Well, I wondered if you were still interested in grabbing dinner some time?" he asked.

"Yeah, that sounds great," she said, forcing her voice to sound casual and forcing her mouth *not* to say, "Yes, Yes! When? Tonight?"

"Okay great!" She could hear the enthusiasm in his voice, and it made her heart do a tiny flip. "How about Saturday night, six o'clock? I was thinking we could go to Sienna. It's a new Italian place in Newmarket, and the food is supposed to be fantastic. I've been hearing about it for months. Can't wait to try it out. And...um...also it will be great to see you again," he added at the end, sounding like a teenager unsure of what to say. "I'll pick you up at six!"

"Perfect, thanks. I'm really looking forward to it," she said calmly, while she silently did a little dance, phone in hand, celebrating.

"Great, see you then!" he said.

Chapter 9

Three days had passed since Eden's encounter with the sad little boy and the drunken father, and though she planned to visit Tommy within the next day or two, she hadn't made it round to his house yet.

At that moment, she wasn't thinking of the unlucky little boy at all. She was sitting, daydreaming about the dinner date, and what on earth she would wear, when she heard a very soft knock at the door. She wasn't even sure she had heard it, but she got up to check.

When she opened the door, there was Tommy Carter looking very small and very upset. Eden looked out into the garden to see if anyone was with him, but he seemed to be alone.

"Hi, sweetheart. What can I do for you?" she asked, bending down to be nearer his level.

"Well...um, can I come in, please?" the boy asked timidly.

"Of course, you can come in. Does your dad know you're here?" she asked.

"No!" he said, sounding suddenly scared. "Don't tell me dad!" he added quickly.

Eden led him into the living room and gave him a glass of milk and a plate of cookies. The milk and all the cookies disappeared in an instant as he hungrily wolfed them down.

"Okay," Eden started. "Now tell me why you're here."

Tommy was very thin and wore clothes that were too small for him and didn't look like they'd been washed recently. Eden started to worry for the little boy.

"Well...um..." He looked very nervous and picked at his fingernails. "Well, you see, it's just me and me dad, and I know Mrs. Welsh is a bit ill, people are sayin'. Plus, you know, she's an old lady, like. I thought maybe you would be better...well, you might understand better. Me dad gets really mad a lot. And he drinks a lot of beer. He says it's cause me mum died and 'cause his back hurts. He's a laborer over on High Fallow Farm. But it's not cause of me mum, 'cause he drank loads before too." The little boy was talking quickly, as if all of this had been bottled up, and now he was finally letting it all rush out at once.

Eden was genuinely concerned. "Tommy, are you all right?" she asked. "Is there no one else who takes care of you sometimes? A granny maybe? Or an auntie?"

The tiny boy's lip started to tremble, and tears ran down his cheeks.

"I don't know, miss. Me dad says it's just me and 'im. I

'aven't got a granny or auntie. Just me and me dad."

"Okay," Eden said. "So, you need help with your dad, that's why you're here?"

"Yes, miss. I can't wake him up. It's been all day. I think he needs one of them teas to help him be healthy."

Eden's heart felt for this scared little boy. It was already very clear that his father would need a lot more than herbal tea to sort out his problems, but she said nothing. She told him she would walk him back home and talk to his dad and see if she could help. Inside she was nervous, her mind was racing.

Was this the appropriate thing to do? Was it the safe thing to do? Should she call the police? But wasn't that being dramatic? Why not just go have a chat with Tommy's dad? Maybe today he would be sober, and it could be handled like adults. Then again, if he'd been asleep all day, as Tommy said, then that was unlikely. Was it safe for her to go alone? It was the middle of the day, and they lived in the middle of a crowded narrow street of row houses. There would probably be lots of people around.

She was still having this conversation with herself in her head when they reached Tommy's door. He pushed it open and walked in.

The first thing that hit Eden was the smell. It was awful. Old food, sweat, she wasn't sure what…a foul mixture of odors made her almost retch. It had been there the other day, too, but for some reason seemed stronger today.

And then her eyes took it in. There were old plates with bits of food all over the place, the counter, the floor, the armchair seat. Cans of beer littered the floor, and ashtrays overflowed on any flat surface that would hold one. The curtains were drawn, and it was dark and depressing, despite it being a beautiful sunny day outside.

Tommy stood in the middle of the room, clearly not realizing how shocking his home was to someone not used to such neglect and filth.

Eden spotted Tommy's father on the sofa. He looked sound asleep. *Passed out drunk, more like*, Eden thought.

She stood in the doorway, still hesitant to get too involved too quickly.

"Mr. Carter?" she called out. Then after a pause, "Mr. Carter!" more loudly. Nothing.

She moved over to the sofa and looked at the man, and her stomach seized.

His eyes were slightly open, and his lips were blue. She reached down and took his wrist in her hand, feeling for a pulse. There was none. Then she felt the side of his neck...nothing. His skin was cold. He was dead. *Oh my God*, she thought. *What the hell am I going to do?*

Eden turned and saw Tommy looking at her hopefully, still certain she could brew him a tea and make all their problems go away. What was she going to do?

She needed to call 999, she needed to start CPR, but she didn't want Tommy seeing any of that.

She grabbed his hand. "Tommy, you are going to Mrs. Welsh's, just for a while, there's a good boy, so I can see about your dad. You know her cottage. She's just down the lane. Now go there and tell her Eden sent you, and that I'll be there soon, okay, sweetheart? You run along now." She shooed the boy toward the lane and closed the front door.

She called 999 and did CPR, using her handkerchief as a barrier, which she thought probably didn't do anything, but it made her feel better.

After what seemed like an eternity, the ambulance arrived. They pronounced Mr. Carter dead at the scene. They said he had been dead for several hours.

As the paramedics loaded him onto a stretcher, covered him,

and put him in the ambulance, driving away without lights or sound, Eden found herself alone in the middle of the filthy house with tears running down her cheeks. Then she remembered Tommy. Poor Tommy, who had already lost his mother, had now lost his father too. And there were no relatives that he knew of. But, certainly, there must be. He was just a small child. What would happen to him if he had no relatives?

She closed the door behind her, said nothing to the several neighbors now gathered around looking and whispering, and walked straight to the little cottage with the blue door.

Eden knocked and then let herself in, which had become her habit by now. She entered the living room and found Tommy seated in front of the fire, eating a big plate of chicken pie with a mound of mashed potatoes next to it. He looked as if he hadn't seen a hot meal in months the way he was going at it.

"Hello, Tommy. Look at you eat! You're going to be a foot taller by tomorrow at that rate!" Eden said.

The boy smiled and went back to the pie, and Eden took advantage of his being distracted and signaled with a slight nod of her head for Mrs. Welsh to join her in the kitchen.

"Oh, the poor, poor dear." Mrs. Welsh said when she heard the news. "Oh, my heart breaks for the wee boy."

"So what should I do?" Eden asked. "I'm going to call the police now. I guess they'll call social services, or however that works here in England. They'll have to find someone to take him. I pray he's wrong and that he does have some family somewhere!"

"Yes, dear. Let the right people know. They will do their jobs and find the best solution. I am sure he will find a good home, I feel that. And who knows, maybe it will be better than the one he had. I think it couldn't get much worse, from what it sounds like he's had this past year since his mum died."

"Yes," Eden agreed. "The house was disgusting. I can't imagine raising a child in that. And the violence. It won't be easy for the poor boy. But maybe, in the long run...I don't know. I think I'm in shock, to be honest. This has all happened so fast."

Mrs. Welsh sat down and let out an almost imperceptible sigh, and Eden realized that her old friend still wasn't fully well. She had sent Tommy here in a panic, because she didn't know where else to send him that was close by. But now Mrs. Welsh looked drawn and tired, and she coughed.

"Thank you so very much, Mrs. Welsh. I'm going to take Tommy to my house while I try to sort this out," Eden said, standing up. "I'll let you know what happens. But you need some rest. You're not well yourself. I promise I'll be back tomorrow to let you know what's going on."

Mrs. Welsh agreed, and Eden and her little companion set out for Eden's house.

When they got to the cottage, Eden lit the fire, to cheer them up as much as to warm them up. She made Tommy some hot chocolate and gave him a big slice of cake she had in her fridge.

As he ate his snack, Eden called the police from the kitchen so he wouldn't hear.

"Newmarket Constabulary," a gruff voice answered.

"Uh, hello. This is Eden Martin in Barton Heath," she whispered into the phone, desperate for Tommy not to overhear.

"You'll have to speak up, can't hear you," the man said authoritatively into the phone.

Eden spoke up. "This is Eden Martin in Barton Heath. I wanted to talk to someone about a child. I mean, I have a child here with me because his father just died, and I don't know what I'm supposed to do."

"Okay, hang on, miss. Let me transfer you to someone who can help you," he said, and after a brief pause, Eden heard a new voice.

"Hello, Detective Constable Perry here. How can I help you?" the new man's voice said.

"My name is Eden Martin. I'm calling from Barton Heath, and I have a young child with me whose mother died last year and whose father just died today. He doesn't think he has any other relatives, and I just don't know what I'm supposed to do with him. I was hoping you could tell me."

"How old is the child, ma'am?" DC Perry asked.

"I think he's six," Eden replied. She peeked around the corner into the kitchen, but Tommy was still happily engrossed in his dessert.

"And his father just died how?" he asked.

"He had a drinking problem. I think that may have led to it. But I don't really know. I had met the boy once before, and he came to me for help because he thought his dad was sick, but, in fact, he was dead. The ambulance took him away an hour ago, and now I have this little boy in my kitchen, with no idea what to do," she said, inhaling slowly to try and remain calm.

"Well, it's very late. We are on a skeleton crew at this time of night. You can bring the boy down and we will contact local services first thing in the morning, but at this time of night, he may end up having to wait here till morning," he said, unemotionally.

Eden imagined this lost little boy spending the night sitting on a hard chair in a police station. "Would it be possible for me to keep him here? I mean, as you say, it's so late, and he's exhausted. I'm just down the road from where he lives. Lived. And he's comfortable with me. Could I maybe bring him in in the morning when the right people are on duty?"

There was a pause on the phone, and then DC Perry said, "Yes, I guess I don't see why not. That would probably be the best thing. Thank you. Let me collect your information. I'll need your name, address, phone number, that sort of thing. You won't have to come here if we wait till tomorrow. I can have someone from child services at your house first thing tomorrow morning to get him," he said, and with that, it was decided that Tommy would stay the night in the cottage with Eden.

Later the next day, Eden could give a statement about finding Mr. Carter to a police officer who would come to her house.

Only after finishing off his treat and coming to sit next to Eden in the living room did Tommy ask questions. His eyes were heavy with exhaustion and the wonderful feeling of both a full belly and a warm house. But he had questions.

"When will me dad be better so I can go home?" he asked,

looking at Eden with such unguarded innocence that it made her heart ache.

Eden wished she'd asked the policeman what to say. Should she tell Tommy his father was dead? That he was an orphan now? She wasn't trained in how to handle this sort of thing, and she was terrified that, if she handled it badly, she could scar him for life.

So she sidestepped and said, "Sweetheart, your dad is with some people right now, who are taking care of him. It's so very late, the best thing is for us to get a good night's sleep, and we can talk all about things tomorrow." *It isn't entirely untrue, I'm sure there are people dealing with Tommy's dad this evening. Just not in the way Tommy is imagining,* Eden thought. "For tonight, we will have a sleepover here, okay?"

The little boy's eyelids were heavy and his belly full, so he simply nodded and followed Eden upstairs. Eden ran a warm bath. She found a long-sleeved t-shirt of hers and left it in the bathroom for the boy to wear to bed. And as he was soaking in the tub, she took his filthy clothes downstairs and threw them in the washer.

Half an hour later, she was tucking Tommy into bed in the guest room and reading him one of the children's books that she herself had been read as a child, *Rikki-Tikki-Tavi*. The boy was enthralled and listened to the classic tale of the little boy and the deadly cobra who lived in his garden. First with wide eyes, then with eyes half-open, and then he couldn't fight it anymore and fell sound asleep. Eden quietly closed the book, leaned over, and kissed his cheek.

"Good night, sweet boy," she whispered, knowing that tomorrow was going to be a very hard day.

Eden barely slept that night. Her heart ached knowing that Tommy would soon find out his father had died. And then he would be taken from the village, the only place he had ever known—his school, his neighbors, his friends—and would eventually be placed with some relative he had never met. And that was the best-case scenario. If he, in fact, didn't have any family, he would end up in a group home. An orphanage.

*

Tommy woke late the next morning, and was so cheerful as he ate his cereal, that it made her even sadder.

Eden handed the boy his clothes.

"Oh, thank you, miss. Wow, these look great. Thank you!" he said, as if clean clothes were a rare treat.

He looked better already, she thought, with some good food in him, bathed, and in clean clothes, even if they were too small.

Then there was a knock at the door. Eden's stomach lurched, and she went to let the social worker in.

They all sat in the living room looking at one another. The woman wore a sensible skirt suit and jacket, with a clipboard and briefcase, and sat in an armchair by the window. Eden and Tommy sat side by side on the sofa.

"Tommy, my name is Jennifer, and I'm here to help you and your friend, Eden, okay?" she asked gently.

"Okay," Tommy replied, unconcerned.

"I know you are wondering where your dad is. And I want to tell you what happened," she went on. "Yesterday, your father got very sick. Unfortunately, there was nothing the doctors could do to save him, even though they tried their very best. Your father died, Tommy. I'm very sorry," Jennifer said with kindness but no sadness, in her voice. Then she waited and watched Tommy.

Eden was relieved that someone who knew what they were doing had told him.

But Tommy's reaction wasn't what she expected. He didn't cry.

"He died?" he finally asked.

"Yes, Tommy. I'm afraid he did," Jennifer replied.

"So, he's with my mum in heaven, right?"

"That's right," she agreed.

He was silent for a long moment, clearly thinking this through. "He wasn't very nice," Tommy stated matter-of-factly.

It shocked Eden, but Jennifer took it in stride.

"Why is that, Tommy?" Jennifer asked.

"He was really mean to me mum. He hit her a lot. Even when she was sick. And then he was mean to me after me mum died. Not hitting me much, but just drinking lots of beer and yelling at me, and he never got me dinner or nothing. He was pretty mean. But I guess I'm glad he's in heaven anyway."

The social worker and Tommy talked for an hour, a combination of letting him express himself and ask questions, and Jennifer expertly getting information that she needed without alarming him.

After the hour Tommy was clearly bored. "Do you have a ball, miss?" the boy asked Eden.

"I told you, Tommy, you can call me Eden," she said, smiling. "And I'm afraid I don't have a ball. There used to be an old cricket set in the garden shed when I was little. It's probably still there, if you want to play with that."

Tommy ran out back to look through the damp old garden shed, while Jennifer and Eden talked.

"We did a preliminary search of council records early this morning," Jennifer said, "but I'm afraid it didn't turn up any relatives for Tommy. When Tommy's mother got very ill, a social worker was sent to the Carters' from National Health to make sure Tommy would have someone to take care of him, in the event that his mother died. Other than his father, there was no other family. She and her husband had been only children, and their parents are dead." She paused and then added, "The social worker had been a bit concerned leaving Tommy with his dad—the place wasn't very clean and there was some evidence of drinking—but, at that time, there hadn't been any reports that he'd abused Tommy's mum, or Tommy himself, and without any evidence of wrongdoing, sadly, there wasn't an alternative. He was left there." Jennifer sighed. "Of course, I'll do a thoroughly exhaustive search to see if there is a family member anywhere, he could go to…a distant relative willing to have him, perhaps. In the meantime, I'll place him in a foster home or group home until we sort everything out," she explained.

Eden excused herself and got up from the sofa and went to the kitchen to make tea. It was a wonderful ritual, making tea. It bought you time, calmed the mind, and gave the hands something to do. She used the time to think.

What can I do? she thought as she filled the kettle at the sink. *I'm a busy working woman—even if work is writing and studying with Mrs. Welsh. I can't keep him. I don't even know him.*

She turned on the stove and put tea bags in the teapot.

And look at my own life. It's a mess I'm barely beginning to sort out. I don't need a child to take care of! But how could I send the little boy off to God knows where to stay with people who may be no better than his father had been? He's had such a hard life already and he's only six.

She put the lid on the teapot, and by the time she had carried the tray into the living room, the decision had been made. In the same impulsive way she'd decided to move to England, she decided to try and keep Tommy. Just for now. Just until they could find a placement for him. And in the same way she had decided to move to England, she knew without question this was the right choice.

"I'd like to keep him, just for now, since he has nowhere to go," Eden said to Jennifer.

Jennifer looked stunned.

"This way, Tommy can stay in his same school, play with his

friends, be in the village that is his home, while he deals with the fact that he has lost his other parent. Then, once something permanent has been lined up, once a relative had been found, Tommy can go to them," she said. "At least then he will be going to a known, safe, settled situation. Not be bounced all over the child welfare system. I don't know much about kids, but I can cook pasta and chicken nuggets, so I think I can manage for a while!" she added, trying to lighten the mood.

Jennifer asked a lot of hard questions, telling Eden that this was not a stray dog she had found (which Eden thought was funny since she had adopted one of those too!).

"This could be very tough," Jennifer said solemnly. "He may seem all right now, but he could have a lot of strong emotions in the coming days and weeks. Not to mention the practical side of taking care of a child his age, which is considerable. Are you sure you're able to take that on?"

"Yes. I'm sure," Eden said, and she was surprised to realize she meant it. "And he must have friends in the village, friends with mums and dads. And I know a few people myself, at this point. I can enlist their help if I need it." She hoped this would bolster her case. "I know it's not ideal." Then she looked into the front garden and saw the little boy with the skinny legs and arms, running around with the cricket bat, a big smile on his face. "But I can't just send him off into the system to an unknown fate. Anyway, it would only be for a few days, a couple of weeks at most, right?"

"It shouldn't take long, yes," Jennifer replied. "There will be reams of paperwork, though. You'll need to take a foster parenting course right away, and have someone approve your home as soon as possible, but all those are formalities, really. If you really think you can do this…" Instead of finishing her sentence, she walked over and hugged Eden. "I'm just beyond words to tell you how glad I am to find someone with such a big heart. This is exactly what is best for little Tommy," she said. "Let's call him in and tell him the news."

Chapter 10

The next morning, Eden was getting ready to take Tommy into Newmarket to get some clothes that fit and a few toys. A soccer ball was top of his list. The boy was clearly not used to being well taken care of, and every hot meal or kind gesture was greeted with a look of astonishment and gratitude that melted Eden's heart.

As Eden gathered her bag and coat, the phone rang. She let the answering machine pick it up, then stopped in her tracks.

James's voice said, "Just wanted to say I'm looking forward to tonight. I'll pick you up at six!"

Eden dived for the phone. "Hello? James?" In all the chaos of the past few days, she had completely forgotten about her date that night. Her heart sank.

Typical, she thought. *A dinner date with a gorgeous, smart, funny guy, and I've decided to take on a foster child. Classic Eden!* But then she looked over at Tommy, who was on the floor playing with Wellie while he waited for her, and she smiled and knew she was doing the right thing.

"Hi, I'm here," James said on the other end of the line.

"Great. Well…about tonight… Oh boy, where should I start?"

Eden said.

James listened silently to the story of Tommy and how he'd ended up at her house. When she was done explaining, there was a long silence, and she thought, *Go ahead, better get out before you get started with someone in the middle of all this*.

And then he said, "Wow. You are an amazing person, Eden Martin. Not many people would do that!"

She brightened.

He continued, "Okay, so how do we make this work? Let's see. Mrs. Innskeep, my nanny, is already lined up to watch Bea tonight. So, let's make the most of that. You go run your errands, and I'll meet you at your cottage at seven. How does that sound?"

"Okay," Eden said, "but I can't go out. I mean, I don't have a sitter, and I shouldn't leave him right now anyway."

"I know," said James. "Just leave it all up to me. I'll meet you at seven. Bye!" he said cheerfully and hung up.

Eden wasn't sure what to think of that, but Tommy was looking up at her expectantly.

"Are we going?" he asked.

"Yes, we sure are," Eden replied. "Soccer ball, here we come!"

Tommy leaped up and let out a cheer. You would think she'd just offered him a trip to Disneyland. The poor boy had had few treats in his life. Eden smiled, and they went out to get in her gran's old car and head to town.

In Newmarket, they went to Marks & Spencer and got Tommy several new outfits, one nice one, and three sets of jeans or sports pants and sweaters. She hated the nylon sports pants that all the boys wore now, but she knew that was the "in" thing, so she let him get them. She got socks and underwear and a pair of pajamas with Superman on them. He looked at the bags of clothes like it was Christmas morning. Then they went to the toy store.

"I 'aven't never been in a toy store," Tommy said matter-of-factly.

"Really?" Eden said. "Well then, let's not wait another minute!"

Half an hour later, they left with two big bags, containing a soccer ball, kite, foam basketball and hoop that could be hung in the living room, several board games, and a stuffed elephant, which he had picked out.

The elephant never actually made it into the bag, Tommy clung to it and wouldn't let it go, which Eden found adorable and sad at the same time. He had had a lot of loss. He wasn't taking any chances with his new stuffed friend.

They got back to the cottage at six, and Eden cooked up some fish sticks and peas, after which Tommy raced out front with his soccer ball, Wellie running around behind him. Eden took the break to head upstairs, wash her face, put on some makeup, and change into a cross-fronted black top with a low neck, which accentuated her good points (her voluptuous breasts), and hid the parts she considered problem areas (her tummy). She squirted on a bit of perfume, added some silver hoop earrings, and headed downstairs to pour herself a glass of wine to steady her nerves.

At seven on the dot, James arrived. She opened the door to find him with two bags full of groceries. Two bottles of wine poked their necks out of the top of one bag.

"I'm going to cook for you guys!" was the first thing out of his mouth.

Eden noticed the bulge of James's muscles under his cotton shirt as he held the heavy bags. He had a five o'clock shadow on his normally clean-shaven face, and his hair had characteristically fallen slightly in front of one eye. His full lips were pulled up at one corner in a half-smile.

Eden felt her breath catch in her throat. She stood to the side wordlessly, afraid her voice might come out as shaky as she felt.

James slid past her, brushing unintentionally against her leg as he did. Eden felt a tingle run through her, and she closed the door and knocked back the rest of the wine in her glass for strength.

Eden introduced Tommy, and then James got busy in the kitchen right away, chopping onions and garlic and sautéing it in olive oil, which instantly filled the house with the most wonderful smell.

Tommy sat on a stool, watching in fascination. "I never seen a man cooking before," the boy said, as if he were witnessing some strange, unnatural event.

"Well, you have now!" James said with a smile. "You can help," he added, and Tommy jumped off the stool, eager to be involved.

James opened the can of crushed tomatoes and handed it to Tommy. "You pour that into the saucepan, okay?" James picked the little boy up, holding him safely away from the hot stove, but close enough to pour the contents in.

"Okay," Tommy said with nervous seriousness. He poured the tomatoes into the saucepan but looked panicked when a big drop of tomato sauce landed on the floor.

James just smiled. "Well done! An excellent cook in the making!"

Tommy beamed. When the meal was done, he ate a big bowl of the delicious pasta.Soon it was bedtime, and Eden took the little boy up to the guest room, tucked him in with Ellie the stuffed elephant, read him a short story, and sat with him as he drifted off to sleep.

She headed downstairs with her stomach fluttering. Now they were alone. She was excited and nervous at the same time.

While she was upstairs, James had set the table. He'd lit the two candles that always sat atop the table, and set out plates, napkins, and two glasses of red wine. The dining room was a small room off to the side of the living room, divided only by one large, ancient beam that ran floor to ceiling on the side of the doorway. There were no walls between the two rooms, which was a cozy layout, allowing you to sit at the dining table and see the fire in the living room's enormous fireplace.

"Wow," Eden said, as she came back downstairs. "You can come over anytime!" She laughed.

James smiled. "I couldn't boil an egg before Jane died. But Bea needed feeding, so I learned fast."

Eden sat down. James served her a big bowl of pasta with

Bolognese sauce and dished some salad into her side bowl. Then he sat down himself.

His dirty blond hair always seemed to flop into his eye on one side, she noticed. That, combined with his handsome face and near-permanent grin, made him both sexy and playful at the same time. The combination completely undid Eden, who couldn't stop her imagination from envisioning tearing off his shirt, even as her mind told her she didn't even know this man. She'd just endured one heartbreak; she didn't need another.

"So how is it going with Mrs. Welsh?" he asked. "I bet you'll have a lot of new stuff to teach those kids in New York when you get back."

The question made her heart sink.

Of course, she thought. *This isn't real. I don't live here. He's already picturing me back in New York. Nothing can come of this. And why do I feel like crying when I think of myself back in New York?*

But she said none of that and instead replied, "I hadn't thought of that, but I guess I will. She is just fascinating, and so lovely. I'm learning a ton and have been writing it all down in a book that's starting to take shape. My dream is to have the book finished before I..." She trailed off.

There it was again, the end of this magical year looming in the distance. It was early December, and before she knew it spring would arrive, and she would need to think about getting back to New York. She had been living in a fantasy these last three months, not thinking about Robert or the university or her "real" life at all. Squashing her old life away and pretending it didn't exist. Suddenly, sitting across from this gorgeous, charming guy, she realized she was lost. What did she want? The thought of returning to New York and the noise, the pollution, the crime, the constant competition at the university to "publish or perish," to secure tenure by edging out other assistant professors…it all felt absolutely horrible to her. Yet that was her life. She would have to go back to it eventually.

"Are you all right?" James finally asked.

She realized she must have looked a million miles away, or three thousand, to be more precise, as these thoughts rushed into her head. "Yes, sorry," she replied. "I guess I just haven't thought much about going back to New York. It won't be easy."

"Yes." He, too, looked away, as if deep in thought for a moment. Maybe it had just dawned on him, too, that he shouldn't risk his heart with someone who was going to be gone in a few months.

After that, they chatted amicably, but both were a bit more

reserved. As if they had both stumbled upon a precipice and realized they had been going a bit too fast and should be more careful.

Eden told him about the unexpected book that was quickly coming together. James told her funny stories of different patients and their owners, and about Bea and what she was like. When they were done with dinner, they moved into the living room with their wine.

Eden threw another log on the fire as James opened the second bottle of wine. At dinner, as the drink flowed, some of the reserve that had crept into the conversation had melted away again. And now, as they sat side by side on the sofa and he poured them another glass each, Eden turned to face him, bending one leg and tucking it under the other. She rested her head on her hand, her elbow on the back of the sofa. James mirrored her and turned to face her, leaving them suddenly tantalizingly close, their faces, their mouths, very near. She could almost feel the heat of him sitting that close to her. She felt flushed and was suddenly very aware of her lips, as if they itched.

"I was engaged," she said, tired of cautious conversation. She realized through a growing haze of wine that she really was a very impulsive person, or at least she was lately.

"Wow. What happened?" he asked, leaning toward her just a bit.

"I walked in on him in bed with another woman. It was the night my gran died, and probably, all in all, the worst night of my life. I got on a plane the next morning and…here I am!"

James looked at her with sympathy. He was quiet for a moment as he thought, and then she noticed him lean just ever so slightly away from her.

Did he purposely move his body away, or was it just his energy? She wasn't sure. But, either way, it had happened.

"I'm so sorry. How awful for you. I can't imagine that kind of betrayal from someone you love. Someone you were planning on spending your life with." He paused. "I hope your time here is helping you heal a little bit." James shifted, turning to face forward, and put down his wine. "Have you spoken to him since? Do you think it's really over?"

Eden realized with a sinking feeling what James must be thinking: *Heartbroken woman, over here hiding from her life for a few months*. She sensed him withdrawing, not so much as to be rude, but the energy that had pulsed between them just moments ago was suddenly gone. She was upset. She wasn't any of those things: heartbroken or a mess or hiding. He had no need for caution.

But, she wondered, *am I? Maybe I am heartbroken, maybe I am a mess.*

There was a long silence, and then Eden had sudden clarity, and said, for the first time in months completely certain it was true, "Actually, I am fine. I haven't spoken to him, but I think I'm just realizing this right now…I'm fine. I'm more than fine. I don't think I've ever been as happy as I am here. I didn't know it until that night, but I didn't love him. Or maybe I did once. But, by the end, I definitely didn't. Not for a—"

She was still talking when James turned suddenly and kissed her. His warm lips pressed hard against hers.

Eden felt a rush, like something sucking the air out of her lungs. Then she leaned toward him and kissed him back. His lips were soft and tender. Her heart was pounding so hard she was sure he could feel it as he moved closer and pressed his whole torso against hers. She could feel the taut muscles of his body, and his kiss grew more urgent. His lips parted just slightly, and she felt his tongue flicker against her lips.

She opened her mouth involuntarily in response and felt like she was melting as the kiss grew passionate.

And then, after a moment, it slowed down, and grew gentle again.

Slowly, James pulled away. When she opened her eyes, James was looking at her with a mixture of desire and confusion.

"I...I'm sorry. I guess I've wanted to do that since that first day I almost ran you over," he said with a little laugh. "I didn't know I was about to do it."

The kiss, and the passion that clearly lay just under the surface between them, had taken them both by surprise. Eden found it hard to formulate a thought. Her head was buzzing. Her lips felt swollen and tingly.

Finally, she said, "I've wanted that too. I'm so glad it happened."

James smiled his lopsided smile and leaned toward her again.

At just that moment, they both heard footsteps on the stairs and Tommy appeared, bleary-eyed and half asleep.

"I 'ad a nightmare," he said, looking small and scared at the foot of the stairs. "Someone was trying to get me."

Eden and James gave each other a quick look full of longing, smiled, and turned to help the little boy.

James soon said his goodbyes. He could have stayed, could have hoped Tommy went right back to sleep and stayed asleep. But the break in the passion had made them both stop and think. And, once their heads cleared, it had seemed a good idea to end the night there. A frustrating, terrible, good idea.

"I'll call you tomorrow," James whispered as he stood in the front door, Tommy in the other room waiting to be tucked back in bed.

"Great," Eden said with a big smile.

James leaned forward and gave her a quick kiss, a soft brushing of his lips while they stood at the door, out of sight of Tommy. Eden's heart went straight back to pounding from just the slight touch. James sighed looking both amused and frustrated, and then he left.

Eden went upstairs with Tommy to get him settled back in bed.

Chapter 11

Mrs. Welsh was sick. For the first time anyone could remember, the woman who healed the village needed healing herself. Friends of hers had driven her into Newmarket to the clinic, where a doctor had told her it was her heart. He had given her some medicine to stop the pain and told her to rest.

She was ninety-three years old. The doctor had said it was time to stop traipsing all over the village at all hours and in all weather, tending to the sick, and time to take some care of herself.

Mrs. Welsh's friend, Esther Perkins, and Esther's husband, Bob, lived in the cottage next door. They had always been a great help to Mrs. Welsh, and when Eden went to visit, she found Mrs. Perkins just leaving. They crossed on the little front path.

"Hello, dear," Mrs. Perkins said warmly.

Eden was thirty-eight, clearly an adult, yet she couldn't bring herself to call this new acquaintance Esther, though she had asked her to do so. She supposed, because Esther was from another generation, it just seemed rude. But then, she wondered, would it make her sound stupid or like a little girl for her to call her Mrs. Perkins? She was all flustered but, in the end, "Hello Mrs. Perkins," popped out of her mouth and she thought, oh well, I guess better to err on the side of caution. "How is she? I was so worried when Mrs. Park told me she was sick. I don't know why Mrs. Welsh didn't tell me herself."

"You know Hazel. She never wants to worry anyone. Never wants to be a bother. I'm just glad she did come and knock on our door before she got too sick to get out of bed. On our way home from Newmarket, Bob absolutely insisted she get a cell phone. He ran into the shop, and we just added her to our plan and got her a phone. She has absolutely no idea how to use it! You'd have thought we were asking her to program a rocket ship. It was quite funny. But it's beside her bed with our number programmed in, and of course, she could always dial 999, so it gives us a little peace of mind." Mrs. Perkins smiled wanly. "We are worried though. I'm glad you're here, dear. You're such a help to her with her work, and I know she cares very much for you. You might need to take on a bit more of her work if you're up to it. She's impossible to slow down, but the doctor did take us aside and say she needs to rest more. You might think about putting your number in her phone too. And let me give you ours. You can call us anytime, day or night, if anything's wrong."

"Thank you, Mrs. Perkins. That's a great idea," Eden said, and the two women stood amidst the winter stalks and dead herbs of the old herbalist's garden and exchanged cell phone numbers.

After they'd said goodbye, Eden knocked and walked in.

"Mrs. Welsh!" Eden called out, so as not to startle the old woman. "It's me, Eden. Can I come up and see you?"

"How lovely," Mrs. Welsh called back, much more softly. "Of course, you can."

Eden mounted the stairs. Mrs. Welsh was sitting up in bed with a shawl over her shoulders and a book in her hand. She marked the page and put the book on the side table as Eden entered.

"I was just about to start some reading. Esther has just left. I feel very popular today," she said with a smile.

"I was so worried. I didn't know you'd been ill until Mrs. Park just told me. I came straight over. What happened?"

"Well, I will tell you, but there is a price for the story," Mrs. Welsh said slightly mischievously.

"Anything!" Eden said.

"I'd love a nice cup of tea, if it isn't too much."

"Of course. What was I thinking? I should have offered right away to make one. I'll be back in a minute." She smiled as she walked downstairs and put the kettle on and set up the tea tray.

What on earth had the English done before tea? It was half-ritual and half-nutritional necessity for the entire nation at this point. And she found herself completely devoted to it now. Such a simple pleasure, a hot cup of tea with milk and sugar. Yet, some days, she thought there was no better treat in the world after a long cold walk with Wellie or a sad moment missing her gran or a troubled day worrying about the future or about her new ward. Yes, tea seemed to take the edge off all things, she thought once again, as she mounted the stairs with two steaming cups rattling on their saucers, going to see her frail friend.

Settled with her tea and a biscuit, Mrs. Welsh told Eden what had happened. "I was in the kitchen making myself something to eat when I got all hot and cold at the same time, and I had a terrible pain down my arm. I stood there, holding onto the counter, sure it would pass, but it didn't. I've never in my life fainted, but I was afraid I was going to, so I just shuffled next door and thought I'd sit on Esther and Bob's sofa for a moment until I was steady. But, of course, once I got there, they completely overreacted—out of love. sweet dears—and took me off to urgent care! I was there for hours, having Lord knows what done to me…tests and blood draws and endless waiting. I guess, in the end, my heart's a bit weak. But I knew that already, didn't I? What kind of a healer would I be if I didn't know my own body?" she asked rhetorically.

"Well, I, for one, am so glad they overreacted, to use your word," Eden replied. "I think it was exactly the right thing to do to take you into urgent care. You may have been on the verge of a heart attack! Did they give you any medication?"

"Yes, dear. A pill to put under my tongue. Some of these pills, of course, are just a compound taken from foxglove, which I have in a jar in my kitchen. I did ask if I could simply make myself some herbal foxglove tea instead. Ooh," she said, starting to laugh, "they looked at me like I had three heads when I suggested that. Silly doctors. They were prescribing me the very same thing. But they made me promise to put a little digitalis pill under my tongue if ever my heart hurts or I get a spell like that. And I have to go see a heart specialist within the month, they said."

"Good. Very sensible. Just tell me when the appointment is, and I'll drive you. Or would you like me to make the appointment for you?"

"No, no, nothing for now, dear. I'm tired. I think I'll rest now. It's been quite an exciting day."

"Of course, it has. Can I get you anything? Oh, I'm going to add my phone number to your phone. Call me absolutely any time at all," Eden said.

After putting in her number and saving it, she let herself out of the house, locking the door behind her with the key Mrs. Welsh had given her the week before so she could mix up a formula, just in case Mrs. Welsh wasn't home and someone needed urgent help.

Mrs. Welsh was sound asleep before Eden had even closed the door behind herself.

*

A week later, Eden dressed in her nicest pantsuit, while Tommy tried to tame his mop of short blond hair with a brush. There were only two inches of hair, and yet it seemed permanently tangled like a rat's nest. Surely, real moms had secrets to keeping a boy's hair looking less wild, but Eden figured that was the least of their worries. They were headed into Newmarket to the social services department for a meeting.

Eden let Wellie out. No home had been found for the dog in the past two months, so Eden had kept him, and she and the dog had become utterly devoted to one another. Tommy knew they were going to meet Jennifer, but like all children, he was so in the present moment, he wasn't worried. But Eden knew she was headed to town with the little boy who warmed her heart, possibly to see him taken from her and sent to a distant relative who knew where.

She watched him tuck in the nice new collared shirt she had bought him, proud to be dressing up, but somehow still managing to look messy anyway, and her heart melted. She realized how much she cared for the little lost boy. She had only had him with her for a week, but to her surprise, she was growing to love him. He had clearly longed for a grown-up who would treat him with tenderness and care, and Eden thought to herself, at her age, the boy had probably sparked her long-ignored desire to be a mother. They were an odd pair, but a good pair, she thought, as they walked out to the old car in the garage and headed to town.

In Newmarket, the social services department occupied an office block at the edge of the quaint town. Eden wondered if it was international law that insisted that government agencies find the dreariest, block-like office buildings to occupy.

A rattling elevator ride later, and Eden took a seat on a plastic chair in a narrow waiting area. Tommy occupied himself by hopping from one colored linoleum tile to another. Eden tried to read an old magazine, but she was nervous. Nervous about what was coming for the little boy.

Finally, someone called Eden's name, and they were ushered

into a small office with a large plate glass window overlooking the parking lot. Jennifer came in and sat behind the desk and gestured for Eden and Tommy to take seats opposite.

"Hi, Tommy. Do you remember me?" Jennifer asked.

Tommy looked at her with his face scrunched in concentration. It had been a traumatic day the day he met Jennifer, and it seemed he was having trouble placing her.

"Kind of," he said finally.

"I came to Eden's house to talk to you last week," Jennifer said.

"Oh yeah!" Tommy said brightly. "I remember."

"How are you?" Jennifer asked, ignoring Eden and talking directly to the boy.

"I'm good," Tommy answered. "Really good. Eden got me clothes and a ball and an elephant! And she cooks real nice things, like meat pies and veg and pudding. And she 'as a dog. I like dogs," Tommy rattled off quickly.

Jennifer smiled, finally turning to address Eden. "And how are things your end?"

Eden thought for a moment, wanting to answer honestly. "Wonderful really," she finally said. "Tommy is a very sweet boy, aren't you?"

"Good. I'm glad you two have had such a nice week together," Jennifer said. "Tommy, I'm going to introduce you to another person, a really nice woman who is a friend of mine and who also works here, okay? Her name is Mary. She wants to have a chat with you, and you can play with lots of toys she has in her office while I talk to Eden. She's going to ask you how you've been feeling since your dad passed away. Does that sound okay?"

Tommy, who lit up at the mention of a room full of toys after the thus-far boring morning, looked suddenly serious at the mention of his father. "All right, miss," he said.

Jennifer took him by the hand and led him out of the room, returning a few minutes later on her own.

"Tommy is with our counselor, Mary Wright. She has a PhD in child psychology, and she'll chat with him and watch how he plays with the things in her room and get a general idea of how he's doing. See what areas he might need help in after having the trauma of finding his dad, moving out of his house, all of it. It's standard procedure with a looked-after child."

"Looked-after child?" Eden asked. "What's that?"

"That's what we call a child who is in the care of the

government, or in foster care, or a group home. Much nicer than the old language, things like 'wards of the kingdom,'" she said.

"Wards of the kingdom?" Eden asked. It sounded horrible and clinical. Dickensian even. She pictured workhouses and Oliver and the Artful Dodger. Looked-after child was much nicer. Still, she started to panic.

"Yes, that's one of the reasons I called you in today. We have done an exhaustive search all week, and there don't seem to be any living relatives of Tommy's, nor was there any will left by the parents to indicate a person to take care of Tommy. So, unfortunately, he is now a looked-after child. We wanted to give you notice, and the counselor will talk to Tommy after you and I have spoken, to tell him he'll have time to go home with you and collect his things, but that he will be moving to a group home in Cambridge in a few days. From there, hopefully, he will find a permanent home. And if not, we will do our best to give him a good home and education at the group home until he's eighteen."

"You mean, you're going to take him and put him in a home? An orphanage? And you're telling him, and me, this today!?" Eden almost yelled.

"Yes. We are so very grateful to you for opening your home to him, barely having met him before the day his father passed. It was so generous. And he'll be fine with us. I know the people over at Chisolm House in Cambridge. They are very caring," Jennifer reported calmly.

"Caring? But how many children are there?" Eden asked, still alarmed.

"There are about twenty-five children there at any given time. With several staff, of course. There are dormitories and playrooms, and they have a television and a garden out back. It's not like living in your own home, but it's the best we can do. We try to keep the homes smaller than we used to."

Eden looked at Jennifer. She looked tired. *It must be a very hard job emotionally*, Eden thought.

Then she thought about the stranger with Tommy right now, talking with him about how he no longer had any parents, and now he had no home and would go live in a different city with a bunch of strangers. Her heart ached.

And once again, in a style that was becoming very familiar to her, Eden made an enormous decision right on the spot, and had total certainty it was the right one.

"What about me?" she asked. "Can I become his…what is it called? A guardian? Can I take him home with me and start the process to have him stay with me? A foster parent, I guess it's called. I mean, at least for now I know I can offer him more than a group home. Most of all, I can offer him love and a home in the village he has lived in all his life, with his friends and school and everything. And, well, he's such a sweet boy. I'm very fond of him, and I can't stand the thought of him ending up in a government home. I want to do whatever it takes to keep him with me. I'm sure there's a mountain of paperwork, but is it at least a possibility?" Eden asked.

"Well, I won't deny I was praying all night that you might say that!" Jennifer said, grinning. "Yes, it is *certainly* a possibility. My one question is, what about when you return to the United States? I don't know much about your plans, but you did mention when we met last week that you were in England on a year's leave from your job in America."

Eden paused to think. She knew she already loved this boy, she knew he wasn't going to an orphanage in a few days. But would she adopt him permanently, move to New York to her tiny apartment and her full-time job with a six-year-old boy who was used to fields and horses and England? Once again, as had happened on the sofa the other night with James, she felt the confusion of her two worlds colliding. And she felt the same cold shiver at the thought of returning to New York.

But this wasn't about deciding whether or not to kiss a man, or to risk her heart. This was a child's life she was talking about. Some common sense must prevail.

"I can't say for sure what will happen next year, Eden said. I do care deeply for Tommy. Can we say, for now, that I'd like to be his foster mother, or whatever term you use here, and sort that all out? And, of course, we'll keep longer-term things in mind. But, for right now, I want to make sure he isn't sleeping on a scratchy wool blanket in an orphanage next week. For now, I know I want him with me. And I'm pretty sure he'd say the same thing."

Jennifer beamed. "Wonderful! Yes, no need to decide anything permanent today. It is, again, so kind of you to take him in at all. I'm afraid you're right about the new mountain of paperwork, home visits, etc., that we will need to complete. But, of course, it's possible for you to keep caring for Tommy. It's more than possible, it's fantastic."

Jennifer came around the table and hugged Eden. "Thank you. You have no idea how many children I can't help. To know that this one sweet boy is safe and loved in a home of his own, even if just for now, is more wonderful than you can know. I'll go talk to Mary and tell her what we've discussed. She and I will have a talk with Tommy and make sure he wants to return home with you. I'm sure that he does, but it's a requirement, of course, to talk to the child. Have a seat, and I promise we'll get you both out of here as soon as we can."

Jennifer hurried out of the room, energized by the good news she had to share.

Eden sat in the hard chair across from the empty desk. *Mrs. Welsh, the herbal practice, the book, Wellie, James, and now, for the moment at least, a son!* These were the most unbelievable three months of her life. Complicated and messy, but wonderful! Her life back in New York, so sensible and organized and seemingly successful, seemed cold and empty by comparison, and she smiled.

*

By the time they arrived back at the cottage it was six p.m. Tommy and Eden were both exhausted and elated. And hungry. There was nothing prepared for dinner, so they decided it was a good day for a treat. They turned to walk down the lane to the pub for dinner.

Tommy had thrown his arms around Eden at the social worker's office when he'd found out he could stay with her, and Eden had burst into tears, shocked at the strength of her affection for the little boy.

Now, as they headed toward the pub, Eden felt a small cold hand slip silently into hers. Tears stung her eyes, and she smiled without moving her gaze. She simply gripped the hand back, with an extra little squeeze, as they walked in silence, twin smiles upon their faces, to the pub.

It was December and the holidays were coming.

"Look at the lights!" Eden exclaimed. The pub had been decorated along the roofline with little white lights, and it looked magical as Tommy and Eden walked down the road, the cold air stinging their faces and hands.

When they got inside Eden said, "Let's sit by the fire." Tommy agreed.

"What will it be then?" Jim asked with a smile.

"I'll have the fish pie, please. And a glass of chardonnay," Eden said.

"And for his royal highness?" Jim asked, smiling.

Tommy turned to Eden and whispered, "Can I get a hamburger and chips and a lemonade?"

"Of course!" she whispered back, winking at Jim, who could easily hear their conversation.

Tommy looked like he'd just won the lottery.

Then he looked up at Jim with a serious expression and said, "I would please like a hamburger and chips and a lemonade."

"Right you are, gov," Jim replied, and he walked off to the kitchen.

Just then, the door opened, letting in a cold blast of December air. It was James and Beatrice. James looked around, nodding to acquaintances. Then his eyes lit upon Eden, and his face brightened.

Eden felt that same feeling she'd had on the sofa, of having the breath sucked out of her when she saw him. Then she regained control and smiled and gestured for him to come over.

Eden had been about to introduce everyone, when Tommy said enthusiastically, "Hi, Dr. Beck. Hi, Bea!"

Of course, they all know each other, Eden thought. *They've all lived in this village their whole lives.*

"Would you like to join us?" Eden asked.

"We'd love to!" James pulled up a chair, as well as a second chair with a booster seat. "Jim, a pint for me and an orange juice for the princess," James called to the barman with a smile.

The foursome talked about important topics, like dogs, Christmas, Santa Claus, princesses, and snow for the duration of their dinner, Eden and James laughing as the children chatted nonstop about these important childhood topics until they started yawning.

"Time to take you home, young man," Eden said to Tommy.

"Time for me to get you home, too, Bea," James agreed, standing and getting Beatrice's winter coat off the back of her chair.

Too bad I'm not going with you, Eden thought, looking at James and smiling.

"What are you smiling at?" James asked as he helped Bea get into her coat.

"Oh, was I smiling?" Eden said, embarrassed. "Um...nothing," she said, looking guilty and blushing.

James laughed. "Hmm...I wonder if you were thinking what I was just now." He winked, and they both laughed together.

Chapter 12

Eden was busy writing the next morning when her phone rang. "Hello?"

"Hi. It's me. I mean, it's James."

"Oh, hi," Eden replied, trying, and she suspected failing, to sound casual. Her heart had instantly started pounding, as it did any time she saw him or heard his voice.

"I can't stop thinking about our dinner the other night. I would really like to see you."

"I can't either," she confessed, smiling into the phone. She had, in fact ,fallen asleep every night since that evening remembering the feel of his mouth on hers, his big hands on her back and hips.

"What are you up to right now?" he asked.

"Right now? I'm doing some writing, why?"

"I have a break between patients at the clinic. Bea is at nursery school. I assume Tommy is at school...so I thought maybe I could convince you to take a break and I could show you something."

It sounded vague, but Eden would have said yes to just about anything he suggested at this point, she realized with a bit of embarrassment.

"Show me something?" she asked. "That sounds mysterious. Sure, I'd love that! Should I come to the clinic?"

"No, I'll swing by and get you. I'll be there in five minutes. Wear your wellies!"

"Okay!" she replied.

She hung up, ran upstairs to change sweaters and brush her teeth, and was back downstairs with her tall rubber boots on by the time his car pulled into the driveway.

"Hi," Eden said as she got in the car.

"Hi," James replied, and there was an awkward moment where they almost leaned toward each other, as if to kiss, then both seemed unsure if that was presumptuous, so they sat in silence instead.

"Well, let's go then," James said. "I have two hours before I have to be back to take some stitches out of a Labrador."

He drove the car out of the village. The December ground was hard as iron. It had been unusually cold for England this time of year. It was gray and misty and cold in a way that seeped into your bones.

James cranked the heater in the little car as they climbed out of the valley in which Barton Health lay nestled, and up a steep, narrow road until they were at the top of an enormous ridge. From there they could see for miles.

Below was their village, tiny stone and wood houses, many with white smoke twisting up from their chimneys, the church tower, the farmlands surrounding, some with fields lying fallow, others with sheep in thick wool coats dotting them. Further on, they could see another small village, and on the other side of the ridge, a larger town. The road ran atop this narrow ridge, and it was like being on top of the world.

Eden realized she hadn't explored much, and she loved the feeling of leaving the village behind for a while. "Where are we going?" she asked with a smile.

"You'll see," James said, looking at her and twisting his lopsided grin, making her breath catch. "It's nothing fancy, just a place I found. Thought it might be fun to show it to you. I thought you might feel about it the way I do."

"Great," Eden said, now more curious than ever.

They sat in comfortable silence as they drove through the ancient countryside. Finally, they turned onto a very narrow road that led down from the high ridge and into a valley, then away from the town there and toward a copse of trees, leafless and stark in the winter afternoon.

James pulled the car over on the side of the road in what

seemed like the middle of nowhere. He came around and opened her door, and as she stood up, he put his arm behind her back and pulled her toward him. Their mouths met, and she felt a rush of heat through her whole body as his lips pressed with urgency onto hers.

She turned to face him straight on and she pressed her body against his, meeting his kiss with an urgency of her own. It was as if her mind had shut off and all that existed were two bodies, lips moving softly, then with force, against each other, two sets of hands caressing and then kneading. His hands tangled in her long hair and hers were under his tweed jacket, on the thin cotton shirt on his back.

And then, slowly, the kiss lessened in intensity. James gently laid his hands on either side of her face. They parted lips and opened their eyes.

Instantly her mind turned back on and it immediately started berating her. *You idiot, you threw yourself at him. I think...did he start that or did I...? I'm so embarrassed.*

And as these thoughts were busy criticizing Eden from inside her head, James said, "Thank God. I haven't been able to concentrate on anything since that night at your cottage. I have wanted to do that so badly."

Her critical mind shut itself up, and she told herself she must stop giving herself these mental thrashings.

Eden beamed into his face. "Me too."

James led her over a low fence and across a field, along a narrow footpath uneven with frozen mud.

"Right to roam," James said at one point.

"What?" Eden asked.

"Right to roam. It's a law in England, there are footpaths like these all over Britain, many of them hundreds and hundreds of years old. If you own property that these paths run through, you must allow people to walk them. The paths themselves are like public property, even if they pass through private land."

"That's fascinating!" Eden said. "In America, you'd never have that. People guard their property lines so fiercely. They'd have barbed wire fences and 'keep out' signs all over here. I love the old traditions here so much."

"So do I," he agreed.

He took her hand and they continued to walk. Eden looked out at the winter scene. Even on a cold, gray December day, England was beautiful to her. The grass was brown, the hay fields mown to hard stubble, but it was glorious in its way. Stone walls divided the fields, and not far away, there was an old stone farmhouse. Eden could smell the wood smoke rising from its chimney. They entered the woods at the edge of the field and Eden felt a tingle through her body, like she had at Mrs. Welsh's house. She was starting to believe there was magic there in England.

As they wound along the path, she could almost feel the history. Who had walked here? Who had hunted in these thickets? Who had farmed this land? The layers and layers of history seemed almost to speak to her through pictures that suddenly appeared in her head. She saw a monk. And heard a bell.

Before she had time to think of where the images had come from, James led her out of the trees. There, in the clearing, were the ruins of a large medieval church. Parts of the walls were standing, she could see the outline in stone of where a tall peaked window had been. But most of the church had crumbled, and in some areas, it was just grass grown over mounds that must have been the stones that had fallen down decades, or centuries, before.

As they approached, a small flock of blackbirds flew suddenly up into the sky, cawing as if in complaint for having been disturbed. It was beautiful and haunting.

"This is incredible!" Eden said, walking down what she realized must have been the center of the church.

As she did so, she, again, began seeing clear images behind her eyes—candles burning; monks walking slowly down the nave of a complete, intact cathedral; women in brown robes, nuns or maybe worshippers. Eden could hear their low chants and smell the incense. She saw candles flickering and faces turned to the floor in prayer.

She felt dizzy and had to stop walking. She shook her head slightly to clear it. What was going on? She wasn't thinking what might have been, or imagining something, she was *seeing* it. It was as real as if she could reach out and touch it. As if she were watching a movie right in front of her in three dimensions.

She turned around and saw James standing behind her, smiling. She decided not to mention the crazy psychedelic show she had just been watching and instead smiled back at him.

"I found this place not long ago," he told her. "I'd always heard about it but had never bothered to come. A few months ago, I was driving by on my way home from a lecture in another town and something made me pull over and look for it. I've been many times since then. It feels...magical to me. I guess..." He paused as if trying to figure out what he wanted to say. "I guess this feels like church to me. I mean, it is, or it *was*, a church," he added with a laugh, "but I guess this feels more sacred than even most standing churches to me, for some reason. Maybe because nature has reclaimed most of it, it's sort of church and nature combined. I don't know. Maybe it's the history. I feel something here. I can't quite put my finger on it, but I can actually *feel* the history here. It's one of my favorite places on earth now."

He grabbed Eden's hand and sat down on a low wall that was clearly once part of the outer wall of the building, pulling her to him. She smiled down at his handsome face, noticing the strong line of his jaw and the blond stubble that was emerging.

"This was the church of an order of monks who had a cloister nearby. Apparently, there's nothing at all left of that. Monasteries usually produced something in the Middle Ages. It's how they helped support themselves. Some were known for their cheeses or jams. Some sold wool or made icons from wood. Guess what these monks were." He paused for effect.

"I don't know. Beekeepers? What?" Eden said, smiling.

"Herbalists!" he declared, looking satisfied.

"No way!" Eden exclaimed. "That's amazing. Oh, I'd love to know more about them." She looked around the church and surrounding clearing and now she saw ancient figures in brown robes, growing and drying herbs, treating the sick with their potions. "Do you know the name of their order or anything? I wonder if I could look them up."

"No idea, I'm afraid. The vicar might. I'm sure there are plenty of records about them around this area if you look into it. They had magnificent herb gardens, apparently, and people would come from all around to get healed. Here." He jumped up and pulled her along behind him with a smile.

At the edge of the ruined church, there was a clear outline of a large rectangle, the edges marked by small square stones. Inside the rectangle were several large circles also marked by stone edges. Many of the stones were missing, but it was clear to see it had once been something intentionally laid out.

"These were their gardens. Some of them anyway," James explained.

Eden's eyes lit up like a child in a candy store. She walked over slowly, as if she needed to show respect to the long-gone monks' sacred gardens. She ran her hands along the dead stalks of weeds growing up in the beds. Her hands tingled wildly. Then she knelt down.

"This is flax!" she said, looking up with an excited smile. "Gosh…I wonder…could some of these plants here be from the original gardens?"

"I don't know," James said, smiling back. "I don't know

anything about plants, I'm afraid. Are some of these weeds actually herbs?"

"This one is," Eden said. "It's flax. Its seeds are used for lots of things. The oil from the seeds was used as a diuretic, and for constipation, and topically to help heal wounds or improve the skin. The stalks can be used to weave fabric." She ran her hand up the thin brown stalks. "In fact, I don't think anyone would mind if I collected some, would they?"

James looked around with a grin smile. "Unless you mean the ghosts of the monks, I can't imagine who would mind. And I should think the monks' ghosts would be thrilled!"

Eden ran her hand up to the top of the stalks and collected a handful of seeds. She put them in her coat pocket and beamed. And again, she saw flashes of pictures in her head as she did it. Monks. A sick old woman lying on the floor of the church under a rough blanket. Church candles. A woman with a bowl of liquid, gently wiping a sick man's forehead. Graves. She shook her head. Then, as she walked back into what was once the church, she saw a nun, clear as day, standing in front of her.

She looked kind and gentle, and she smiled and said very clearly, "Welcome home, sister."

And then she turned and walked into the woods, seeming to slowly fade, till she vanished just before reaching the trees.

Eden looked around wildly. She saw nothing else, no one else. James walked in the ancient cemetery, reading gravestones, but he looked relaxed and unconcerned. Clearly, he hadn't just been spoken to by a nun from beyond.

Welcome home, sister? Eden thought with a mix of fear and irritation. *What is that supposed to mean? Sister as in fellow human being who is female? Or sister as in a nun? What is going on here? I'm just imagining things.*

She walked toward James. But then she felt it. The *knowing*. No, she wasn't imagining things. She had been here before. To Barton Heath, to this church. Or maybe it wasn't that *she* had been here before, but that she was meant to be here now. It didn't seem to matter.

"That's right," said a voice that seemed to come from inside her head and outside in the air at the same time. "It only matters that you're here now. Home."

She wasn't sure if she heard it, saw it, felt it, imagined it, or all of the above. But she knew it was real, whatever it was. And when she allowed herself to feel that welcoming, she wasn't scared or irritated anymore.

She smiled and said, "Thank you," softly into the mist.

James and Eden strolled around the pretty church in the clearing of the woods for a little longer, until it was time to head back, to the Labrador with the stitches, and to collect Tommy from school.

As they turned to go, James kissed her again. "When can I see you again?"

"This weekend maybe?" Eden suggested. "My mother is coming back to Barton Heath for Christmas. She gets in later this week."

"Oh, that's nice," James said.

"Yes, I can't wait. But it also means, once he's spent a few days with my mom and gets to know her, I can leave Tommy for an evening with her, and you and I can finally have that dinner out," she said.

"I hadn't thought of that. I like your mum already," he said with a grin.

They walked back to the car, hand in hand. They kissed again, this time for longer, Eden leaning back against the car, James leaning the weight of his body against her. This time the kiss felt more playful, as if they were relaxing a bit, exploring. Then they straightened themselves up like a pair of teenagers and drove, smiling, back to the village.

Chapter 13

It was the week before Christmas. Barton Heath looked like something out of a holiday card. The houses had little white or colored Christmas lights along fences, around rooflines, or wrapped artfully around the empty winter branches of trees, lighting them up in great detail in the long, dark evenings.

In the town of Newmarket, there were even more decorations. Eden was in town with Tommy, doing some Christmas shopping and waiting, with great excitement, for six p.m., when she would meet her mother's train from London. It was going to be the best Christmas in years, Eden was sure of that. She had told her mother about Tommy and Susan had tried to hide the surprise in her voice, and saying that it was a lovely thing to do, to take the boy in. Eden figured her mother was probably waiting to see her in person before asking her what the hell she was up to.

In the oldest part of Newmarket, there were winding, ancient cobblestone streets lined with centuries-old buildings, some at raking angles, perched atop other buildings like they had been thrown up there haphazardly. Amazingly, they remained, hundreds of years later. Plate glass windows let off a warm glow of light in the darkness that fell by midafternoon now. Toys, sumptuous food, wine, tinsel…all of it sparkled and glowed, drawing Eden and Tommy to peek inside, and sometimes even go inside, to see what delights were to be had.

"Ooh, look at that," Tommy said, eyes wide as saucers. He pointed in the window of the greengrocers. It seemed he was pointing at a large pineapple.

"What are you seeing, Tommy? The pineapple?" Eden asked.

"Yeah. Look at that!" he said in amazement. "Like in the tropics!"

"Have you never had a pineapple?"

"No. I mean, yeah, I 'ad some one time at school, from a tin. It was lovely. I ain't never 'ad a real one, though. Seen pictures. But never 'ad one."

"Well, we will have to rectify that immediately!" she declared.

They went into the shop and, three minutes later, walked out, Tommy proudly carrying a large pineapple.

At ten minutes to six, Eden, carrying several heavy bags filled with food, wine, and gifts, and Tommy marching with his pineapple in his arms, loaded their purchases into the trunk of the car and drove to the train station. They stood on the platform with folded arms trying, unsuccessfully, to shield themselves from the bitter wind. Finally, they saw the train approach. Eden smiled, looking eagerly at each person who stepped off the train. Then she saw a familiar figure.

She couldn't place the man at first. Then she realized it was Peter Penley-Smith. As soon as he had stepped down, he turned back toward the train, held out his hand, and it was taken by a woman who stepped down after him. It was her mother.

"Mom!" Eden yelled and waved her arms.

Her mother broke into a joyful smile and they ran to each other and hugged.

Lord Penley-Smith collected their bags and paid a valet to take them to the car, then strolled over to Eden, Susan, and Tommy. Eden gave him a big hug.

"So good to see you again," she said, and she meant it. Peter turned and held out a hand to Tommy, greeting him as a grown-up would greet another grown-up.

Tommy straightened up and looked almost comically serious and shook his hand.

"Very pleased to meet you, Tommy," the lord said. "I've heard so much about you, young man."

"Thank you, sir," Tommy said.

"Call me Mr. Penley-Smith, my dear boy. None of this 'sir'

nonsense," Peter said, with such a boyish grin that Tommy broke into a smile and visibly relaxed.

"I didn't know you were coming on the train too," Eden said to Peter. "Did you meet Mom at the airport in London?"

Susan and Peter looked at each other and both broke into mischievous grins.

"Not exactly," he said ambiguously. "Let's get home out of the cold, and we'll tell you all about it."

With Eden intrigued, the group went to the little car, squeezed in, and drove to the cottage. When they arrived, Peter insisted on leaving Susan's bags in the car, saying he would unload them later.

"Okay, well, sit down you two," Eden said as she lit the fire. "I'll just grab a bottle of wine and something to nibble on, and then you can tell me everything that's been happening!"

She went into the kitchen and laid cheese, crackers, and olives onto a platter, and carried it back in. Susan and Peter sat next to each other on the sofa. Tommy was playing with a toy fire truck, pretending to fight the fire that raged in the enormous fireplace. Eden sat in an armchair.

"We have something to tell you," Eden's mother started.

Again, Susan and Peter shared their secret smile. Then Susan held out her left hand, palm down, for Eden to examine.

On her mother's third finger was a wedding ring and a sapphire ring atop that, presumably an engagement ring.

"Oh my God!" Eden jumped out of her seat. "Are you married?!" she asked, stunned.

Susan and Peter broke into laughter as if delighted they'd finally been able to spill a delicious secret.

"Yes!" exclaimed Peter. "We are! I cannot believe she agreed to it, but she did!" He beamed proudly.

Eden rushed over and gave her mother, then Peter, enormous hugs.

Tommy looked up from his truck. "Who got married?" he asked.

"My mom and Mr. Penley-Smith did!" she replied. "Isn't that wonderful?"

"Yeah," said Tommy, not nearly as enthralled as the grownups were with the news. He went back to his fire truck.

"Oh my gosh, when did this happen? And where? I thought you'd been in Rhode Island all this time, Mom. What is going on?" She laughed as she asked.

"Well, I came home from work one day in November, and

found a handsome man with a handful of flowers on my doorstep." Susan turned and looked at Peter with a look that melted Eden's heart.

"I couldn't stay away for two whole months," Peter chimed in. "Not when I was sitting over here, thinking of nothing but your beautiful mother. And when she was just a short plane ride away."

"So, he's been staying with me all this time, almost two months. And well..." Susan hesitated, "I suppose it must seem crazy, but we just knew. We knew. So, we went to town hall one day and got married! We had a few of my friends come round afterward for drinks. And there it is. Done. Married!" Susan and Peter both beamed like proud children. It was irresistible.

Eden raised a glass and made a toast. "Congratulations. I am so thrilled. Here's to the happy couple!"

And they all drank some wine.

"Now," Peter said, "we will have to have a party!"

*

It was a party no one in Barton Heath soon forgot. They held it the following week at Peter's manor house and invited everyone they knew, and since Lord Penley-Smith had grown up there, that was most people in town and others from as far away as London and Edinburgh. He was very unlike upper-class gentlemen of even a generation ago, or, in fact, many of his own peers, in that he had total disregard for class differences. And in a country whose entire history, and some of its present, was based largely on what class you were born into, it made him a rare breed. It wasn't something everyone agreed with, and the snobbier of his friends avoided his big parties, as they had no desire to rub elbows with the gardener and the cleaning woman. But, for most people, they thought it was wonderful, or at the very least interesting, and they accepted his invitations with alacrity.

Eden had been so busy, between Mrs. Welsh, Tommy, her book, and now her mother and Peter, that she hadn't managed to see James at all in a week. When Eden told him about the party, he asked if she would make him the envy of the county and go as his date. She was thrilled and accepted right away.

The manor house was a stately Georgian home, which sat at the end of a long gravel drive, with manicured gardens on either side, and rolling green hills behind. It was made of the yellow stone typical of Georgian architecture. Its simple, square and symmetrical design was impressive and elegant. And the golden shade of stone made it seem always to be in a glow of evening sunshine.

There were three large windows, each at least ten feet tall, on either side of the door, then a second story with seven similar-sized windows, evenly spaced across the facade. A third floor above, with seven smaller windows, had housed the servants' quarters in former days. A large veranda sat on one side of the house, made of the same stone, and with a stone railing around the edge.

The house had been decorated like something out of a film. Evergreens hung around the front door and draped along the walls of the terrace. White lights followed the greenery, lighting up the contours of the veranda and the door. An enormous wreath with a large red bow hung on the front door, and all of this was lit beautifully by carefully placed spotlights shining upon the impressive home.

Eden had been absolutely tickled watching her mother play lady of the manor, ordering food and champagne and wine for the party, while Peter climbed up ladders, hanging the sharp, pine-scented boughs of fresh greenery and the white lights himself.

"Money pit, this old house is," he would say with a smile, doing as much of the work as he could to be frugal. He complained, but he clearly loved the place dearly. It had housed his family for generations, and he cared for it as he would an elderly relative, gently and lovingly.

He hired a local company to cater the party and supply a few people to help keep wine glasses full and dirty plates cleared away. But he wasn't extravagant, and the party managed to feel intimate, even though there were over a hundred people attending.

James pulled up to Eden's cottage a few minutes before the party was due to start.

James walked to the door and rang the bell. When the door opened, he felt his heart skip a beat and he felt suddenly hot in the face.

"Wow," was all he could get out at first.

Eden beamed, taking his shocked expression as a compliment. She looked stunning. Her thick brown hair hung in soft waves around her face, her eyes shone. She had bought a new dress for the occasion, a dark green velvet dress with a deep V neck that showed off the tops of her beautiful smooth breasts. The material clung to her hips, then flowed to the floor. She had on black heels and clutched a tiny black bag.

James couldn't speak. She sensed that he wanted to grab her and kiss her and run his hands all over her.

"Are you all right?" Eden finally said with a laugh.

James shook himself and managed to whisper, "You're so beautiful. And sexy. That dress is making it a bit hard to breathe at the moment."

It was said with such simple honesty, combined with desire,

that Eden felt her defended heart soften and open even more. She leaned toward him and laid a gentle kiss on his mouth, which made her lips tingle like a tiny bit of electricity was running through them.

Realizing this could get out of control very quickly, she stood back and called to Tommy, who raced out past them to the car and hopped in.

They all made a good-looking group. James wore a dark blue suit with a light blue collared shirt and a tie with a small purple and green pattern. The suit fit his muscular build perfectly, and his hair was slicked back slightly, out of his eyes for once. He looked straight out of a magazine, Eden thought. Bea was in a red velvet dress with a wide black satin sash. She had on white tights and black patent leather shoes with a strap and was clearly thrilled to be so dressed up. Tommy was dressed in khaki trousers, a new navy blazer, collared shirt, and red tie...an outfit which seemed to make him equal parts proud and embarrassed.

As they turned into the driveway of the manor house, Eden felt she was dreaming: the gorgeous stately home was decorated and lit, guests arriving by car, some already gathered on the veranda with glasses of champagne.

Surely this is not happening, she thought. *Am I really on my way to a Christmas party in a manor house in England, thrown by a lord, who is now my stepfather, with this gorgeous Englishman at my side?* She almost laughed out loud at the insanity of it all.

When she looked in the back seat, she felt flooded with affection. Tommy's eyes and mouth were both wide with disbelief.

His world has gone even more crazy than mine, she thought. *Here he was, a poor boy with an alcoholic abusive father a few weeks ago, now dressed up in a jacket and tie and headed to the manor house.* Life was unpredictable, that was certain.

In the great hall, there was a twenty-foot Christmas tree lit up with hundreds of white lights and decorated with large red bows. The whole room sparkled with lights and ornaments and candles and champagne bubbles and diamonds, some real and some fake, but sparkling bravely, nonetheless. King's College Boys' Choir was streaming through speakers, singing traditional Christmas carols in clear, high voices, and everyone looked beautiful because they were so happy.

This was why Christmas is my favorite time of year, Eden thought. *Because everyone shines, everyone's heart is open, everyone feels a common bond in celebrating this ancient holiday.*

A waiter passed by with a tray of champagne flutes. James and

Eden each took one, looking at each other with a mix of desire and simple childish happiness. Tommy and Bea went straight to a table laid with a white linen cloth and pretty little china dishes, containing chocolates, tiny cakes, and peppermint sticks.

"Eden!" a voice called out as James was taking their coats.

Eden looked into the crowd and saw Tara smiling and waving. She walked over.

"Isn't it magnificent?" Tara said.

"It's like a fairy tale," Eden said. "They've done an amazing job." She looked up the enormous winding staircase, with a banister wound round with evergreen the whole way up, candles flickering in the windows, people laughing and talking.

James walked up behind her. "Hi Tara. You look lovely as always."

"Such a charmer. There are many broken hearts in this village you know, thanks to you, Eden," her friend said, winking at Eden.

Eden blushed.

"Is Martin here?" James asked.

"No, working tonight, unfortunately," Tara replied.

"Ah well, the price you pay for dating an ER doctor, I guess," James said with a smile.

Just then a hand slapped James on the shoulder, and a man asked loudly, "How are you then?"

James turned and smiled broadly. "Dave, how are you? How is that ewe of yours? Infection gone, I hope?"

"Aye, after you drained the abscess, she were much better after that. A bit of thick, yellow stuff came out for a few days, smelt something awful, but antibiotics you gave me helped with that," the man replied.

James turned to Eden and Tara whose faces were scrunched up in disgust at the conversation over abscesses and pus. James laughed, "Maybe not cocktail party chitchat, is it?" he asked. "Eden, this is Dave Thompkins He and his wife own a lovely sheep farm just up the road past the church."

"Nice to meet you," Eden said with a smile. "I'm Eden Martin."

"Very nice to meet you," Dave said. A woman, presumably his wife, waved from another part of the crowded room, obviously unable to get away from a conversation just then.

Eden thought to herself, *This is no corporate chitchat about tile and renovations...I'm having a conversation with a sheep farmer about an abscess. And I love it.*

About halfway through the party, Eden felt James's large hand slide onto the small of her back as they chatted with the Parks. Her heart did that funny flip it did so often these days. For the rest of the evening, his hand stayed there, as if it was the most natural thing in the world. Warm and exciting, like a secret invitation. Eden, too, rested her hand on his arm and thrilled at the feeling of his solid arm under his clothes. If there had been any doubt in the village about whether or not the vet had recovered from his loss and was seeing the American, it was dispelled at that party and many an old lady chatted with her friend about being glad to see "that nice young man" looking so happy again.

Throughout the whole evening, there were light touches, stolen smiles, and a growing tension building as Eden watched his handsome, rugged face laughing, and how he flicked the hair out of his eyes that had fallen into its usual place, despite the pomade.

Chapter 14

It was eleven o'clock and slowly, reluctantly, people were heading home.

"We should go," James said to Eden, who had been talking with her mother.

"Yes, we should. Oh, wow, I didn't realize it was eleven already!" she said, looking at her watch. "Poor kiddos have been sound asleep on the sofa in the other room for hours."

"It's adorable," Susan said. "I keep going in and checking on them, but those two are out for the night."

"Big night for them. I saw them in and out of the house, checking out everything from the Christmas tree to the garden. And I think they ate most of the sweets on the dessert table themselves. I'm not surprised they're passed out," Eden said, laughing. She hugged and kissed her mother on the cheek. "Good night, Mom. Good night, Peter," she said, doing the same to him. "Thank you so much. Tonight was absolutely wonderful. And congratulations again."

"Yes, good night, Susan," James said kissing her cheek. "Good night, Peter." He shook hands with his host. "It really was a perfect evening. Thank you."

"You are so welcome, both of you," Susan said. Peter seconded the sentiment, and then the host and hostess turned to say goodbye to other revelers heading home.

James and Eden scooped the sleeping Bea and Tommy up from the sofa in the manor house's living room and buckled them in the car. They drove back to Eden's cottage, Eden's hand resting on James's knee as they drove in happy but charged silence.

When they got out of the car, the children still asleep, James pulled Eden to him and kissed her. She leaned back against the car and wrapped her hands around his neck. James moved his mouth to the side of her neck, and she let her head fall back. They both glanced at the children sleeping in the car and clearly had the same thought.

They carried Tommy and Beatrice into the house. Eden put Tommy in his bed, took off his shoes, and covered him with his blankets. James did the same with Bea, putting her in what had been Susan's room. Then, without waking the children, they tiptoed into Eden's bedroom.

Eden had imagined this moment countless times, her first time making love with James. In her imagination, there was tension, embarrassment, but now that it was happening, there was nothing but desire. No room for doubt or questions.

As soon as the door was closed, James pressed her back against it, ran his hand slowly up her neck, cupped her chin, and softly kissed her mouth. He then dragged one finger very gently from her chin, down the side of her neck, to the rise of her breast. Then he slid his lips down to the tender skin on the side of her neck and kissed her there until her breath was fast and ragged.

Her hands went to his belt, and she untucked his shirt and ran her hands up his bare back, which made him arch just slightly with the pleasure. James slowly bent and lifted the hem of the dress, lifting it slowly to reveal her shins, knees, thighs. He stood, and in one quick movement, pulled the dress off over her head and threw it on the floor. She lifted his shirt over his head without stopping to unbutton it. He reached out and guided her over to the bed, where he lay her back and gently lowered himself on top of her. His fingers, woven with hers, held her hands above her head as he kissed her with both tenderness and hunger.

*

In the very early hours of the morning, James woke with a start. He looked around for a moment in confusion, then saw Eden's sweet face sleeping peacefully beside him. He lifted the covers and drank in her beautiful body in full view in the light of the bedside lamp—soft, milky skin, curves at her hips, and the magnificent crest of her full breasts. He traced a finger from the hollow of her neck down through the valley of her breasts to the inside of her thigh.

Eden stirred and woke, smiling sleepily up at James.

"God, you're beautiful," he said, and he gently kissed her.

"So are you," she said back.

"I have to get up. I need to get Bea back to the house before she wakes up," James said. "We shouldn't let them see us like this. I mean, not yet, don't you think?"

He stood, making it Eden's turn to take in the full measure of his body. He was tall and broad-shouldered, with just a little hair on the center of his chest. His chest was muscular and there was a clear line running straight down his middle, past the ripple of stomach muscles, to the tuft of hair at his groin.

"Do we have to be so mature?" Eden asked jokingly.

"Believe me, I want nothing more than to get back in that bed right now," he said with a smile that turned from playful to longing. He shook himself. "No, I have to go now, or else I never will!"

He pulled his trousers on and buckled his belt, pulled his shirt over his head, and stepped into his shoes, stuffing his socks in his coat pocket. "I'll call you later today," he said. He paused, as if he wanted to say more. But he didn't.

He kissed her lightly on the lips and tiptoed out to lift the still sleeping Bea back into his car and drive her home.

*

A few days later while Tommy was at a friend's house, Eden and her mother went out to dinner. They had both been so caught up with their new lives that they hadn't had time for a really good chat since Susan had been back. They went to a cozy bistro in a nearby village.

When the glasses of wine were in front of them, Eden started with a big smile. "So? How is life as lady of the manor?" Then she added, "Seriously, Mom, you look so happy, but I have to ask, how did this happen? You are the most sensible person I know. You could have knocked me over when you got off that train with a ring on your finger!"

Susan smiled back, a slow, happy smile. "I know," she said. "It's absolutely crazy. I'm totally aware of it and I don't care. Isn't that wild? It's so not me. But I think I loved that man from the first day he wandered into the cottage to offer his condolences. I can't explain it, I just knew."

Eden did understand. For the first time in her life, she

understood that.

"He was on my doorstep in Rhode Island when I got home from work one day, and that night, over dinner, he proposed, and I said yes, like it was the most natural thing in the world. When, really, it's the craziest thing in the world!"

She laughed, and Eden thought she had never seen her mother this happy in all her life.

"Of course, there were lots of practical things to work out. There still are. I'm not selling my house. I have taken a leave of absence from work. But I'm sixty-five. It's time for me to retire and enjoy myself, so I probably won't go back to the hospital. That said, we won't spend all our time here. We think we'll be here during the winters, and spend summers in Rhode Island. The weather and the beaches are so beautiful then. And that way we can see my friends, be in my life there some of the time too." She sipped her wine, grinning like a teenager with a crush. "And" she added, "we have come up with a plan these last few weeks."

"Ooh, do tell!" Eden said with a smile.

"Well, Peter is obviously retired, and I guess I am now too. Or will be soon. But we don't want to sit around on our rear ends till we fall off our twigs," she said.

Eden smiled at another darkly humorous English saying.

"So, we have decided to restore the manor house gardens." Susan looked at her daughter with a proud smile. "So many old stately homes have house and garden tours. They're big attractions here. There were once stunning gardens there. And you know how much I love gardening, and Peter does too. We are going to hire someone to help. Obviously, we won't do it all ourselves. But we are going to do a lot of it ourselves. And it will be a wonderful thing for us to do with our time. And, also, wonderful for the home, so that when it gets handed down— I think it's Peter's niece who is in line to inherit—it will be even more lovely. Each generation does try to leave its mark. And this will be Peter's. Plus, there will be a nice little income from the tours. We'll probably have a tearoom off the veranda for visitors. It will be great fun!"

"That sounds wonderful, Mom. You're such a good gardener. What a great project and, as you said, good all the way around!"

"Yes," her mother replied. "And we were thinking, that maybe in the kitchen gardens out back, we might plant a big herbal garden. We thought you might help us decide what to plant."

"That would be so much fun, I'd love to!" Eden said. "In fact, wouldn't it be neat to do tours of the herb gardens and then sell little sachets—some for the bath, some for the common cold, or for different little health problems? Maybe in the tea shop. Herbs you could take home and make a little tea with. I bet people would love that!"

"That's a wonderful idea. We should definitely do that. Maybe you and Mrs. Welsh could give little lectures there sometimes. You know, more and more people are really going back to the older cures these days, having had enough of antibiotics every time they sneeze. It would be fun and might turn a little profit too."

Eden got excited as she started envisioning orderly rows of raised bed gardens with linden for fever, garlic for sore throat or infection, mint for upset stomach, borage for depression or "lowness of spirit."

Then, seeing her mother look at her with a smile, her thoughts returned to the here and now. After a pause, she said, "Well, certainly seems like you have worked it all out. I'm so happy for you, Mom. I really am," she said and smiled lovingly at her mother, who had worked so hard to take care of Eden and provide for her as a single mother for so many years. She was so happy that Susan was now being showered with affection and luxury. She deserved it.

"And how about you, Eden? Your life has changed almost as much as mine! What a year. What are you going to do? James seems like such a nice man. I can tell youre very fond of him. But what about New York and your teaching position, your apartment? What about Robert? Have you resolved all of that? Have you talked to him?"

Eden's mind drifted three thousand miles away to gray, concrete New York. To Robert, slick and successful, handsome, but not very kind. She saw cars and skyscrapers and people rushing by, no one noticing anyone else. She felt very sad just imagining it.

"I don't know what I'm doing, Mom. I'm so confused. I..." She paused before she said something too dramatic. "I really like James. A lot. And I love my life here. I think I have had love at first sight, too, except it's with this place. I mean, obviously, I've been coming here my whole life. But this time, for the first time, I had this instant feeling like I was home in a way I never have before." She stopped and took a sip of her wine, then continued. "But I don't know. I worked for years to get that teaching position. I have a future, a career, friends. My apartment. Do I really want to give all that up, or is this just playing house? Playing at a fantasy? I don't know." She looked at her mother who smiled with both love and concern on her face.

"And Robert?" Susan asked again.

"No. I haven't spoken to him. I know it's silly. I know I have to. It was so awful. So painful and humiliating. But at the same time, ever since I got here, I just really don't seem to care. It's another thing I don't know if I can trust. I mean, I was prepared to marry the man. Can I really not care?"

"You were *prepared* to marry him. Not a phrase that sounds like you were wildly in love, sweetheart," her mother said gently.

"No, it doesn't. And I wasn't. I think I knew it even then, but I wasn't really in love. At least I don't think I was. And now, after that night, when he calls, which he still does at least once a week, I just can't be bothered to dredge it all up. I just want to stay in my little fairy bubble in my fairy cottage and ignore it. I guess that's probably very unhealthy!"

She and her mother laughed at that, and Eden felt more relaxed.

"I guess it will work itself out in time. I know, at some point, I will have to face it all. Have to make some decisions." She paused, recognizing how strange it felt not to really care what happened to Robert or to her job or to her apartment. It was a peaceful, but very odd, feeling. And unsafe, as if the detachment was covering something messy and dangerous. "But for now, the most pressing decision I have to make is whether to go for the shepherd's pie or the risotto," she said, smiling, and her mother let it drop.

*

Friday nights James usually went to the pub for a drink to end a busy week. He most often went alone, Bea still with Mrs. Innskeep, and then he went home to take care of his daughter for the weekend. Tonight, Felicity Poolbridge was in town, down from her fast-paced life in London to stay with her parents for the weekend. She was twenty-six, blond, successful, and ruthless, both in business and in love. To stave off the boredom of being back in sleepy Barton Heath, she went to the pub. Her slightly too-high heels clicked coldly on the sidewalk as she approached the door of the pub. She tugged at the slightly too-tight dress she had on, then flung the door open and marched in as if she owned the place.

She was not the sort of girl you took home to Mum, but the men all took a good look as she walked in, and she knew it. And she liked it.

She was sipping a prosecco at the bar when James walked in, and she decided that he would be as good a diversion as any. He was a widower, probably hadn't gotten any action in a while. He was handsome and looked like he'd be good in bed. She perked up a great deal now that she had a plan.

"Pint please, Jim," James said, and he sat down heavily on a stool and ran his hands through his hair, exhaling.

Felicity observed him from her stool at the other end of the bar, planning her approach. By the end of his first beer, James seemed to be discussing something serious with Don Topper, a farmer from the village.

Felicity decided to make her move. She got up and sauntered over to the other end of the bar and gave Don a hard stare over James's shoulder. A quick jerk of her head toward the door made it clear she wanted Don to leave. He looked almost scared as he left some coins on the bar, drained his drink, and said a quick goodbye to the vet.

Felicity reached out and put a hand gently on James's shoulder and then ran it down his arm. He turned in surprise and Felicity smiled. She had soft gray eyes and an inviting mouth. Yet, somehow, she managed to look cold, despite her sensuous features.

"Hello, James," she said, breathily.

"Oh, hi, Felicity," James replied. "I haven't seen you in a while. Down from London for the weekend?"

"Yes, it's Mum's birthday tomorrow, so I felt I had to come home," she said with a hint of resentment.

"Hmm," James said vaguely, turning back to his beer. There was silence as it seemed James was not going to start up the conversation.

"How are you? You're looking very good, as always," Felicity said with a flirtatious smile.

James looked serious and stared into his beer. "I'm all right. Rough day."

That was more of a response than she usually got out of him on the rare occasions she saw him. In fact, she decided it was a downright invitation to conversation.

"Oh no, I'm sorry to hear that," she said, intentionally sounding casual. "What happened?"

"Oh, nothing really. I mean, not *nothing*. But nothing too bad. It was Mr. Jenkins down the alley," he said.

The alley was the oldest part of the village. It was a narrow, dark street on the far side of the church, with cold, damp stone row houses, two rooms downstairs and two upstairs. Tiny, cramped, dark and, most of them, crumbling, they were largely uninhabited at this point, most low-income villagers having moved to the modern, comfortable council houses that had been built on the other side of the village in the 1970s. But a few old-age pensioners wouldn't give up the homes they'd lived in all their lives, and they had stayed on in the miserable hovels. Bert Jenkins was the last surviving one of those pensioners.

"What happened?" she asked with insincere interest.

"It was his dog, Maisy. Poor old bugger, he has nothing. His wife died two years ago, and it's been just him and his old dog. She's everything to him. He called today saying it was urgent, and when I got there, I could see the dog was on its way out. It had a huge mass on the side of its throat, and it was having terrible trouble breathing, had stopped eating. Cancer, I'm sure. In the end, the only humane thing I could do was put the poor dog down. Mr. Jenkins went into the kitchen so I wouldn't see him, and I heard him cry in there. Broke my heart," he said, staring at his glass the whole while. "I mean it happens. I'm a vet…it happens. I just wish I could do something for the old man. I think he's the last one left down the alley now. I'm surprised he's allowed to stay there. The conditions there are medieval."

"Oh, that's just awful. So sad!" She said, pretending to care, but not caring at all about the stupid old man who was too idiotic to help himself and move into a council house. "I'm so sorry." She laid her hand on his forearm. He didn't move away. Another big victory, she thought to herself. She had heard that James's father had died the year before. She wondered if that was making him more gushy about this dim-witted Bert.

"Jim," Felicity called softly to the barman. She didn't want to break the spell of intimacy she felt she had with James just then. "Another," she said, nodding at James's glass. "And another prosecco." She turned back to James. "It's so hard to see people suffer, isn't it?" She racked her brain to try and think of what sympathetic, weak people in movies said in situations like this. Inside she was thinking, *Oh my God, get over it. It was an ancient dog in a smelly hovel. It's his own fault, that old man.*

But she knew this would be the wrong thing to say, so she let the vet take a deep pull on what was now his third beer. She sipped her wine and pouted in what she hoped was a look of deep concern. Taking it a step further, she very softly laid her hand on the nape of his neck and stroked his hair that gathered at his shirt collar.

*

That night, Eden was at home with Tommy, her mother, and Peter, having dinner and lingering over dessert at the dining room table. There was a pathetic little noise coming from the living room.

"That's Wellie whimpering again," Eden said.

"He's been parked by the front door for half an hour," Susan said with a smile.

"Everything has been so busy lately, I don't get him out for long walks as much these days." Eden got up from the table. "I'll just take him for a little walk now. Poor boy. How's that, Wellie? You want to go for a walk? Want to go for a *walk*?" Eden emphasized the word "walk" and, clearly, the dog knew what it meant, as he leaped up and started wagging his tail wildly.

Eden took down his leash, put on her coat, and announced, "Be back in a little while." She headed out into the evening.

She walked briskly to fight the cold, and to exercise the dog. Up the lane, past the Parks' shop, now closed for the night, along the sidewalk past the pub.

And as she walked by The Horse and Cart, thinking of nothing but what a beautiful cold night it was, she happened to glance in the window and see James seated at the bar, his back to the window. She stopped and looked in, smiling at the sight of him.

Then she noticed a woman next to him with her hand on his arm.

Eden felt a rush of anxiety and told herself to stop it. It could be anyone. It could be his cousin, for all she knew!

Then she saw a manicured hand slowly reach out and stroke the back of James's neck. The woman gently raked the hair at the base of his neck, as she half-stroked, half-massaged the skin there. Then she did it again. This was no cousin.

Suddenly, the image of Robert and the young woman at the party flashed in her head and her stomach lurched. She recognized that feeling of anxiety, of feeling like she was seeing something that meant something. Then she saw Robert and the woman, making love, before they realized she was there.

Eden felt like she was going to throw up. Her eyes stung with tears, and she yanked at the leash and raced back to the cottage, her mind reeling.

Eden walked in the door of the cottage, flustered and upset.

"You're back soon," Susan called from the kitchen where she and Peter were washing up the dinner things.

"I suddenly don't feel well. I'm going to lie down." Eden unhooked Wellie's leash with shaking fingers. "Will you get Tommy ready for bed, Mom?"

"Sure, no problem," her mother said, coming into the living room, drying her hands on a tea towel. "Are you all right? Gosh, I hope it wasn't something you ate, or we *all* ate, I should say."

"I'm fine. Sudden headache. I'll see you in the morning." Eden bolted upstairs.

A few minutes later, lying under the down comforter, she tried to calm herself. Deep breaths, she told herself. Eden knew she was someone ruled more by emotion than logic, so she let the waves of panic and sadness wash over her. But soon there was room for clear thinking, so she had a talk with herself.

Okay, Eden, she said to herself, *you saw James in the pub with a woman. It didn't look good. But you know him. He's not a liar.* Then the other Eden replied in a hysterical voice inside her head. *What the hell do you know? You don't really know him. And men are men, he was in the pub, drinking, with a woman's hand running through his hair. I love that hair, I love to do just that and run my fingers through it myself while his mouth is on mine. Okay stop it,* the logical voice said. *Just go to bed. The truth is you haven't known him that long. Maybe he isn't the man you thought he was. You'll be ok. No matter what, you'll be ok. It's not as if you're engaged to him. He isn't Robert.* Robert. Again, the thought of Robert. *At some point, I'm going to have to talk to him. Have to deal with everything,* she thought. *My gosh, it's almost the new year, I'm supposed to be back in New York in a few months.*

The thought made her so sad and tired that she lay her head down on the pillow and slept.

Chapter 15

The next few days were spent at Mrs. Welsh's while Tommy was in school. Sadly, Mrs. Welsh hadn't felt well enough to come to the Christmas party celebrating the marriage of Peter and Susan. But she was up and about at home, at least, which was good because it was the busy time of year for her—flus, coughs, pneumonia, bones that ached in the cold. And Eden was happy for the distraction.

Eden had put the image of James in the pub out of her mind. He had called her once when she was out, and she hadn't called him back. She would, she thought. Just maybe not today. She was wary. She couldn't handle getting hurt again. Not this time. This time, she really cared. It surprised her. because she hadn't known James very long. But it was different. She felt that he could hurt her in a way that was both exciting to realize, and very scary.

So, she put it out of her mind and welcomed the diversion of the work at Mrs. Welsh's.

That day, there was a knock at the front door. Eden opened the door to find two young men holding large boxes.

"Shipment for Mrs. Welsh," one of them said.

"Oh goodie," Mrs. Welsh said, coming out from the kitchen.

"Some more herbs have arrived. Put them in the kitchen, if you would be so kind."

Once they had left, Mrs. Welsh opened the boxes. "Midwinter, I have to order herbs, as I've usually run out of things I've collected from my garden by then. Let's get these sorted."

Eden smiled at how much she looked like a child on Christmas morning.

Eden felt the same way.

The two women began sorting the herbs into glass jars: valerian, lavender and chamomile for anxiety and sleeplessness; turmeric, cat's claw, and ginger for arthritis; goldenseal for canker sores; echinacea for bad coughs; and many others.

The feeling of the brittle leaves in her hands, the rich varied smells. Some, like lavender, were lovely. Others, like valerian, unpleasant. They all mingled together in the air to produce a magical, soothing feeling. Eden always tingled as she worked with the herbs, something she had come to accept. She even enjoyed the fizz of energy in her hands as she sorted, ground, and jarred the remedies.

There was another knock on the door, and Mrs. Welsh bustled off this time. She had told Eden that this was common, especially this time of year.

This time it was Mrs. Harrington, who was seventy-six, but looked much older. She was slightly bent, and her hands were gnarled with arthritis. The cold, damp weather was a torture for her aching joints, and though she took a painkiller, she came around every few weeks for a balm that Mrs. Welsh had taught Eden to make—ground ginger and lavender and eucalyptus oils cooked in a beeswax base, then put into a small jar to harden. This salve would be rubbed on her aching fingers and provide instant, if temporary, relief. Collecting the salve was also a great excuse for a cup of tea and a chat with her old friend, Hazel, and now her new friend, Eden.

No sooner had Mrs. Harrington left, then there was another knock at the door.

Mrs. Welsh laughed. "We'll never get the herbs sorted at this rate."

A moment later, she returned to the kitchen with raised eyebrows and a little grin. Behind her were James and Bea.

"Come in, my dears," she said to her visitors. Then she quickly added, "I'm so sorry, I've been working here with my wonderful assistant all morning. I'm feeling a little peaked. I'll just put my feet up for a moment, if you don't mind."

She disappeared quickly upstairs to her room, with Eden

staring after her, knowing exactly what she was trying to do.

In the kitchen, James put Bea up on a tall stool by the counter and turned to Eden.

"I called you a couple of times, but didn't hear from you. Everything okay?"

Logical Eden was telling her to be calm and not make a drama. Crazy Eden was telling her not to trust him and to tell him to get out. Logical Eden won.

"I'm fine. I'm sorry. I've been busy and...I guess..." She wanted to elaborate, but Bea was right there. She motioned with her head to Bea and James got the hint.

"Hey, Bea, why don't you go play with Whiskers in the living room, okay?" He hoisted her down from the stool, and she ran off to find Mrs. Welsh's cat. James sat on the stool.

"Well," Eden started. "I don't know, I guess I've just been busy...and also, just, confused a little. I mean, I'm a little freaked out by how much I like you, and I'm supposed to go back to New York in a few months, and I just got over this horrible breakup with Robert and..."

She looked away, out the window, across the winter garden, to the village houses, cozy and familiar now. She wondered how she would ever leave.

"I just don't know if this is so smart. I don't know what I'm doing." There was a long silence, and Eden looked up to see James looking serious.

"Ahh...are we having the 'it's not you, it's me' talk?" he asked, looking straight into her eyes.

Eden was surprised at the strength of feeling that instantly rose up in her chest.

"No!" she exclaimed, wishing, as always, that she was better at playing it cool. "No," she repeated calmly. "Not at all. I think it's almost the opposite of that, and that's why I'm confused. I don't want to get hurt again."

James looked at her with a small smile on his lips, then hopped off the stool. He crossed the kitchen to her and kissed her, slowly and expertly, pulling on her lower lip just slightly as the kiss ended.

Eden's head was reeling.

"I don't know what's going to happen either, Eden. All I know is that I want to do that all the time. It's almost all I think about. That...and much more. And it feels amazing. I've been hurt too. Differently, but badly, and I am loving feeling happy and alive and..."

He paused. "Just *feeling* again. Let's not stop something that feels this good. You don't have to be back in New York tomorrow, do you?"

"No," she conceded.

"Good. So that's all we need to know right now." He smiled and put his hands on her hips, hoisted her onto the stool, and gave her another long, slow kiss.

Eden desperately wanted to leave it there, but she didn't know where this was going. *I'm going to do this right this time. I'm not going to keep my thoughts and feelings hidden to make things easier.*

James turned to go look for Beatrice, but Eden stopped him. "There was something else."

James turned back around, still smiling. "Okay."

"I was walking Wellie the other night, and I saw you through the window of the pub and..." She wasn't sure how to phrase what she'd seen, because she wasn't sure exactly what she *did* see. She went for honest accuracy.

"I saw a blonde woman running her hands through your hair. I don't know who she is, but it freaked me out. I mean, I know we never actually said we were going to be exclusive, and I haven't known you that long but—"

"Oh my gosh, you saw that?" James exclaimed.

Eden's stomach tightened. So, he *had* been trying to hide it!

"Yes, I saw it," she said, her voice harder now. "Is that another lucky lady you are also seeing?" She instantly regretted the sneer she let cross her face.

"Are you crazy?" James let out a laugh. "Okay, first of all, that is Felicity Poolbridge. I've known her since she was born. She is not the nicest person in the world, and not someone I would be interested in under *any* circumstances. She tends to come on strong, as she did that night. But nothing happened. She was flirting, so I quickly finished my beer and left. I was probably gone about two minutes after you looked in the window. But more than that, as anyone in the village can tell you, I have been living more or less under a rock since my wife died. There is no way in hell I could be dating two women right now. I find it terrifying enough to be dating you!"

Eden softened instantly at the look of vulnerability and affection in his eyes.

"I'm sorry!" Eden threw her arms around his neck. "I knew that. I mean, in my gut I knew that, but sometimes my head does a number on me. I guess, once bitten, twice shy. After Robert, I guess it's a bit harder for me to not worry that I'm being a fool again."

"Eden, you aren't being a fool. Or maybe you are, but if you are, then I am too. I feel sort of like a fifteen-year-old fool around you. But in a good way," he said with his sexy half-smile. "I don't know what's going to happen here. I wish I did. You have a whole life in New York. We never really talk about that. But as far as I'm concerned, you have nothing to worry about. To make it clear—I'm yours, if you'll have me."

Eden answered by kissing him softly, deeply, her heart tight with emotion.

A few minutes later, they went into the living room to find Bea, but she wasn't there. She had wandered out into the back garden and was wandering slowly, almost meditatively, through the dead winter garden, running her tiny hands along the stalks of herbs.

She turned and saw them, and stood there for a long moment, staring with such a serious expression that it made Eden wonder what she could be thinking.

Then Bea grinned and raced back into the warm house.

*

Two days later, Eden and James were having dinner at the pub. Tommy was spending the evening playing with Bea at James' house, Mrs. Inskeep watching the two new friends for the night. James seemed distracted.

"Penny for your thoughts," Eden said.

James smiled. "Sorry. I didn't realize I was so tuned out. I just can't get poor Mr. Jenkins out of my mind. He's the old man with the dog I had to put down last week," he clarified. "He lives down the mere, which is what we all call that row of ancient houses down the narrow lane past the church. They're just so dismal. They were nice little homes at one point. It's sad that they've been so neglected. But they're horrible, dark little places now. I know Mr. Jenkins stays out of nostalgia. He and his wife, Patty, raised two sons in that house. Both are grown and gone now." James paused. "Now that I think about it, I wonder why neither of them ever comes back to make sure their father is okay. But Bert really shouldn't spend another winter in that place in the state it's in. And now he's truly alone. His dog was the only company he had."

Eden looked away for several long seconds, before turning back "Well let's help him then."

"Ha," James laughed. "That is so very AmericanThat instantly jumping to action. The confidence that, for every problem, there is a solution and that one can fix any problem themselves. So, how are we going to help him, then? He flatly refuses to leave that little place."

"Let's start by going to see him. I want to see how bad it is.

Maybe we can fix it up a bit. We love a good fixer-upper story in the US," she said with a smile.

"Okay, let's do it this weekend," James said.

"I know, I'll make a big pot of beef stew or something, and we can take him some dinner," Eden said. "Saturday night? If it works for Bert."

"It's a date!" James said.

*

Late Saturday afternoon, Eden and James walked down the uneven cobbles of the mere. There were rows on either side of the street with six houses on each side. Eden could see they must have been very sweet homes in their time. They were made of gray stone. Plate glass windows looked into what must be the living rooms. Each had a walled garden out back, where, no doubt, people had grown vegetables and kept some chickens or pigs, as many villagers used to, and some still did today.

All the windows were dark along the street, except for one. James had told Eden that Mr. Jenkins was the last hold-out resident of the old homes.

They knocked on Mr. Jenkins's door. James had asked if it would be all right for them to visit on Saturday, so the old man was expecting them.

Bert Jenkins greeted them warmly and opened the door to the small sitting room. Mr. Jenkins had a small fire going in the fireplace, but it did little to take the cold out of the stone walls, so they kept their coats on. The room was tidy, but poor. There were two very worn armchairs beside the fire. Mrs. Jenkins's chair had sat empty for a long time, but he hadn't moved it. There was a thin rug on the floor and a bookshelf full of old books. And not much else.

In the kitchen, there was similar sparseness. James and Mr. Jenkins sat at the plain wooden kitchen table, while Eden unpacked the big bag she had brought. It contained a large pot of beef stew, still warm, a bottle of whiskey and a large loaf of crusty bread. In a small tin, there were chocolate cupcakes for dessert.

"This is ever so nice of you two," Mr. Jenkins said with a sweet smile. His eyes were pale blue and watery, and his hands had a slight tremble. "I don't know what makes you want to come down here and have dinner with me, but I'm thrilled that you did!"

"Well, I have been thinking of you since Maisy had to be put down, Bert. I've been worried about you all on your own down here," James said.

"Oh, I know. Everyone keeps telling me I'm mad to stay here.

But it's home. I don't much want to move to some strange place at my age. I'm alone, but here I have a house full of memories everywhere I turn to keep me company."

Eden said she could understand that completely.

James had told her the houses had been fitted with indoor plumbing and heating in the late fifties, but it didn't do much to take the gloom off the place. Still, Eden could see why Mr. Jenkins might not like to leave the memories of his wife behind.

Mr. Jenkins devoured his stew, and Eden made a mental note to bring him some dinner once a week. Something that would last him several nights. While they ate and chatted, she looked around, deciding what needed doing to the little home. First was a deep clean...the place was filthy. She could tell Bert was a tidy man, but he had neither the energy nor, probably, the skills to keep a home deeply clean.

Then paint. A bright color on the walls would do wonders. More lighting...yes, Eden was quickly seeing how this could be made into a pleasant, cozy home with mostly elbow grease, and just a little bit of money.

After dinner, Bert—as he'd invited them to call him—made everyone coffee, and they sat in the living room by the tiny fire.

"Would you get another dog, Bert? It's such good company to

have a dog," James asked at one point.

"Well, I wouldn't mind a dog, I must say. They are the best company in a long evening. But at my age, it'd have to be an old one, like myself," he said with a little chuckle. "Maybe someday, if the right one comes along."

James made eye contact with Eden, and she knew he must be making a mental note to keep his eye out for "the right one."

After a lovely evening, James and Eden said a warm goodbye to Bert, and Eden promised to have him to her cottage next time. He seemed thrilled.

James and Eden walked back up the tiny street, arm in arm, both silently lost in their thoughts.

"I will tell you what. If I spent £500 and had a weekend in that house, I could transform it, you know," Eden finally said, as they turned onto the village sidewalk, ready to relieve Susan from her babysitting duties.

"Could you really?" James asked.

"I could. With your help, if we could get a few things secondhand. And do a bit of painting. It could be lovely. It's just filthy, and dingy. And cold. Okay, it has a lot of things wrong with it," she conceded with a laugh. "But they're all lovely little houses. I wonder who owns them? It's a shame to see them all crumbling. They're probably historic. They would make great weekend homes for Londoners. They'd probably sell for a pretty penny, in fact."

James laughed. "Yes, a true American. Always seeing bigger and better. I thought we might go around with a rag and bucket one afternoon. You're seeing a street transformed into holiday homes!"

"Guilty as charged," Eden agreed. "I love a good project. And why not? People pay a fortune now to have a little place to get out of the city. Two or three bedrooms. Garden. In this gorgeous village. Anyway," she reined herself in. "To start with, why don't we see if Bert is willing to let us have a go at his place. Maybe he has a friend he can go stay with for a weekend, and we can get in there and fix it up a bit. Poor old guy. That's no way to live. I need a hot bath after just one dinner there. That cold gets in your bones!" she exclaimed.

Chapter 16

Christmas was coming, and Eden decided she wanted to have Mr. Jenkins's home done before then. As a gift to the old man. So, they convinced Bert to go visit his cousin, Annie, several villages away. They paid his bus fare and saw him seated on the bus and then went to the house.

Mrs. Innskeep would watch the children during the days on Saturday and Sunday. Eden had spent the previous week online shopping and attending estate sales and, with an additional trip to a home center, she was fully supplied and eager to get started.

As soon as they walked in, the reality of how much there was to do hit them. Eden had bought a small woodstove that could be inserted into the fireplace. The little Norwegian stove would heat the whole house with a wonderfully toasty warmth, so much more efficient than the old fireplace. There was someone coming from Newmarket later that day to install it to code.

"Well," Eden said, looking around, "we better get started!"

They first dragged out the thin, filthy carpet, and the two armchairs. They beat the armchairs to clean them of dust and left them out in the sun to breathe. The rug went in the garbage. They set about with mops and brushes and buckets of hot soapy water, cleaning decades of grime off the walls, windows, and furniture.

After a quick lunch in the pub midday, they went back and felt heartened when they walked back in.

"It already looks much better!" James declared. And it did. With the windows clean and the wooden floors scrubbed and shined, it already seemed lighter and roomier.

"You're a tough boss, Eden," James said, several hours' of work later. He put his scrub brush down and laid down on the now-clean floor with a loud groan. "My back is killing me. God, that's depressing. When did I turn into such an old man?"

He grinned up at Eden, who stood over him. His boyish smile, along with the flat stomach and broad chest visible under his shirt, made her think he most definitely did not look like an old man.

"Lie down, woman! Take a break just for a minute. Out of pity!" He laughed and reached for her hand.

She put down her broom, then let James pull her down on the floor next to him. Looking up, she realized the ceiling would need a coat of paint too and she said so.

"Stop! You're killing me. Close your eyes so you don't see anything else that needs fixing." James laughed then pretended to snore loudly, and Eden playfully kicked him.

She rolled onto one side, her head on her elbow, and looked at him. He turned and looked back, eyebrows raised, with the slight grin he always seems to have.

"Do you think I'm crazy to do this?" she asked. "I mean, sometimes lately, actually a *lot* lately—" she laughed, thinking about the last few months of her life, "—I find myself in the middle of things and don't really know how I even got there! I mean, I don't even know Bert." Then she added, with a hint of defiance in her tone, "I mean, I want to be here. I really want to do this for him. But *you* don't have to be doing this, you know. I could do it on my own."

His lopsided grin grew a bit bigger. "Oh, I have no doubt in my mind you could do this on your own. And anything else you set your mind to! I don't know if it's an American thing, or just who you are, but you seem to feel you can do anything you like. I mean that in a good way. It's not very British. We tend to be better at doing what we're told," he said with a laugh. "But you do it the other way around. You seem to decide you want to do something and then just do it, no asking, just doing. It's amazing."

Eden looked away for a moment and thought. *How incredible. That's not at all how I see myself. I've always considered myself rather meek. Someone who always felt I should fit in, but he's right. I am that person. How funny I hadn't seen that before.* Eden looked back at the handsome face, rugged, dusty, with a streak of white paint along one side of his nose.

"Strange, but you almost seem to know me better than I know myself. I mean…that sounds pathetic. That's not what I mean," she said.

"Okay, what do you mean?"

"I guess I *am* that person. I do see something I want to change, something that's not right, and I try to change it. At least, inside, that's who I am. But I guess it's only since coming here that I'm actually becoming that person. Not just thinking things but doing things. Not always in my head now, but in my body. I hadn't realized it till you said that. But I feel actually pretty good about that!" She smiled.

"Well, you should," James said. "Look what you've done for Tommy. No matter what happens down the road, you've given him more peace and comfort and affection these past few weeks than he's probably ever had, even though his mother did try. And then you meet Bert and, without a second thought, you decide to spend your own money and break your own back, and mine, and totally transform his home. For no reason! Except that it's a kind thing to do. It's amazing really. *You're* amazing," he added. He strained up to kiss her, groaning again at the ache in his back and falling back on the floor.

"Thank you," Eden said, blushing. "You're pretty amazing yourself. ou help out so many people here, all the time, with the work you do. Pets are like family members to a lot of people, especially some of the older people in the village. Some of their pets are the only family they have. You go way above and beyond the call to help the people here. I've seen it. Working all hours. And I've seen you treat pets and charge the owners way under what the actual fee is. Just enough so they save face, but not so much that it would be hard for them. And the way you care for Beatrice. It's beautiful. I really mean it. You are such a wonderful father."

James looked toward the window when she said this, suddenly appearing far away. "When Jane died. I didn't know how I would go on. Not for a single day."

Eden stayed quiet. James hadn't opened up in much detail about Jane's death, and she didn't want to make him stop by saying the wrong thing.

"I loved her. I really loved her. And then when Beatrice came along, we had everything we'd ever dreamed of. And then she got sick. And it all happened so fast. She was gone in a matter of months. Those last months were so awful. Just so awful."

Eden saw him reach up and wipe the corner of his eye.

"And there had been so much to do, her getting so sick so fast. Doctor visits and chemo and taking care of her. And Bea was just a baby. And then suddenly, she was gone. And there was nothing to do at all. It was done. Over. I'd never understood before that…that it isn't the death part, or even the dying part, that really gets you. That really rips your heart out. It's not those concrete events. It's the afterwards. It's the huge, gaping absence of where the person used to be. This enormous, palpable, permanent, irrevocable absence that kills you. The huge hole where a person, a life, was. It isn't gone. It's still there, it's just empty. Forever. That's the part that undid me. Almost undid me."

He rolled onto his side to face Eden.

"I think Beatrice is what saved me. I had to get up. I wanted to stay in bed and hide and sleep for days on end, but I couldn't. She was a baby, just barely one, and she needed to eat—all the time—and have her diapers changed—all the time—and play—all the time. God, it was exhausting." He smiled. "But she made me get up. Made me make breakfast. Learn to cook. Learn the words to silly songs. Learn how to raise a child on my own. I don't know if it's good or bad, but she was so young that she's sad thinking her mother is gone, but she was too young to get really hurt by it. She asked for her right afterwards, all the time. And I'd have a little one-year-old-level chat with her about Mummy being in heaven. Then I'd go in the bathroom and bawl my eyes out for two minutes, then come back out and start dinner. But kids are so in the moment, and so quick to move on, she was all right pretty quickly. Thank God. And then...then days just started passing. And the forcing myself to take a shower and get dressed and go to work got a tiny bit easier. And then months had gone by. And then a year had gone by. And then two. And life goes on," he said with a sound of resignation.

He smiled again at Eden. "And of course, I've met a few women here and there. It has been three years, after all. And sometimes a man just needs...well, you know," he said, looking down a little bashfully, "some companionship. But it took a long time for me to feel it might ever be possible to really care about another woman. A very long time. In fact, I was mostly resigned to the fact that it would probably never happen. Not in any way that really...I don't know, made me want to crawl out from under my rock." He laughed, as he reached up and cupped Eden's face in one hand. "Then I was driving down the road one day and I almost ran you over, and you stormed up to me and yelled at me. And by the time you showed up in my clinic that afternoon, sick, pale, with a red, runny nose, trying to help some homeless dog you'd carried for a mile in the rain, I was already a goner."

Eden felt her eyes sting with tears. "I was too," she said, and she leaned over him and kissed his mouth.

James pulled her on top of him and pushed her hair back from the sides of her face with his hands while he kissed her softly.

"Miss Martin, if it weren't completely inappropriate, being in Bert's living room, and if I didn't think it would actually, truly break my back, I'd make love to you right here and now on this cold, hard floor."

"And I'd let you." Eden returned his smile. Then she rolled off him and stood up, offering him her hand. "All right, old man. Get up. Back to work."

The woodstove was installed that afternoon while they were cleaning the kitchen, scraping and scrubbing away layers and layers of grease that had accumulated from years of smoky cooking. By late afternoon, they got out the paint, just slightly off white. They painted the entire downstairs, then got a little start cleaning the two bedrooms and bathroom upstairs before they were so tired, they couldn't go on.

The next morning, they were back, bright and early. They

finished scrubbing and painting the upstairs, carted out the lumpy, ancient mattress Bert had been sleeping on, and laid down the clean comfortable mattress and box spring Eden had gotten secondhand. They put on all new bedding, clean and cheerful, and hung a picture on the wall that Eden had found in a closet—a lively watercolor of the seaside somewhere. A new rug on the floor, two lamps on side tables, and this room, too, was transformed.

Downstairs, Eden got out a lovely, thick, dark red and blue rug she'd found at an estate sale, and she and James unrolled it across the living room. They brought back in the two chairs and fitted the new blue slipcovers over them. Then added side tables and two bright floor lamps. They filled the wood basket with wood and then added the final touch, a small Christmas tree that they proceeded to hang with tinsel and little lights.

James and Eden stood, arms around each other, beaming with satisfaction at their work. They were sore, exhausted, and starving, but it was amazing. The dark, damp hovel was now a clean, bright, cheerful little cottage. The outside of the building was still dark and could use a wash, Eden decided, and the little patch of grass out front would need planting in the spring. Maybe a window box of red geraniums. She laughed at herself. She really was American, always thinking of bigger and better.

"I wonder who does own these cottages," she said to James, as they walked toward home. "I bet we could find out in the village records somewhere."

James, so tired he could barely stand up, looked wary. "Oh boy. What's going on in your head? Going to transform the whole street singlehandedly, are you?" He laughed.

"No, of course not." She shot him a huge grin. "You're going to help!"

*

Three days before Christmas, Bert got off the bus after a lovely visit with his cousin. James and Eden drove him to his house. Eden couldn't resist doing something to the outside, so she'd added a flower box and filled it with holly with shiny green leaves and bright red berries. She painted his front door bright red and hung a wreath. It looked very festive.

"Oh, my goodness, this is too much!" Bert exclaimed, just seeing the holly and the door.

Eden and James just smiled. Bert opened the door and took a step inside, his mouth falling open. His clear, light blue eyes grew wide as he took it all in. They had a fire crackling in the woodstove, and the house was dry and toasty warm. The beautiful, colorful rug covered shining wood floors. The walls were white and clean, and the furniture all looked like new. He took in the little sparkling Christmas tree, and he began to cry.

Eden rushed over and gave him a hug. "Please don't cry. This is supposed to make you happy!"

He looked at her tenderly. "My dear, you have no idea how happy this has made me," he said, wiping his eyes.

Just then, something moved, and he noticed a brown mass of hair rising out of the corner of the room. It was a dog. His eyes grew wide again.

"Oh, my goodness, who is that?" he asked.

James smiled. "That is Trixie." He paused to let Bert take it in. "Her owner moved to a nursing home recently and couldn't keep her. The dog has been at the shelter in Newmarket for weeks, but most people want a puppy. She is very sweet, very calm. She's four years old, so she's not going to be bounding around. I asked at the shelter if we might bring her here just for a trial. I hope you don't mind, Bert. Of course, it's entirely up to you. There's no pressure to keep her. But this is a lovely home for a dog, and she needs a home. So, if you want to, you can keep her for a week and see how it goes."

Eden saw Bert look around, then go upstairs and see it too was clean and bright. Trixie had gone back to the dog bed that had been set by the chair and was asleep already. Bert told them this was the happiest Christmas he had had in many years and none of them had a dry eye by the time the new friends parted.

*

Christmas morning started early in Eden's little cottage.

"Wake up! Wake up!" Tommy yelled, running into Eden's room and jumping on her bed. "It's Christmas! Let's see if Santa Claus came!" With a broad smile, he raced down the stairs.

Eden smiled, pulled on her dressing gown, and phoned her mother.

"Hello?" a sleepy Susan said from the other end of the call.

"You said you wanted to know when the action was starting over here. Well, he's up!" she said, smiling into the phone. "I won't be able to hold him off for long, so if you want to come over for presents, I'd come now!"

"What time is it?" Eden's mother asked.

Eden looked at the bedside clock. "6:03 a.m.," she replied. "I'll put the coffee on."

Tommy told Eden he had had a few gifts at other Christmases.

His mother had done her best to make it a special day in years past, but funds had always been tight, and his father usually ruined the day by starting a fight or getting drunk.

Eden found Tommy in the living room with a pile of shiny packages and ribbons all for him.

Eden's mother and Peter showed up a short time later for the fun, and Tommy ripped open his boxes with wild excitement. The biggest thrill of all was the bright red bike with a huge bow on it. It was his first bike, so it had training wheels, and Tommy burst into tears when he saw it, he was so overwhelmed.

After all the gifts had been opened, he put his winter coat on over his pajamas and took it out to ride up and down the lane until he was half frozen and had to come in and sit by the fire.

Eden got a beautiful cashmere scarf from her mother and Peter, and a gift certificate to a very nice restaurant in Cambridge. She found a box with a tag saying it was to her from James. She smiled in surprise, realizing he must have slipped it under the tree without her noticing. It was a book of English poetry from the Middle Ages. Eden didn't know why this made her want to cry. Then she realized it was because the gift was so perfect. Not huge. Not expensive, but it showed that he knew her, he saw her. And he cared for her.

When it seemed everything had been unwrapped, Tommy walked over to the sofa with a little crumpled pile of wrapping paper and handed it to Eden.

"This is for you," he said with a sweet, tender look on his face.

Eden opened it carefully. Inside was a small handmade clay pot. Around the sides of the pot in red paint it said "I love you" in sloppy, yet just legible, block letters.

Eden looked up and tears welled in her eyes. It was so unexpected. She thought it might be the nicest gift she had ever received.

"Tommy, this is for me?"

"Yes. I made it in school. And I do. Love you," he said, and he threw himself into her arms and started to cry.

The day had been a lot for him to handle, she thought as she hugged him tightly. All the excitement, mixed with the sadness of his first Christmas without either of his parents.

"I love you too, sweet boy," she whispered into his ear, and she felt his face smile against her cheek.

Carols played cheerfully on the radio as Eden and Susan prepared Christmas dinner. They had a big roast turkey, stuffing, Brussels sprouts, lots of wine. After the meal, Tommy and Peter brought in the Christmas pudding, with a holly sprig atop the black mound. It was doused in brandy and lit on fire. There were Christmas crackers, and everyone wore their paper crowns and read the silly jokes from the little slips of paper.

Finally, everyone was so full, they moved into the living room, where Peter threw a log on the fire. The grownups all fell asleep on the sofa and chairs, while Tommy played with his new toys.

Chapter 17

A few days after Christmas, Eden brought sandwiches to James's clinic for lunch. They closed and locked the door, and James flipped the sign on the door to "Back Soon."

They sat in his office, sharing a beer and ham and cheese sandwiches. They didn't have much time to be truly alone, with no children, parents, patients, or neighbors around. In fact, it was such a rare event that just sitting across James's desk from one another, eating and chatting, felt sexy to Eden.

As they finished their lunch, there was a pause in conversation. James watched Eden take a long drink from the beer, looked at the front door, locked tight. Eden caught his eye and instantly read the desire in it. Her stomach did a little flip.

She watched him get up, without saying a word, eyes locked on hers. He closed the door that separated his office from the waiting room, then turned back, lifting Eden out of her chair, kissing her before she was fully upright.

He had his hands in her hair, and their kisses were instantly hungry. He lifted Eden effortlessly and sat her on his desk. Eden pushed her hands under his shirt, hungrily running them over his back.

They moved to the sofa against the wall in his office, pulling off their clothes while kissing.

When they were both spent and satisfied, they lay together on the sofa, wrapped in a blanket, happy and tired. James played with a long piece of Eden's hair that fell onto his chest as her head rested on his shoulder. He twirled it around his finger and looking down at her with a look of affection—and surprise—on his face.

He ran a rough finger along the edge of her chin and whispered into her hair, "You mean so much to me, Eden. So much." He kissed her head softly.

Eden raised herself up onto her elbow. His square jaw was covered in stubble, his full lips, which were usually smiling, were serious now. As were his eyes as he looked at her with intensity and vulnerability at the same time.

She reached down and ran a finger along his face, before leaning close and whispering into his ear, "And you mean so much to me, James Beck. So much."

Half an hour later, a bit late, and with two clients already waiting outside, James unlocked the front door. Eden, now pulled together, hair brushed, and clothes back in place, left with a forced casual goodbye as she passed the people waiting to see the vet.

When she was down the hall, she turned back just as James ushered the people and their animals in. Their eyes met. She smiled and bit her lip. James closed his eyes and exhaled, a smile on his lips too.

*

As winter wore on, cold and gray, Eden worked daily at either researching and writing her book, or with Mrs. Welsh, making tinctures, preparing herbs, recording stories and remedies, or out on calls, healing the unwell. And working with social services to finalize becoming Tommy's official foster parent.

There had been many colds and flu to see to. A few cases of insomnia. One of depression. And even a couple of exciting cases.

One woman, pregnant with her fourth child, went into labor so quickly, there was no time to get her to the hospital. Mrs. Welsh, with Eden watching, had delivered a baby right on the living room floor of the woman's house. They then cleaned the mother and baby up and waited until an ambulance came and took them off to the clinic to be checked out by the midwife. It had been terrifying and thrilling at the same time.

Eden had watched as Mrs. Welsh, who had done this several times over the years, encouraged the woman and helped ease a new life into the world, just as, no doubt, her ancestors had been doing in this village for centuries.

Once the woman had been taken to the clinic, Mrs. Welsh and Eden cleaned up and then brewed a strong tonic tea. They'd also made a simmering pot of chicken soup, filled with ginger, sage, rosemary, and shepherd's purse seed, to build her strength, warm her and make sure her milk came in. Mrs. Welsh explained that she thought it was terrible that women now got sent home from the hospital with a new baby and nothing else. As if their bodies hadn't been through war getting the child out. A woman needed herbs and soups for at least a month following childbirth, and many young mothers in the village, though they went to the hospital and had a modern, conventional delivery, paid Mrs. Welsh in advance for this month's supply of healing food and drink to be delivered starting as soon as they got home.

Another time, a man cleaning his gutters had fallen off his ladder and hit his head. An ambulance was called but, in the meantime, Mrs. Welsh held a rag steeped in yarrow and St. John's Wort to the wound. It miraculously stopped bleeding, possibly saving the man's life.

But, most of the time, they treated things like an old woman's arthritis, a baby's rattling cough, or an infected finger. Still, all of this got Eden and Mrs. Welsh out about the village with their baskets of herbs and teas. And Eden loved it.

But the work and the cold weather, combined with Mrs. Welsh's weak heart, began to take a toll on the old woman. There were several days that, stubborn as she was, Mrs. Welsh had to admit she wasn't up to going out. She left the herbs and patients in Eden's hands.

"I trust you fully, my dear," she said. "You've more knowledge in some things than even I do, and you have the touch. You go on and make a remedy, and I'll be here waiting to hear all about it when you get back."

One day, while Eden was mixing a remedy for a woman having panic attacks, Eden remembered her day at the church in the woods with James. "Mrs. Welsh? Have you ever been to that old cathedral in the woods? It's half fallen down now, but the skeleton of the building is still there."

"Certainly," she said. "My mother took me there as a child, and I've been a few times since. Though I don't think I'd be up for the long walk there now, I'm afraid. Why, dear?"

"James took me," Eden told her. "And it was beautiful. It definitely felt sacred and….and also strange."

Mrs. Welsh smiled as if she knew something Eden didn't. "Strange? In what way?" Her smile grew playful, which Eden knew meant she already knew the answer.

"Well, I saw things. Or heard things. Or both. I think I saw things and heard them, even smelled them…as if I was really there. Okay, let me clarify that. I saw things…I saw monks in robes, and women chanting. I smelled candles burning, and incense. And I saw the cathedral fully standing, and one nun even spoke to me. I know that sounds absolutely crazy, but it was as clear and plain as you are sitting there right now. I know I didn't make it up. But I can't explain it."

"Oh, how lovely, dear," Mrs. Welsh said in that friendly but totally unimpressed way that instantly put Eden at ease any time these strange, magical happenings made her nervous. "You found a *knowing* place. Always good to have one or two of those."

She wandered into to the kitchen to slice some pound cake for tea. Eden followed her.

"Sorry, what's a knowing place?" Eden asked.

"It's a place to get the knowing. You get…well, information, I suppose. Sometimes it's a bit choppy and hard to explain. Other times it's very clear. Every healer has a few places they feel the knowing the strongest. Mine happens to be right in the herb garden at the back of my house. Very convenient," she said with a smile. "You have some places where the knowing is very strong back in your country. Some are very famous. Sedona, Arizona…that's a well-known one. I've always wanted to go there and see what it felt like." She looked off into the distance as if picturing it. "I doubt I'll make it in this lifetime. But there are lots of them. Sounds like yours is the chapel in the woods, dear. How nice." She filled the kettle to make tea.

A knowing place, Eden thought as she walked home that afternoon. *My knowing place.*

That evening, after she put Tommy to bed, she wrote about the knowing place in her book, adding magical, mystical experiences taking place in the mist, as they had to her.

*

The next day, after dropping Tommy at school, she drove herself back there. She wanted to sit in the cathedral alone, not worried about looking or sounding crazy in front of someone else. She drove the same route James had driven her, pulled onto the same shoulder of the road, and walked along the narrow path into the woods.

When she arrived at the clearing, it was bitterly cold, and she was glad she'd worn her thick coat and gloves. As she entered, she was disappointed to find she felt nothing.

She sat on a stone wall, but still heard and saw nothing out of the ordinary. It was very peaceful, but nothing beyond that.

She stood and walked out to the ancient herb garden. There, she felt a slight rumbling. She wasn't sure if it was inside or outside her body.

She took her gloves off, knelt down, and touched the dead stubble of herbs and weeds on the ground. She felt the tingle then, all the way up her arms. Then she saw a light, flickering. It was a candle— lots of candles lining the walls of the cathedral. And she heard chanting again.

Instead of being scared, she sat down, hands still on the cold earth, legs crossed. She closed her eyes. *Yes, there you are*, she heard, or felt, or imagined.

A vision of herbal gardens, full and blooming, came into her mind. She saw her own hands picking a certain herb: yarrow. She recognized the feathery, fern-like leaves and tiny white flowers.

Yes, that's right, she heard and felt again. *You will need that soon*. She opened her eyes. *Incredible*. She looked over the dead garden and wondered what it would look like in a few months when the plants started coming up.

I will have to keep coming here and see what these monk ghosts are growing in their garden, she thought with a smile.

She collected some seeds from a few other dry stalks and

carefully wrapped each little pile in separate small pieces of paper.

"Thank you," she said out loud, smiling at the garden and hoping someone heard her. "I'm going to plant these in the spring. I'm going to start my own healing garden. You're welcome to visit it any time."

She laughed out loud at how crazy she would have looked to herself just a few months ago. And how crazy she would probably look to most of the world right then. And she didn't care at all.

*

Tommy settled in happily to life at the cottage with Eden, and they both fell into the routine of school and work till the afternoon, followed by homework, dinner, and playing till bedtime. They took Wellie for long chilly walks on the wind-swept hills above the village, and on days when needed, Tommy even accompanied her as she took herbal remedies to sick villagers, feeling very proud and important as he did so.

All the while, Eden had those row houses in the back of her mind. One day, she decided to go and see if she could figure out who owned the cottages on Mere Lane after all. She felt sad thinking of Bert there, with all those empty houses falling down around him, but also curious to see who owned them and why they weren't doing anything with them. As someone who had lived for the past twenty years in New York City, she knew valuable real estate when she saw it. Why didn't someone, or even the town, spruce the little homes up to rent or sell?

So she went to the little building that housed the village hall and talked to the young clerk there. He looked about eighteen years old and bored to tears. *He must spend hours sitting here with nothing to do in such a small place, poor guy*, Eden thought.

When she said she was looking for the owner of the houses down the lane, he seemed almost as interested as she was to find the answer. Clearly, it had never occurred to him to wonder who owned them.

After a trip to some dark shelves in the back of the building, the clerk supplied her with several large ledgers and told her to start looking, while he looked through some different files.

Two hours later, feeling very dusty and tired, Eden's eyes grew wide with shock as she came across the information she wanted. The owner of those cottages. She had to read and reread the entry to believe it.

The owner was none other than Peter Penley-Smith!

Eden didn't tell the clerk she had found the information, thinking that Peter might not want the news spread around the village that he was a slumlord. But she thanked him profusely and walked out, blinking in the sun.

Next stop, the manor house.

Eden rang the bell at the front door and waited. Without a butler standing by to open the door, it often took a while for Susan or Peter to answer.

Eventually, the door opened. "What a lovely surprise!" Her mother stood aside to let Eden in.

Eden asked if Peter was home, and Susan said that he was in the library reading. Susan went to fetch him. She made a pot of tea and they all sat down at the kitchen table.

"The reason I'm here is that, well, you know how James and I cleaned up Bert's house for him?"

"Indeed, we do!" said Peter. "Such a lovely thing to do. Very good of you."

"Well." Eden paused, suddenly afraid she might offend Peter if it seemed she was confronting him. Then again, it really wasn't okay for him to let an entire neighborhood of historic cottages crumble to the ground, especially while Bert was still living there, and she was interested to hear what he had to say about it. "Well," she started again, "after we did that, I got curious as to who owned those houses. I know

Bert owns his. But the others must be owned by someone."

"Yes, good point, dear girl," Peter said. "I hadn't given it much thought. I assume the town owns them, and as they built all those comfortable new council houses, they just let them go to pot."

"The thing is," Eden said, relieved to realize Peter didn't know who owned the houses, "it turns out they aren't owned by the town. It turns out...they are owned by someone in the village."

"Well, I never," said Peter, with only mild interest, turning to pour himself a new cup of tea.

"Actually...the owner of those houses is you, Peter."

"What?" Peter almost shouted. His eyes grew wide, and he spilled a little of his tea. Eden wasn't sure if he was angry or just surprised. Or both. "I say, that's not possible. I have nothing at all to do with those houses. Never seen one scrap of paper anywhere about them!"

Eden could tell he felt insulted that she could think he would let something of his fall into such a state of disrepair.

"I thought that might be the case," she went on. "I mean, I thought you might not know you owned them. That was the only explanation I could think of! I knew you'd never let them crumble all around Bert without any upkeep at all. But, the fact is, you do own them."

Eden looked over at her mother, who also looked surprised. But her feathers were not easily ruffled, so she also looked slightly amused and entertained by it all.

"Your grandfather apparently sold a few to individuals and planned to sell the rest to the village. At least, he almost did. The sale was drawn up, and the village council was going to take them over and sell them. This was before the new council houses were built. Anyway, I found in my research that, just days before the sale was final, your grandfather died. And not long after that was the great fire of Barton Heath, where so many homes were lost. Somehow, in all the ensuing chaos and the rush to rebuild, the project fell through the cracks. Your father had likely been told that the estates were being sold and, well, I don't really know. Somehow, everyone thought someone else owned them, and then the council houses were built. No one needed the row houses anymore, or almost no one did, so they just sat there. But they are, in fact, yours! Well, most of them."

There was a long pause as Peter sat with his mouth still agape and tried to take it in.

"My dear, you're telling me that the houses on Mere Lane are mine?" He looked exasperated. "Those falling to bits old row houses?

Good Lord! What on earth am I going to do with a dozen falling-down row houses?"

"Well…I have an idea."

*

Two hours later, a plan had been hatched. Peter would supply the funds, while sticking to a fairly strict budget, and Eden would do the work. She would gradually go over all the houses, as she and James had done to Bert's. Then a few would be sold, advertised to Londoners looking for a quaint weekend getaway, and the rest would be rented out as permanent homes or holiday homes. There was plenty to see in the area for tourists, from those wanting a simple quiet village getaway, to horse enthusiasts eager to be near Newmarket, the horse capital of England, to amateur historians eager to see the few local castles and historic homes.

To start, Peter would hire a building contractor to inspect each house, its plumbing and electrical wiring, its soundness, and if anything beyond soap and paint was needed, the contractor would take care of it. Eden thought, if they were anything like Bert's, the run-down look was likely mostly cosmetic.

Eden would scour the countryside for secondhand woodstoves, paintings, and rugs. Beyond that, the houses would be sold unfurnished. They would all need a deep clean, a fresh coat of paint to brighten them, some new updates in the kitchens, and a shiny red painted front door with a window box of geraniums.

All three thought the plan was quite exciting. Peter insisted he would give Eden a portion of whatever he made out of the various leases and sales. She protested strongly, but he wouldn't be swayed. It had been her idea, and she was planning on doing most of the work. In fact, he would likely never have even known he owned them without her. She would be compensated.

Eden left feeling energized and excited, ready to get to work. But first, she'd have to wait for the all-clear by the contractors. So, she went home to draw up plans and look up paint colors.

By the following week, a contractor had been in to see each of the eleven uninhabited houses and listed the things that needed repair. Some electrical work needed doing in a few of the cottages. The stone wall out front had tumbled down and needed fixing at another. And there were several other small jobs. The contractor would have the various masons and technicians in to do those things.

Eden drove up to the manor house late one evening to collect Tommy, who had been watched by Susan and Peter.

"I drove all the way to Tewksbury because a large bed and

breakfast was going out of business there. I got four woodstoves and three great rugs at a steal!" she exclaimed as if she'd won the lottery.

"Wonderful!" Peter agreed. "You do move at lightning speed, I must say. I think that's an American thing. Or maybe a New York thing. But whatever it is, it's impressive!"

"I'm scrubbing and painting every morning now, just a couple of hours, so I have time for Mrs. Welsh and a bit of writing before I collect Tommy from school. But they're really coming along!" she said, still flushed with excitement. "I guess I do love a good fixer-upper. Maybe I feel a bit like one myself. I just need a little work and a little love and I'm good as new."

The houses were starting to look different very quickly, and Eden loved the almost instant gratification of seeing each house start to take shape. As soon as a house was finished on the inside, the last thing she did was hang a wooden window planter and add the evergreens, which would be replaced by geraniums later in spring. Then she'd paint the front door a shiny bright red.

One by one, the little houses seemed to stretch and yawn and open their eyes and look around. Bert came out every morning that Eden was there, Trixie trotting at his side, and bring big mugs of sweet milky tea to Eden. Grass seed was tossed in every little square patch of front garden, behind each stone wall, as the weather shifted and nurtured the lawns perfectly with its constant move between rain and sun. Life was returning to Mere Lane.

Chapter 18

In the early spring, English weather was predictably unpredictable. One day was lovely and warm and everyone would have tea out in sunny, protected corners of their gardens. The next day it might be pelting down cold rain.

Every spring, the village held its annual animal show. Sometimes Eden thought the Brits did so many outdoor activities, despite the terrible weather, just to prove they were tough. Either way, each year, crowds of people gathered on the village green with their animals to see who would win best in their breed.

"Pigs over there," one volunteer yelled to a farmer with a pig that must have weighed several hundred pounds walking behind him on a thin string leash.

"Daniel, take Spot over there with the other dogs," a mother said to her son.

There were stalls of prize cows, sheep, pigs, horses, and of course, all the village children—and several of the village adults—brought in their dogs, washed and brushed, or their rabbits in little portable cages. Even a goldfish made it onto the table in its round bowl.

The judge was always the village vet.

James had told Eden he'd been judging the event for several years and always looked forward to it. For the more serious large animal categories, always entered by farmers who knew more about animals than he did, he had to draw on his professional knowledge, as well as opinion, to decide the healthiest and best specimen in the category.

The scruffy dogs on leashes, were held by excited little children looking up at him with nervous and expectant expressions. He always took plenty of time on the children's pets, so they all felt they'd had a fair share of attention. He made sure he found things to compliment, about even the scrappiest, mangiest dog, brought in by the poorest child in the village. A dog like that might even win for "best personality" or "sweetest eyes."

Eden, Tommy and Tara arrived at the fair when it was in full swing.

"Let's look at the pets first. The children are so sweet, with their happy dogs and their cats looking miserable in crates," Tara said with a smile.

"Sounds good," Eden said.

They walked over to the area with a banner reading

"Household Pets" swaying overhead in the breeze.

A little girl in a sparkly dress stood proudly beside a cage that contained a rabbit with a large bow around its neck. The rabbit was shaking its head and kicking with its back legs at the pink bow, trying to dislodge this annoying new appendage. The little girl was oblivious to her pet's discomfort and stood next to the cage with a proud smile. This had been her handiwork, clearly.

"Poor thing," Eden said with a laugh. "I'm sure half these pets have been tortured all morning."

Near the rabbits, they found a girl with a poodle who had been dyed purple and its hair brushed and teased till he looked like an enormous purple ball of fuzz.

"Oh my God! Now that should get you disqualified." They giggled seeing the ridiculous-looking dog.

Eden saw James a few times in passing. In the pigpen, where he was deciding between six different, impressive-looking pigs. Then, at the tea tent when he took a break.

"It looks so fun. Is it *actually* fun to do, to be the judge?" Tara asked him.

"It is," James replied. "It's a lot of fun. But also, a bit hard, because someone is always disappointed. Especially the kids. They usually take it well though. And it's all part of life. We can't all win every time. But that part can be tough. Last year, one boy cried. Then his father yelled at him for crying! I felt terrible." James grinned. "I snuck him a lollipop as consolation."

Later in the morning, James had just begun inspecting the dogs, the largest category at the fair every year. There were seventeen dogs, all of whom James knew from his practice.

He was petting a pretty yellow cocker spaniel when all hell broke loose. There was a loud banging sound and then some commotion and then someone screamed. One of the horses had spooked and kicked its flimsy travel pen door open. The owner still had the horse by the reins, but it was an enormous workhorse, and it reared up, pulling on the rein, eyes wild in panic. People yelled and rushed around, trying to get out of the way, but it only made the animal more frantic as they did so.

Finally, the horse reared up, and the farmer lost hold of the reins. The horse took off.

James sprang to action. This could be dangerous. Deadly even. An enormous farm horse bolting through a crowd, with most of the village's children in it.

Several other men ran toward the scene, but many of them

were farmers and knew horses and knew not to run over and scare the beast even more.

The horse raced around, unsure where to go with so many people on all sides. James saw the horse spot a fence. *Oh no.*

The horse suddenly ran flat out at the fence and tried to jump it. But it panicked at the last second, hesitated, and went down across the fence rails, landing back on the green, neighing wildly.

James arrived next to the animal, calling out, "Okay, everyone, just give him some space. Back away slowly. It'll be all right."

"He's Toby," the horse's owner said, coming up beside James. "That's his name. One of the best horses I've ever had. No evil in 'im. That's a good boy, Toby," the farmer said soothingly.

James and the farmer, a man named Ted, walked toward the huge animal. It had a large gash in its neck and was bleeding profusely.

"Ted, go to the tent, behind the microphone, under that table. You'll see my black bag. Bring it here fast as you can."

The farmer took off quickly, as James observed the scared, injured horse, whose eyes were so wide James saw mostly white, rolling wildly around in his head. He put his arms out, hands toward the horse, and spoke softly and soothingly.

"There, Toby. Hush. Hush. You're all right." As he said this, he walked slowly closer.

There was a large crowd now standing silently, mouths open, watching the excitement. Eden and Tara were among them.

A dog barked, and the animal thrashed around, trying to get up. James could see the reins had gotten caught on the fence. Soon, Ted was back with James's travel bag. James took it and took the last few steps toward the horse, who now lay still, breathing heavily, eyes still wide.

"Okay, Toby. There's a good boy," James said again.

Eden felt a flood of worry for the horse, and for James, and pride watching him calm the huge, injured animal. James knelt down, opened his bag, and took out a long needle and small glass vial. He put the needle into the vial and drained the clear liquid. Then he slowly reached a hand out toward the horse.

"Hush now. Okay, you're okay," he repeated over and over. He got near to the beast and was able to lay one hand on its neck.

The horse flinched but didn't struggle or thrash. James ran his hand up the enormous neck until he found the spot he was looking for. Then he very slowly moved the needle toward the spot and quickly slid it through the tough skin. The horse reared and neighed wildly. It was in pain and scared and it tried to stand to get away from this new assault, but its head was still tied to the gate by the tangled reins. He looked like he might break his own neck if he kept thrashing.

"I'd 'ate to lose him, James. He's a good one," Ted said.

James didn't turn around. "I know, Ted."

In another few seconds, the horse stopped struggling and laid peacefully on the ground, this time staring ahead unseeing.

"I've sedated him," James said. "I need to stitch the wound right away. He's bleeding badly. That's the real danger here. Then, we can get him up and home, and I can really examine him."

James reached into his bag and took out a suture line and needle and, after pouring disinfectant liberally into and around the wound, he began to sew the gash back together. For several minutes, everyone watched as James's expert hands, now bloody, deftly sutured the horrible injury closed. He was so calm and tender, though he'd had to face the enormous, dangerous animal head-on.

Eden felt her heart swell as she watched.

A short time later, James wiped the wound down with more disinfectant, and the horse was transformed. Where, just a little while before, there had been a gash, bleeding heavily, there was now a neatly closed line of stitches. He applied a thick antibiotic ointment to it and bandaged the wound. Then he carefully stood up and unhooked the reins from the fence and after another injection, the horse staggered to its feet.

James slowly led the horse back to its temporary stable, where he examined it thoroughly and declared that the cut on the neck had very luckily been the only injury. The farmer was thrilled. James looked thrilled. Only the horse didn't look thrilled, but, rather, groggy and unsteady. But he would be fine. And no one had gotten hurt.

A voice over the loudspeaker tried to restore the mood. "After a short break, our very able veterinarian will be judging the dogs!"

James was walking toward a hose spigot to wash the blood off his hands when Eden ran up to him. She beamed at him, and he laughed.

"You were amazing!" she said, planting a long kiss on his lips. "You were like…I don't know…it was amazing. Is it awful that I found that sexy? I mean blood and an injured horse, and I was thinking, God he's sexy. Is that awful? That's pretty awful." She laughed.

"I'm glad you think so. Maybe for our next date, I'll find a cow with a compound fracture to set, instead of cooking you dinner," he said with his sexy smile. "Anyway, just doing my job." He leaned over while his hands were under the frigid stream of water from the spigot and kissed her back.

*

Life with Mrs. Welsh continued to be a lesson in both history and reality. Eden met her old friend almost every day and marveled at how much knowledge Mrs. Welsh's mind contained. She felt she could visit with her for years, and the fascinating and vital information would pour forth completely uninterrupted the whole time. This week, she was teaching Eden about herbs for coughs.

"There were different kinds of coughs, distinguished as separate ailments in the sixteenth century, not so different from how they are categorized today," Mrs. Welsh explained. "Dry cough, wet cough with phlegm, etc."

Eden was mixing up a recipe for a dry cough so they would have it on hand. The old healer read out the ingredients, and Eden ground them together in a bowl. Celery seeds, anise seeds, and violet seeds were ground and then mixed with honey. This was the failsafe over-the-counter cough mix of the 1500s, Mrs. Welsh told her, and Eden almost wanted to catch a cold so she could try it.

She never had long to wait before someone else needed it, though. Someone in the village, and occasionally from another village, was always getting sick that time of year, and it was often with coughs.

Mrs. Welsh was mixing a cough syrup of her own, containing licorice, vinegar, and honey, when Eden's cell phone rang. As expected, she was given a chance to try out her remedy on a patient almost immediately. It was the village school, and Tommy wasn't feeling well.

"Poor dear," Mrs. Welsh said. "Bring him here, and we'll sort him out, and then you can take him home and put him to bed."

Eden wrapped a scarf around her neck, having learned from healers of the Middle Ages never to "catch a chill on the back of the neck" unless you wanted to catch cold yourself. She hurried off to the school on the other side of the green. She was back shortly afterward with a miserable-looking Tommy. His eyes were watery, his cheeks flushed, and he was coughing and sneezing.

Mrs. Welsh sat him in front of the fire and handed him a mug of tea, and then gave him a big tablespoon of the violet seed syrup. She sent Eden home with a jar of the very mixture she had just created, and Eden bustled Tommy off to bed with a hot water bottle.

*

When Tommy was well and back in school, two days later, Eden made another trip to the chapel in the woods. She went as often as time would allow, always bringing offerings when she went. She wasn't sure why, or to whom she was offering them. But she felt drawn to do it. Often it was a candle. Once, a handful of seeds of wildflower she scattered outside the stones. Once a small cross she'd made of two twigs tied with yarn.

She liked to light a candle and just sit in the peace of the ruins, listening to the voices, seeing the sights that came to her, but now, somehow, seemed just as they should be. No longer frightening or crazy.

That day, she saw again the garden with the yarrow and made a note that she'd been shown that twice.

As the vision cleared, suddenly, with absolute and complete certainty, she knew that something had happened to Mrs. Welsh.

It wasn't a subtle knowing. And it wasn't vague.

Eden jumped up and ran all the way back to the car, driving top speed to the little cottage with the blue door.

When she got there and banged on the door, there was no answer.

She used her key and entered, calling out, "Hello! Mrs. Welsh? It's me, Eden!" But there was no reply.

She searched the house, to no avail, before running next door to knock at Esther and Bob's cottage. Bob answered.

"Hi, Mr. Perkins. Do you know where Mrs. Welsh is? Is she all right?" Eden asked, in full panic.

"Yes, love, she is in the hospital. I'm so sorry. We had to call an ambulance this morning. Esther is with her there. They aren't sure if it's her heart or her lungs, but she's terribly short of breath and was feeling very ill this morning. Esther is giving me constant updates."

"Oh my God," Eden said, her hand flying to her mouth. "Is she going to be okay?"

"I certainly hope so, very much. Esther called me a few minutes ago saying that she's stable, and they're observing her till tomorrow, but that Hazel is insisting they let her come home. Stubborn old woman wants to treat herself here at home rather than stay in the hospital. I don't know if they'll let her though."

"I need to go see her. What hospital is she in, where is she?" Eden asked.

"She said she doesn't want anyone visiting her at the hospital. Esther says she's quite adamant about it. She wants to get out of there as soon as she can and come home."

"But I need to see her!" Eden almost shouted. "Can I at least call her?"

"I think what she needs this evening is just rest, my dear," he said kindly. "Why don't you come by, or call, first thing in the morning, and we will let you know what's going on. If anything changes at all, if she takes a turn for the worse, or anything like that, I promise I will call you, even if it's the middle of the night. But let's wait till tomorrow and see where we are, all right?"

It wasn't all right at all with Eden, but these were Mrs. Welsh's own requests, so she had to respect them. "All right," she agreed. "Thank you, Bob. I'll see you first thing in the morning. And make sure you call me if anything changes," she added.

"I will, I promise," he said.

Eden told her mother what happened, but they kept it to themselves. If Mrs. Welsh didn't want visitors in the hospital, the news needed to stay quiet for now.

That night, Eden barely slept a wink. At one a.m., her phone rang. She leaped out of bed and answered it, sure something terrible had happened to Mrs. Welsh. She was half right.

"Eden, it's James. I need you to come over. It's Beatrice," he said, voice tight with panic.

"What's going on?" Eden asked.

"I've called an ambulance. She had a fever all afternoon, but it suddenly spiked an hour ago. I gave her Paracetamol but she's 40. Oh my God, Eden, I don't know what to do. She's having convulsions. What should I do?" he almost yelled into the phone.

"Put her in a cool bath. I'm on my way!"

Eden hung up and pulled her boots on over her pajamas, grabbed a sleeping Tommy, and carried him to the car. Eden made a quick stop at Mrs. Welsh's house, empty now that the old woman was in the hospital. *Now I understand*, she thought, as she grabbed a jar containing tincture of yarrow.

"Thank you," Eden said into the dark night air.

Yarrow was excellent at bringing down a high fever. She had been shown this herb twice.Now she knew what the message had been for. It had been for Beatrice.

Eden pulled into the driveway at James's house and coaxed a confused, sleepy Tommy out of the back seat.

"Beatrice is sick, sweetheart. Come lie down on James's sofa while I help her, okay?" she said.

" Okay," he replied, following her to the door.

Eden let herself in and called out, "James?"

"Upstairs!" he called back.

Eden laid Tommy down on the sofa and covered him with the blanket that was folded over the arm of a chair. By the time she'd put the blanket on him, he was already asleep again.

She ran up the stairs two at a time. She opened the door to the bathroom and saw James on his knees next to the tub, cradling Beatrice's head as she lay back in the shallow water. When he looked up, Eden saw his cheeks were stained with tears.

"Her fever hasn't gone down, and she's unconscious. Every few minutes..." He trailed off. It was unnecessary to finish his sentence.

Convulsions gripped Bea just then. Her back arched, and her head, arms, and legs shook.

"Help her!" James said desperately.

"They're febrile seizures," Eden said calmly. "They'll stop as soon as we get her fever down. Hold her head, like you are doing, and I'll try and help."

She reached inside her little canvas bag and pulled out a tiny lancet, a disposable small plastic handle with a tiny, razor-sharp blade on the tip.

"Let me have her hands," Eden said.

James held his daughter's tiny hands as they shook with the convulsion.

Eden took the lancet and cut a tiny prick in the tips of all ten of Beatrice's fingers. Within a few seconds, the convulsion stopped. Eden squeezed each finger to encourage a few drops of blood to come out of the cuts. As she did, Bea's breathing became more regular.

"Take her temperature," Eden instructed, as she reached back into her bag.

James put the digital thermometer in Beatrice's ear, and when it beeped, he held it up, looking shocked. "It's 38. It's down two degrees already. How did you do that?"

"Bleeding the fingertips. Medieval, but effective. It works to instantly reduce high fever. At least temporarily, so we can keep her safe till the ambulance gets here. Now let me add this to the bath." She poured the pungent tincture of yarrow into the bathwater.

Eden then took some of the tincture and poured it into her hands, putting one hand on Beatrice's tiny forehead, one on her stomach.

Slowly, a glow appeared in the tub. At first, Eden wasn't sure she was seeing it. But the glow grew in intensity until it was a bright golden light.

It started in Eden's hands, then spread to Bea's forehead, then her stomach, until finally, her whole body shone with a golden light. Eden felt her hands and arms tingle wildly as the light pulsed between them. The bathroom had been almost dark just moments before, but was now lit up as if by lanterns.

Eden turned to look at James. His mouth was hanging open.

"Eden, what is happening?" he said softly.

"It's the healing, James. It's the light. The energy that heals. It's in the herbs. It's in our bodies. It's everywhere. It's concentrated so much right now that we can see it, but it's always there."

As she said the words, she was amazed at her own explanation. Eden had talked with Mrs. Welsh many times about the healing and the knowing. But these were her own words now, and she knew they were true. She hadn't mentioned the magical side of her work with Mrs. Welsh to James before, but clearly he knew about it now. She wondered how he would react.

He reacted sensibly.

"Let me take her temperature again." He did so, then removed the thermometer to read. "36 This is incredible." he said with almost reverence in his voice. "You two are glowing, Eden. I've never seen anything like it."

"I haven't either," Eden said.

Slowly, Beatrice's breathing steadied, her muscles relaxed, and then she groggily opened her eyes.

"Beatrice," James said softly, so as not to startle her.

"Daddy," her tiny voice said weakly. "I don't feel good."

James lifted her slightly out of the tub and hugged her soaking wet body, nightgown clinging to her thin frame. "I know, sweetheart. We'll get you better soon. Eden is helping you." James looked up at Eden, as tears ran down his cheeks. "Thank you."

Just then, they heard the wail of the ambulance siren in the distance, and within a minute two young men with medic bags were at the front door, with the stretcher ready to take Beatrice to the hospital.

James called Eden two hours later to say it was pneumonia and that she had been right. The seizures were from the high fever and were gone now that her temperature was down. James was sure Eden had saved his daughter's life.

"I will never be able to repay you, as long as I live, Eden," James said into the phone. "She's on IV antibiotics and fever reducers, and is sitting up and having a ice lolly But God knows what those convulsions and that fever might have done to her without your help. You saved both of our lives tonight, because I know for sure I couldn't survive losing her."

"I just did what I'd been taught," Eden reassured him. "And what the knowing told me to do. But I'm so very, very glad she is all right, James."

*

At 8:30 the next morning, Eden stood knocking on the Perkins' door.

Esther answered. "Hello, dear. We expected you early."

"I'm sorry," Eden said, seeing Esther still in her nightgown. I can come back. I wanted to come over at 5:00, but I made myself wait till now. I couldn't wait any longer," she admitted.

"No, come in. We've just put the kettle on. I'll fill you in."

Seated around the kitchen table with scones and mugs of tea, Esther said, "It's pneumonia. She's had a bit of a cough for a while now, as I'm sure you know, but it didn't seem like much. But, suddenly, she was having trouble breathing, and it seems to have gotten worse quite quickly. Apparently, several people have had pneumonia in the area lately."

Eden knew she was right about that.

Esther continued, "She's on a strong antibiotic and is responding very well, as she has rarely ever needed to take one. Mrs. Welsh is absolutely insisting, of course in her usual kind and sweet, but fiercely determined, way, on being released today. Her doctors have to concede she is doing much better, so they're going to send her home by ambulance this afternoon."

"Oh, thank God!" Eden said. "I'll make sure to be here when she gets home so I can look after her."

"I'm sure she would find great comfort in that, dear," Esther said.

Eden exhaled for the first time in a day.

Eden went home and arranged for Susan to move into the cottage for a few days to watch Tommy. Tommy loved Susan and thought this was a fine setup, especially as Susan often gave him a second serving of dessert.

"I can't take him to Mrs. Welsh's cottage with me, as it could be contagious," Eden said when her mother reported for duty at her cottage. "But I need to be there for her for a few days, especially at night, so thank you, Mom. This means so much to me."

A few hours later, the ambulance arrived, delivering Mrs. Welsh back home. Eden had come in and cleaned the cottage and lit fires in the living room and bedroom fireplaces to get any spring chill out of the house. She stocked the kitchen and made elderberry syrup and chicken soup and was ready to become healer to the healer herself.

"Eden, how lovely of you to be here," Mrs. Welsh exclaimed as the men helped her into the chair by the fire. There were discharge papers to be signed, and then the medics told Eden that Mrs. Welsh needed to follow up with her doctor in two days to keep an eye on things. They left a large bottle of antibiotics on the table, and then they were gone.

"Thank goodness!" the old woman exclaimed. "Good Lord, how anyone gets better in those hospitals, I cannot understand. All noise and bright lights and awful food. I cannot tell you how happy I am to be home." She stopped as a coughing fit shook her whole body. She was able to stop it only by breathing in in little spurts through her nose.

Eden didn't like the sound of it. Then the herbs came back into her mind as clear as day.

"Horehound and licorice?" Eden asked.

"Yes, dear," Mrs. Welsh said with a smile. "You are exactly right. I'll have that and some elderberry syrup up in bed, if that isn't too much trouble."

"Of course, it isn't too much trouble. And just so you know, I'm staying for a few days. Don't even try to stop me," Eden said, interrupting the refusal Mrs. Welsh tried to get out. "Sorry, but you have nothing to say about it. I have already installed myself in the guest bedroom, and my mother is looking after Tommy, so anything you need…I am at your disposal," she said, happy she was able to offer this small gesture of her affection.

Mrs. Welsh suddenly looked very pale, and she frowned. "My tablets please," she said to Eden. "The ones next to my bed, in the bedside table drawer." Her hand went to her heart, as if touching it might soothe it.

Eden raced up the stairs two at a time and came bounding down with the digitalis. Mrs. Welsh took one pill and put it under her tongue, breathing through her nose so as not to set off another bout of coughing. Slowly her frown eased.

"Oh, that's better," she said, exhaling deeply. "Thank you. This pneumonia isn't helping my heart any. Poor old me. I seem to be falling apart these days," she said with a weak smile.

"Are you sure you should be home?" Eden asked, worried at how frail her friend seemed.

"Yes, dear. I've never been more sure of anything. And when my time does eventually come, whether it's right now, or years from now, it will happen with me in my warm bed, in my lovely home. Not under beeping machines and bright lights, with strangers poking me and yelling and rushing around. But, for now, I think I might ask your help up to my bed. I think I'll take a little rest."

Eden walked her friend up the stairs slowly and helped her into bed. All through the day, she brought up juice and broth and toast and the horehound and licorice tea she made, and then she would sit downstairs and read and listen to her poor dear friend racked by the deep, angry cough. By evening, Mrs. Welsh was pale as a sheet and had a fever.

"I'm calling the ambulance," Eden insisted.

"No, dear. No, it's all right. It's *all* all right," Mrs. Welsh said, placing a hand on Eden's hand to keep her there. "This is where I want to be. Right here. This is right," she said, her eyes now watery and tired, but kind as always.

Several times that evening, Eden went to the kitchen and asked the jars on the wall to talk to her. She thought of some helpful herbs and brought up echinacea and goldenseal, bad tasting but good for fighting infections. Slippery elm to soothe the cough and the throat. She saw the jars sparkle at her and added honey, peppermint, chrysanthemum, and oregano.

In the early hours of the morning, Mrs. Welsh finished a tea Eden had made her after a particularly bad bout of coughing, and then called Eden to her bedside and thanked her.

"My dearest one," Mrs. Welsh said, her voice now very weak.

"There is something downstairs I would like for you to bring to me. In the dresser against the wall. In the drawer. Thank you."

Eden went downstairs to a dresser against the wall and opened a little drawer. She pulled out a necklace. Curious, she took it upstairs and Mrs. Welsh held out her hand for it. Eden placed it in her palm and looked down at the beautiful old hands, joints swollen, skin creased and thin as paper. They were the most beautiful hands in the world, Eden thought. Their story was a lifetime of service, and healing, and kindness. She felt her eyes fill with tears.

"Eden, my dear," Mrs. Welsh started, looking up, "this necklace has been handed down for generations. I'm not sure how many, to tell you the truth, but certainly for hundreds of years. It is a locket." She put a fingernail against the edge of the long oval shape and pulled it open. "Inside is a tiny leaf. I don't know what it is. When it was given to me as a young woman, I was told it was from an ancient remedy. It could be anything. It's just a piece of a leaf. Might just be from an elm tree, for all I know," she said with a smile. "But it is handed from one herbalist to another. And now it is your turn to have it, my dear."

She said it with such softness and kindness that, again, Eden's eyes stung. She looked into Mrs. Welsh's face and saw tears there too.

"Why are you giving it to me now? I don't want it right now. You can give it to me later," she said, with rising panic, as she realized Mrs. Welsh was setting her affairs in order.

"Everything happens in divine timing, my dear. Once we accept that, life is much easier. And more fun," she added with a twinkle in her eye.

Then she was overcome by another fit of coughing that lasted almost a full minute. Eden poured a small glass of water from the pitcher into her glass.

"This is my gift to you," Mrs. Welsh said.

Eden looked down at the locket, and Mrs. Welsh placed it in her hand. It hung from a long thin chain. The locket itself was metal, with an engraving of a leaf and flower on the front. It was beautiful.

Eden closed her hand over it. "Thank you, Mrs. Welsh. I will cherish it forever."

"Not forever, my dear," Mrs. Welsh corrected her. "One day, you will pass it on to the next healer. As I have today. You will know her. But, someday, years and years from now, you will know when the time is just right, and you will pass it on then."

Eden felt confused, trying to imagine handing down both this beautiful precious necklace and the whole legacy she was now a part of.

"Then, thank you, Mrs. Welsh," Eden said. "I will be the keeper of the necklace until I pass it on. Though I have no idea to whom that will be. But I know by now, you will tell me to trust that when the time is right, I'll know."

"That's right," her old friend said with a smile. "And until then, I will be here. Remember, Eden, no matter what, I will always be here. You have been so very good to me, my dear. Please remember, that all is well." Her beautiful smile made her sick, pale face glow for an instant.

As another coughing fit took over her frail body, Eden ran downstairs to get some tea and some lozenges and the next dose of antibiotics, which was due to be taken soon.

She climbed back up the stairs, glad to hear the coughing had stopped, but when she got to the doorway, she dropped the cup of tea. The delicate little cup and saucer smashed on the floor.

She ran to the old woman's bedside. "Mrs. Welsh!" she called out in desperation.

But her friend was gone.

"Mrs. Welsh!" Eden yelled. "Oh my God," she said out loud to no one. "Oh my God, I was supposed to be taking care of you! You trusted me. Oh my God, I've killed you!"

She was about to start performing CPR and call an ambulance when she remembered that Esther Perkins had told her that Mrs. Welsh did not want extraordinary measures taken. She had told them she was at complete peace with passing when it was her time and not to fuss about trying to bring her body back when her spirit felt it was time to leave.

So, Eden stood at the bedside, crying and wringing her hands, to keep them from trying to resuscitate the frail little body.

"James, I've killed her," Eden sobbed into the phone a few minutes later.

"What!?" he asked, concern evident in his voice.

"I've killed her. Mrs. Welsh, she's dead!" she yelled into the receiver between sobs.

"I'm on my way."

Five minutes later, James walked in the door and grabbed Eden, pulling her to him and letting her tears fall against his chest.

"I'm so sorry, Eden. Shh. It'll be all right. I'm so sorry," he said over and over, stroking her hair and letting her cry.

Finally, she stood back, wiped her nose on her sleeve, and said, "Who am I kidding. Herbalist! What a joke. I let her die in my care. The village's healer put her life in my hands, and I let her die!" Tears ran down her face anew.

"What are you talking about?" James asked. "She was ninety-three years old! And she had a bad heart and pneumonia. How on earth can you think you killed her?"

"She came home to heal, and I failed!"

"No, Eden," James said firmly. "She came home to die. And you let her."

Eden looked up, sadness and confusion mingled in her expression.

"It sounds very much to me like she was ready to go," James said gently. "And you let her. Sometimes that is the most beautiful thing a healer can do. Letting someone go. Peacefully, at home, surrounded by loved ones. None of us can ask for more than that," he said gently.

Eden took in his words, and knew deep down he was right, but she shook her head, as the feelings of guilt and failure rose up in her. She pushed James away. "I have to go. I need to get out of here."

Eden ran to her car and drove down the narrow, winding country lanes until she came to the spot on the side of the road, parked her car, and ran into the woods. She ran straight through until she reached the clearing. She knew this was where she had to be, right that very moment.

When she got there, she sat down in front of her makeshift altar and said through streams of tears, "I'm so sorry, Mrs. Welsh. I failed you. Please forgive me! Please tell me you forgive me!" There was no answering voice. No vision of Mrs. Welsh, just silence.

Then a bright yellow light began to emanate from the ground outside the crumbling walls. Eden could see it shooting skyward.

Slowly, she stood and moved toward the source of the intense, comforting, light coming from the garden. It was yellow and white combined, it was blindingly bright, yet didn't hurt the eyes to look at. Eden felt drawn toward it, and as she stepped into the garden, this energy rushed up through the soles of her feet and through her whole being, sucking the breath right out of her.

She was frozen in that spot, unable to breathe, as the light rushed through her. She felt the most wonderful, blissful, and complete sense of peace, more complete and comforting than she had known it was possible to feel. This energy was complete…it made *her* complete, a part of everything that is, or ever was, or ever would be. She felt knowledge, wisdom, the history of all the healers before her, rush into her body and fill her with light, with love, with knowledge, with information about herbs and plants, entering her mind at such a speed that she couldn't consciously pick any of them out. But she felt them being transferred into her body, into her mind.

She was filled with this brilliant light until it was shooting out her fingertips and out the top of her head. And Eden knew one part of that light was Mrs. Welsh, and she knew that her dear friend's spirit had gone.

Slowly, the light receded and went back into the earth. Eden was able to breathe again, and open her eyes, and move again, but she was so awestruck that she stood there for several minutes, not moving.

Then she took that sense of peace and connection and spirit, and she walked back to her car.

*

One week later, Eden sat in the front row of the church with the Perkinses and a few other of Mrs. Welsh's dearest friends. The church was packed. The old woman had helped almost everyone in the village at one point or another. From easing a headache to saving a life. And everyone turned out to pay their respects and share their stories over tea and wine and sandwiches at the reception held at Eden's cottage afterward.

Eden was still racked by guilt, certain that if she had mixed just the right herbs, she could have helped her dear old friend fight off her infection and live to heal another day. Everyone told her what a beautiful thing she had done to be with Mrs. Welsh at home when she passed, but, inside, Eden knew they were all wrong and that she had failed. She was no healer. But she kept her mouth shut and nodded and simply said, "Thank you."

Chapter 19

A week passed, and Eden tried her best to take over at Mrs. Welsh's. People were kind and came to the door offering condolences before they told her of their aches and pains and asked for a remedy. Eden cringed at each kind word, feeling inside that she had let Mrs. Welsh down in her hour of most desperate need. But she soldiered on in the British way, working to fill the hours of the day and keep the guilt at bay.

One day, there was a knock at the door, and Eden opened it to see James standing there.

"Can I come in?" he asked.

"Of course." She stepped aside.

"How are you doing?" he asked gently.

"I'm all right, I guess. Trying to stop feeling like I've killed a close friend. But other than that, I'm all right," she said with a macabre smile.

"Well, the thing is, I wanted to ask you about our weekend. I mean, I know the timing isn't good, but we are never, ever *alone*." He emphasized the word alone, so that it contained all his frustration and desire. "And we set this weekend up ages ago, so we could finally be on our own for two whole days…and nights. I know the timing is pretty bloody awful, but I wondered...do you still want to go ahead with it?" He stepped towards her, putting his hands on her waist.

Eden felt she should say no, as someone mourning a good friend, but her body betrayed her as soon as she felt James's hands on her hips.

Maybe a weekend of lovemaking would be just the thing to help my heart, she thought. *At the very least it would be an amazing distraction.*

So, she said, "Yes, let's keep our plans. I want to." She smiled as she said it, realizing it was true.

The weekend plan was confirmed. Susan and Peter were taking the children to London for two days, to see a play, and then to visit with James's mother. They would stay at a nice hotel and live it up. The children were buzzing with excitement. So were Eden and James.

Eden kissed Tommy goodbye and handed him his little suitcase containing pajamas, a change of clothes, a toothbrush, and Ellie the elephant. Susan, Peter, and Bea were waiting in the car to whisk Tommy off on his first weekend trip to London.

Eden had a lump in her throat as she kissed him goodbye, but

Tommy raced off, a huge smile on his face, jumping in the car and buckling in his seat belt, ready for the adventure. Eden waved till the car was out of sight, then turned to go inside and get ready for her own adventure. A whole weekend with James.

She had just gotten out of the bath and was in her robe, looking for something to wear to dinner that night, feeling both jittery and already full of desire. Just knowing there would be no one home all weekend was a delicious and intoxicating feeling. The weight of Mrs. Welsh's death was still there, but she allowed herself to get excited for the rare treat of two days completely alone with James.

James picked her up at six, and they drove the forty-five minutes to Cambridge for dinner. Without having to worry about time, they thought it would be romantic to walk along the river, and then eat in one of the many cozy restaurants near the famed university.

They parked the car and stepped out into a beautiful spring evening. It was unseasonably warm, and the sun shone on the old buildings, giving them a buttery glow. The streets were narrow and winding with centuries-old buildings on both sides, street after street of them.

They made it to the campus of Cambridge University. Though James had been there many times, and Eden had visited a few times herself for research, standing together, holding hands and looking up at the huge golden stone buildings, with their steep shale roofs and spires twisting to the heavens, there seemed something more magical about it that evening.

"I'm sorry I've been such a downer lately. But I have a little good news," she said, almost shyly.

"What is it?" James asked, smiling at her as they walked.

"Well, I'm really superstitious…too much studying medieval life, I guess." She laughed. "So I wasn't going to tell anyone but…I finished my book." She smiled up at James.

"Oh my God, that is incredible!" he exclaimed. "When did you have time to finish the book?"

"I don't know. It was the strangest thing. It was almost like it wrote itself. I guess having studied the period for twenty years beforehand didn't hurt. But then I'd get these amazing ideas from stories Mrs. Welsh would tell me, and I'd go home, and it would just roll out of me onto the computer screen. I sent it off to a few publishers in New York. I mean, I don't expect to get published. It's my first try at a novel. But I don't know, I wrote it, so I thought I'd better at least send it off." She suddenly felt a bit unsure again, just telling him about it.

"That's amazing, Eden. And I am absolutely sure it will get

published. When you let me read some of it, it was a total page-turner. We'll order champagne to celebrate!" he declared, and they strolled on, smiling, arms around each other's waists, toward the restaurant.

"I'm off to London next week," James told her over appetizers.

"Oh, that's fun. What for?"

James leaned over and offered her a small stuffed mushroom with his hand, and she opened her mouth, feeling almost obscene it felt so intimate. He slowly placed the delicious morsel in her mouth while smiling into her eyes.

"Just for a visit," he said. "Bea has a break from school, and I'm taking her to see my mum. We're going to drive out to see her sister in Dorset for a day or two. I'll be back by the end of the week."

"That will be great," Eden said. It was funny, this feeling for James. It was all happiness. It was smooth and light. There were no sharp edges. His going away didn't make her jealous. She didn't feel insulted that she wasn't invited. She was just happy he was going to have a nice week. It felt so luxuriantly simple.

"What are you smiling at?" James asked with his sexy half-grin.

"You," she said, grinning back with a twinkle in her eye.

"Mmm. I like the sound of that. And just what were you thinking, Miss Martin?"

"Just that I like you. Pure and simple. And it feels so nice. I'm not a simple person. I can make the littlest thing into a mess. But I just like you. That's it. It's nice."

"Well, that sounds a little boring," he said with a laugh. He took a long pull from his beer. "But, really, I know what you mean. I feel it too. Simple. I mean, I want to rip that silk dress off you and have you right here on this table. But the rest of it. Yes. Simple. It is nice. I hadn't really thought of that."

Eden reached over and ran her hand up his arm. Their smiles turned serious as they both imagined what lay ahead, a weekend with no one but them.

"Let's skip dessert," James said with a laugh, though his voice was raspy.

"Yes," she replied slightly breathlessly.

They drove back to Barton Heath, talking about the children, the village, their work, but both had only one thing on their minds: getting upstairs, if they made it that far, and pulling each other's clothes off.

Both of them also carefully avoided talking about anything too far down the road. Even the summer, fast approaching, was off limits, as they realized that Eden might not even be there by then.

They pulled into the driveway, and James leaned over and kissed Eden with a soft, but deep, kiss that grew in its hunger until they both had their hands in each other's hair and their tongues in each other's mouths. They broke the kiss and got out of the car, into the dark, warm evening, thrilled at the thought that no one would be in their way.

They had their hands around each other's waists, and James rubbed his hand over Eden's hip as they turned from the small garage to the path to the cottage, walking fast so they could get inside and close the door. It was like there wasn't another soul on the earth.

And then they saw him. A big figure sitting on the front step.

James pulled his hand from around Eden's waist and stepped in front of her slightly, naturally protective.

"Hello?" James called out, putting a hand behind him to stop Eden where she was.

They were in an English village, not some gang-infested city, still, one would just be cautious when a stranger on the doorstep.

Then he stood up and Eden gasped.

"Oh my God!" she exclaimed. James turned around and

looked at her, as she said, "Robert!"

Chapter 20

"Hi, Eden," he called out casually, like it was no big deal that he was sitting on her doorstep, uninvited, three thousand miles from home.

James turned to face Eden and spoke softly, so Robert couldn't hear. "Is this okay? Believe me, I'd be more than happy to get rid of him. What's he doing here anyway?"

"I have no idea at all," she whispered. "I haven't even called him back since I moved here. I'm as shocked as you are. And yes, I want him to go away. I have a weekend with you. A rare, beautiful weekend with you. Screw Robert. He's not going to ruin it!"

James turned back to face the figure in the doorway. and said, politely, "Ili. I guess you're Robert. I'm James, I'm a friend of Eden's."

"Yes, I can see that," Robert replied coolly, moving towards them.

James took a few steps forward. too, like two bucks in a mating tussle.

"Eden has just told me she'd like you to leave. Right now isn't a good time. I'm sure she'd be happy to talk to you later." James paused. When there was no response, so he added, "So if you'd be so kind…" He let the sentence trail off.

"Well, I don't think I can do that," Robert replied, rudely. "Eden, you're my fiancée, and I haven't been able to get you to return a single call in all the months you've been here. What else was I supposed to do?" He looked like he genuinely felt sorry for himself.

Eden stepped in front of James. "I am *not* your fiancée," she said firmly. "We ended that arrangement the night I found you in bed with another woman. We're not engaged, and I haven't returned your calls because I don't want to talk to you! I have nothing to say to you, so please leave."

"But, babe," he said with sugary sweetness, "there is so much to talk about. It can't be over just like that. I was so wrong, but it was one mistake after…how many years together? Come on, let's go inside and talk."

"Absolutely not!" she yelled, feeling stony and determined.

She pushed him out of the way as she opened the door to the cottage. James followed her inside, and she closed the door with a bang and locked it.

They heard Robert yelling from outside, "I'm not going anywhere. I'll stay here all night if I have to. You can't just walk out on your whole life, Eden. Stop playing this childish game and come talk to me!"

James put his arms around Eden, and she rested her head on his shoulder. "You're shaking," he said, leading her over to the sofa.

"I'm just in shock. And I'm so angry. I'm so damned angry I could scream. He has always been a bully. How dare he try to burst into my life like this?"

James was quiet for a moment, then said, "I guess he just wants to talk to you. Not that I want you to talk to him right now! But, I mean, you haven't called him even once?" He looked sympathetic but questioning.

"No, I haven't. I just never knew what to say. And truthfully, I don't have *anything* to say. We are over. End of discussion."

James rubbed her back gently, soothing her like he would a scared dog in his practice, she thought, suddenly irritated. "Why? You think I should talk to him?"

Just then they heard another yell from the front yard. "Eden, I'm not going anywhere. You can't just never speak to me at all!"

"Look, we can't enjoy ourselves with your ex-fiancé in the front yard shouting down the house," James told her. "I'm going to go to the pub for a pint. You talk to him. I mean, at some point, you have to talk to him. There must be a lot to discuss. There must be feelings in there to sort out. You were about to marry the man. Maybe you have avoided it all because it's so confusing and overwhelming. And I care about you so much, but I only want you if your heart is free. I..." He stopped and looked into the distance for a moment. "Truth is, I don't think I could take getting really hurt again. Not now. I know you're probably going back to New York in a couple of months. But if you're going to go back to your old fiancé, that's different. If you are, I need to know that now. And if you definitely aren't going back to him, then hallelujah! But I think you need to settle that for yourself too. I mean...I don't know what I mean. But what are you doing, Eden? People's hearts are at stake here." The pain in his eyes was evident.

For the first time, Eden felt guilty. This was a widower. A man whose wife had *died*. He was opening his heart and body to her. Did she actually know what she was doing? Was James right? Was she avoiding Robert, in case she found she still had feelings for him? Why couldn't she even answer his phone calls?

Before she had time to reply, James leaned over and kissed her tenderly. "I'll be back in an hour. Or call me if you need me sooner. I have my phone. I hope you can sort some things out, Eden. I really do." He walked out and closed the door behind him.

Eden sat on the sofa and burst into tears. Tears of frustration at the letdown. After waiting and deliciously anticipating this night with James for so long, to have it ripped away from her by idiotic Robert infuriated her.

Then the tears turned to tears of confusion and fear. Mrs. Welsh was dead, Robert was here, James was pulling away, she'd need to go back to New York soon...she hadn't made any decisions about anything. Suddenly, the simple life she had been living, in peaceful bliss for months, was falling apart around her.

Typical, she thought critically. *Your life is always a mess. Did you think if you ran away it wouldn't be? You've managed to screw it up royally here too. Nice work.* Her tears became those of self-pity.

Then she heard a knock on the door, and anger made her dry her eyes and let Robert in.

He stepped toward her, as if to kiss her, and Eden backed up in disgust. "What are you doing?"

"Eden, my God, I've been so desperate to talk to you. My calls, my emails, you didn't answer anything. I didn't know what else to do but come here." He sat down on the sofa and exhaled loudly.

For the first time since the night she had walked in on him in bed, she remembered that he had been someone she loved. She saw in his tired face the Robert that she had kissed, that she had laughed with.

She felt confused.

"I'm sorry. I guess I should have called you back at some point. I think I didn't call you because I didn't want to get confused. I saw what I saw, and that was all I needed to know. So, I left. Then I just didn't want to feel the pain of dredging it all up again." She stood by the window and looked out into the dark night, thinking about James arriving at the pub. Wishing she were with him.

"I still love you," Robert said.

Eden turned to him, her momentary feeling of tenderness for him passed. "Did the young girl dump you?"

Robert looked shocked at the question.

"You didn't love me, Robert. I guess I'm only really realizing it now, but we didn't love each other. We stayed together because we'd been together so long. You needed a wife to fit the picture of the successful banker with a family. You needed me as an accessory. I needed you because I felt lonely. But, clearly, you found a younger, slimmer model. I assume, if you're here, that she dumped you."

When Robert looked up, the sheepish expression on his face told her she was right. What a jerk, she thought.

"She didn't dump me. She moved to Los Angeles. And I'm sorry, Eden. I didn't love her. I don't know what I was thinking."

Eden hated that she was starting to feel compassion for him, for what a mess he was too. It was easier when he was three thousand miles away, frozen in that moment in bed with the tart from his office.

"I don't know what to say, Robert. I have a whole life here. A pretty complicated one, actually," she added, thinking about her mother living here now, and Tommy, and, of course, James. But seeing his familiar face had cracked her glass wall. It let her old life in, and in a flood, she found she was confused, scared, and unsure of herself for the first time in a long time.

She started to think about the safety of New York. The few good friends she had there, whom she missed. Her enviable job. Security. Here she had what...a relationship with James? But who knew where that was going? Her mother was happily married now and didn't need her around. She was clearly no healer. She had killed Mrs. Welsh, for God's sake! What was she doing here, pretending to be a part of this place?

She shook her head, trying to get the frustrating thoughts out of her head. "This is why I didn't call you!" she yelled at Robert. "This is why I don't want you here! You get me all confused. Just go, Robert. I want you to *go*," she said emphatically.

"That's it? After everything we've had, you're saying you've moved on and telling me to go?" he said loudly, clearly more insulted than hurt.

"Yes. I am. I caught you having *sex* with another woman. Please don't act like the injured party here. The truth is, we broke up because we don't really love each other. At least, I don't really love you, and I assume, by your behavior, that it's mutual. But either way, I don't care. It's over. So, please go," she said.

She stood and opened the front door.

Robert strode to the door then stopped, inches from her face. "I think you're wrong. You can have it all as my wife. Beautiful life, all the money you could want, your career in New York. I'll leave now, but come back to the city. Come see me. Your life is there. A life you want. This is a fantasy. This isn't the real you."

He leaned forward quickly and kissed her before she had time to react, then he turned and walked away into the night.

Eden closed the door, leaned back against it, and let out a huge sigh. But, inside, she felt dread and confusion creating a knot in her stomach. What *was* she doing here? She felt like Cinderella at midnight. Poof, the illusion was over, the carriage turned back into a pumpkin. As her life in Barton Heath would suddenly disappear too.

She went to the sofa and sat down, putting her face in her

hands.

"Eden," James said, letting himself into the cottage a short while later. "Are you all right? I saw Robert out the window of the pub, walking down the road so I came back." He saw her sitting on the sofa crying and rushed to her side. "What did he do?" he demanded. "I'll kill him!"

"Nothing, James. He didn't do anything. I just...I just wish he had never come here!" she said angrily. "Why couldn't he leave me alone? I'm just so confused. I hate that he came here and ruined my little bubble. It's all falling apart now, being here, Mrs. Welsh, and..." She trailed off.

"And what?" James asked, both worry and defensiveness evident in his voice. "And me? Was I part of your *bubble*?"

"Yes," she said before she could think. "I mean no! Not you. I don't know...I've ruined things. I always do. I couldn't save Mrs. Welsh. What kind of herbalist was I pretending to be? I killed her! And I don't know what I'm doing. I've got a foster child, for God's sake. What the hell am I doing with a foster child? And then there's us. I don't know what's going to happen with us. And what else do I have here, really, with everything such a mess now?" She started crying.

"Eden," James said softly as he sat down beside her. "I love you." He lifted her chin with his hand and looked into her eyes.

Eden paused and then said, "I...I think I...just...I'm sorry, James, I just don't know what I'm doing right now. I'm so scared. I don't want to get hurt and I'm just so confused."

Eden started crying again.

James silently rose from the sofa. His face was tight with pain and disappointment and even anger. He bent over and kissed her on the forehead and, without saying a word, he let himself out of her cottage and walked home.

*

James found himself walking through the dark, silent village, a storm of frustration, anger, and grief raging in his head. He got to his house and stood outside. It was empty. Dark. Sad. He let himself in, closed the door, and stood there, not moving, for several minutes.

Slowly, he walked down the hall to the living room, turned on the light, and slumped into his favorite chair. Next to it, on a small table, was a photo of Beatrice and Jane. Jane was laughing, wind whipped her hair, and she was holding onto their baby daughter, only a few months old in the photo. James remembered every detail of that day. It was a warm summer day and they had gone for a walk with this new creature, who had joined their lives, and with whom they were both madly in love. It was just a few weeks before Jane had gone to the doctor and gotten the terrible diagnosis. It was one of the last totally happy days of his life. Until recently.

Of course, there were countless joys with Beatrice, but for his own heart, a man's heart, and a man's body, there had been a sadness that only in the past few months had finally been replaced by happiness. First by a hint, then a flicker of something sweet, then to a kind of joy he thought he would never feel again.

Sitting there, looking at Jane, her sweet face, her smiling eyes, he smiled, and then he felt a tear escape from the corner of his eye. He couldn't bear to lose love twice. He didn't think his heart could take it. Part of him was angry. He wasn't sure at whom. Most of the anger was toward himself, for getting so involved with someone whose life was in turmoil. And a little part of the anger was toward Eden, for playing a game here in England, like they were all quaint characters in a TV show, instead of real people.

And now she would probably flit off back to her real life.

He would wait for a while, though, pray that Eden would sort things out and come back to him, make his life feel complete again. But he wouldn't wait forever. He knew, eventually, he'd have to close his heart back up, fold it up like a piece of tattered paper, and tuck it back in his pocket. Just so he could do what he needed to, be there for Bea, for his work. Just so he could survive.

*

That night it started to rain. Then the wind picked up. Eden had worked herself into an emotional storm equal to the lashing rain and wind outside.

She had kept all those feelings about Robert, about New York, and, to an extent, even her feelings about losing Mrs. Welsh, bottled up. But they all came rushing out that night, in wave after wave of confusion and anger and frustration, all aimed at herself.

Tommy was away in London, having a happy weekend and knowing nothing of the chaos that now engulfed life at the cottage. Eden needed to get out, needed to move. She walked to the car in the wind and rain and drove out to the path into the woods. To the ruins. The chapel.

She parked the car on the side of the road, got out, and leaned forward to fight the howling gale blowing against her. She liked it. Its strength and fury matched her emotions, and she pushed against it, walking toward the clearing in the woods.

When she got there, she fell to her knees inside the ruins. She cried all the tears she'd not let out in months. Tears she had avoided with work and new love and change.

And then she was quiet. She sat in the rain, totally still, totally quiet and listened. Desperate for the knowing. Desperate for some divine wisdom to sort all this out for her.

But there was nothing. Just darkness. Just wind.

In frustration, Eden looked to the sky and yelled, "Where are you? What do I do?"

Still, there was nothing. Not even the *sense* of a presence. She felt, perhaps, more alone than she ever had, feeling that now even the spirit world had abandoned her.

"Mrs. Welsh?" she yelled through tears. "Can you hear me? I'm sorry! I'm sorry I couldn't help you! Mrs. Welsh, what do I do?" she asked, face lashed with rain and wind.

But there was no reply. There was no tingle and buzz, no visions, no voices.

And then there *was* something. A knowledge creeping into her. She wasn't sure if it was from the other side, or from her own head. Or body. But it told her what she most did not want to hear.

Some answers can only come from within. Some answers you have to find alone.

She realized that, whether this came from the spirits, or from herself, didn't matter. She knew it was true.

No other visions came. No sounds. No wisdom to suddenly clarify everything.

Hours later, cold, muddy, and soaking wet, she walked back to the car and drove home.

Chapter 21

And then, almost as quickly as Eden had come, she left. Monday, Susan, Peter, Bea, and Tommy arrived back in the village from their weekend away. Bea had been dropped off first, and Tommy raced in the door, talking a mile a minute about all the exciting things they had seen in London.

"I saw Big Ben with my own eyes!" he exclaimed. "And they're right. It's really big!"

On and on the stories poured out. Eden listened with a smile, and lots of questions, and finally, exhausted from the retelling, and from the trip itself, Tommy went upstairs to play with some toys by himself.

Eden asked her mom if she would help her in the kitchen to make some tea.

Once there, Eden started to cry.

"He came here, Mom. Friday night, when James and I got back from dinner. Robert was here," Eden said through her tears.

Susan's eyebrows lifted, but she didn't say anything.

"I told him to go away, but he wouldn't," Eden continued, "so eventually, James left, and I let Robert in. And it's all awful! I'm so confused, and I don't want to hurt James, and I don't have any idea what the hell I'm doing with my life. Once again, I have royally screwed everything up."

"Okay, first of all, you haven't screwed anything up. Take a breath. Of course, Robert showed up," her mother said gently.

Eden showed her shock, eyes wide, mouth open.

"Whose side are you on?" she almost yelled at her mother.

"Yours, Eden. Yours. But you were engaged to the man. You could have at least returned one phone call. He's a liar and an ass, and you're well rid of him. But, of course, eventually, he needed to see you, or at least talk to you."

There was a long pause, then Eden replied softly, "I guess you're right. Would have saved me a lot of trouble to have just called him once, I guess." She smiled a little.

"So, what did you tell him?" Susan asked.

"I told him it was over."

"And did you mean it?"

Eden didn't respond right away, and her eyes filled with tears again. "Mom, can you tell me what I should do?" She felt like a small child rather than a grown woman.

Her mother gently shook her head. "No, sweetheart. Only you

can do that I'm afraid." She gave her a big hug.

Eden dried her eyes on her sleeve. "I've made a mess of things, but I know you're right. No one can tell me what I should do, what I need to do to get my life sorted out. Not Robert, not James, not Mrs. Welsh, or spirits from the other side, or even, hard to believe as it is, even my mom," she said, smiling at her mother. "I got myself here, and I'm the only one who can sort this all out. I guess it's time to pull on my big girl pants and get my life together."

Susan threw her arms around Eden. "I'm so proud of you. You've had a hell of a year, but you're right, you can sort it out yourself. You can. I know you can, sweetheart."

"So...the big question is Tommy," Eden said.

"Yes," Susan agreed, "the big question is Tommy."

"Do you think you and Peter could watch him, and Wellie, just short-term?" Eden asked. "I know it's a huge thing to ask. You're both over the age of wanting a small child running around, and of course, I'll go talk to Jennifer at social services tomorrow. But I wonder if you could, at least until...well, I don't know. Maybe I'll come back. But I really might not, not permanently, I mean. And if I don't, of course I would come back to talk to Tommy and help his transition, but maybe you could take care of him until they at least find him a foster home, instead of sending him to an orphanage. Or until I figure out what the hell I'm doing. Just for a while."

"Well, I'll have to talk to Peter, of course," Susan said after a moment's thought. "And you'll have to find out if that's even possible in terms of social services. But, yes. I will watch Tommy. If Peter really isn't up to it, I would understand that completely, but I could stay here with Tommy for a short time, if that's the case. That said, Peter is the most generous and good-natured man I've ever met, and if I know him at all, he'll think of it as an adventure." She smiled kindly at Eden. "But you will have to figure out what you're doing fairly quickly. You can't have half of England putting their lives on hold. It's time to face the music, sweetheart."

"I know," Eden said, and she gave her mother a long, hard hug. "I know."

*

A few days later, Eden was on a plane. Leaving early in the morning and, with the time difference, arriving back in New York at almost the same time she left London.

She stepped out of the airport and felt a shock almost like a physical blow. Horns blared, people pushed, and everyone walked very quickly, with a look of grim determination on their faces. She felt hopelessly lonely and out of place. But she had lived in this city for twenty years, so she knew the ropes.

She got a taxi back to her apartment and found herself standing on the sidewalk outside her building, staring up at the beautiful gray stonework of the early twentieth-century building. She had rented it out for the fall semester, but hadn't rented it out for the spring term, thinking at the time that racing off to England with two hour's forethought might not turn out to be as brilliant as it seemed. She figured she might want to come home by the New Year. She'd been wrong. Mostly.

She lugged her suitcases up the stairs, put the familiar key in the familiar lock, and entered her apartment. She felt a jolt of unexpected emotion as she did so. Like returning to the scene of a crime, or some other trauma, for the first time.

She had raced out of this apartment heartbroken, lost, and angry. Now she stood in the doorway and looked around with a feeling of sadness. Sadness at what she had lost here, and now what she was losing in England. But at least she had some space. Some space to think and figure out just what the hell she was doing with her life.

*

After a day of settling in and battling jet lag, Eden called her old friend Bob at his history department office, and they made plans to meet for lunch. They met at Asia, their favorite sushi restaurant on the Upper West Side.

After greeting each other with a big hug, they sat down on the clean wooden floor on bamboo mats, cross-legged, to eat at the low Japanese-style table.

"It's so great to see you," Bob said. "You look amazing. Fit, healthy, and, I don't know, is it a cliché to say you look like you're glowing?"

"Really? Thanks," she replied. She thought for a second, then added, "You know, I feel great. In fact, I'm probably the happiest I've ever been. Or at least I was, over there. Now…well, I have some things to figure out."

"Well, I want to start," Bob said. "I have news. I was going to call you this week, but I'm so glad I get to tell you this in person. Eden, the department doesn't want to lose you. We want to offer you a position as a full-time tenured professor!" He stared at her, with a wide smile, as if awaiting her scream of excitement.

Instead, Eden just looked confused and said nothing.

Finally, Bob asked, "Eden, what's wrong? This is the job you've wanted for years, that you've worked toward for twenty years.

Tenured professor at Washington. That's the professor jackpot! What's the matter?"

"I don't know," she said, honestly. "I mean, first of all, thank you! Oh my gosh, that is so incredibly nice of you all, and I am so flattered, I can't believe it. But...wow. Okay, one more massive thing to throw into this crazy mess I have to sort out."

"Mess? How are you not jumping at this?" Bob said, clearly shocked. "Do you know how many excellent, highly qualified assistant professors would kill for this offer? I mean, I'm not saying that as a threat, I just mean, this is a big deal, Eden. I know you got hurt by Robert. I know you were upset. I know you've really enjoyed the past few months in England, but this is Washington University. This is your career. This is a life changer, Eden. You can't give this up to go make teas in a village in England."

She thought for a moment, and then said, sadly, "I know I can't." Then she paused, frowning, before looking at him again. "Wait a minute. Who says I can't?" She shook her head. "Listen, Bob, I'm here. I'm in New York. I've got a ton of things to sort out. Yes, this is an amazing and incredibly flattering offer. I sort of can't believe you're saying it. Just give me a minute to catch my breath, okay? I just need to think things through. I promise I'll let you know soon. I'm sure the department will want an answer. Just…just let me catch my breath."

"Fair enough," Bob replied, but clearly it hadn't been the reaction he was expecting, based on the disappointment on his face.

They managed to enjoy the rest of the meal, anyway, old friends catching up on what each had been doing for the better part of the past year. Eden mentioned James, but only in passing. She wasn't sure why. Somehow, she felt she didn't want people to know too much until she knew what she was doing with her life.

*

The next morning, Eden looked out at the drizzle, the taxis speeding by, the excitement and bustle of New York, and remembered that she did love this city. In some ways, she did.

She picked up the phone and dialed.

"Robert Nagle's office," a woman answered.

"Hi. Is Robert in, please?" Eden asked.

"Please hold," the woman replied.

Then there was another pickup.

"Robert Nagle."

Her heart skipped a little at the sound of his voice, but she realized it was from nervousness rather than love.

"Hi, Robert. It's me."

There was a long pause, before he replied. "Wow. Eden. I sure as hell didn't expect you on the other end of this line in the middle of a workday. How are you? *Where* are you?"

"I'm okay, thanks. I'm in New York. I wondered if we could meet," she said.

"Now?" Robert asked. "I'm actually heading into a meeting in ten minutes, but—"

"No, not now," she interrupted. "Just...soon. Maybe this weekend. Go for a walk or something. If it ever stops raining."

"Eden, I've missed you so much," he said.

"How about Saturday?" she said, ignoring his declaration. "Entrance to Central Park. Ten a.m.?"

"That sounds great. I'd love that. And Eden, it's really great to hear your voice. I'm so glad you're back."

Eden wasn't sure what he meant by "back." In New York? With him? But she didn't ask.

She just said, "Great. I'll see you then. Bye."

*

The rest of that week, Eden went for long walks and runs. Around Central Park, up the West Side trail along the Hudson, across to the East River, down to SoHo and the Village, all over the city, feeling more and more at home again as she did, and finding herself surprised at how happy she felt there.

It seemed that, even after everything—the confusion, leaving England and James, all of it—she found herself in the middle of New York still feeling…happy. Confused. Exhausted all the time. Upset. But under all that, happy.

She walked for miles every day, familiarizing herself with the city like it was an old…well, an old acquaintance, if not friend. And as she did so, she thought. She thought about the cottage, the professorship, Robert, James…James. She talked in circles in her head. She made lists. Pros and cons. Robert or James. Who did she want to be with? Or neither? Where did she want to be?

As the days passed, and she walked, or sat in coffee shops, or laid on her sofa under a blanket, she realized that this New York was different. The city felt different. The friends she met with here felt a little different. Talking to the guy working the food cart felt different. *She* was different.

And suddenly, in one single moment, sitting on a bench outside the Metropolitan Museum of Art, it all became clear. She got it. The big point. The reason she felt so happy, even here in New York, where she was increasingly sure she didn't want to stay. She realized it wasn't about whether she wanted to be with Robert or James. Not even about whether she wanted to live in New York or Barton Heath. Teach huge university classes or deliver jars of herbal tea and write. All that mattered was that somehow, in all those months in England, she had found happiness.

And it didn't have a thing to do with anyone or anywhere on earth. It was her. It was inside *her*. Happiness wasn't something someone could give her. And so, it was not something someone could take away.

It was the most freeing feeling she had ever felt.

She actually looked around her, surprised that no one had noticed the huge revelation that had just dawned on her. Eden realized she hadn't gone to England to find love or her calling. She had gone and found *herself*. She didn't need to think and think and think about what to do. Once she went into that place in herself that she had just discovered, the place that was happy, and calm, and unshakable, she knew all the answers with total clarity.

Her true *knowing* place was inside her heart and her body.

And she finally, finally, knew what she wanted.

Chapter 22

Back in Barton Heath, James went on with his daily life. He treated sick and injured animals, he took care of Beatrice and watched her, almost astonished at how much he was capable of loving her.

But there was an empty place inside him. He went to the pub but often left early. He and Bea went to the Penley-Smith Manor for dinner with Susan, Peter, and Tommy now and then, and Susan and Peter would give each other glances full of sympathy for the obviously miserable James.

One such evening after dinner, when Peter was outside with Tommy and Bea and his motley pack of dogs, Susan laid her hand on James's arm. "Have you talked to her?"

"No," James said. "I told her when she left that I would wait to hear from her. I would give her some time and some space. But I can't deny, it's very hard. I haven't heard a word. She's back in her life in New York City, the greatest city on earth, her home, her career, her fiancé. It's incredibly hard not to let my mind make up all kinds of disastrous scenarios. And each day that passes, I must admit I feel more and more sure that she isn't coming back."

"I'm so sorry, James," Susan said. "This must be so awfully

hard for you. I know she isn't a cruel person; she would never mean to hurt you. But I don't really know what is going on in her head, either, I'm afraid. When she does call, she's always very quick to get off the phone. She mainly just wants to speak with Tommy and then quickly tell me she's all right, but I don't know anything else, either, I'm afraid." She wished she had something to offer James that would give him hope.

As James walked home that night, Bea skipping ahead of him down the sidewalk, he wondered if that would just be it...would he really just not hear from her? Would she do to him what she had done to Robert and simply disappear?

Or maybe he'd receive some pathetic letter, months from now, saying sorry, that it had been a hard time in her life, and thanking him for everything.

Spring was turning to summer, the grass was deep green, the lambs had been born, cricket matches were returning to the green, the pub had put the tables and benches back outside in the sun, but James didn't feel the usual elation all of that normally brought him.

One evening the following week, James was putting his instruments into the sterilizer, getting ready to head home when he heard the bell tinkle above the door, signaling a client had come in.

He yelled into the waiting room, "Sorry, I'm done for the day. Unless it's an emergency—" He stopped cold when he turned around and saw Eden standing in the doorway.

Eden stood, feeling almost fearful, trying to read him.

Finally, she spoke. "James." She exhaled and let her shoulders relax. She took a deep breath and smiled at the rugged, kind, gorgeous face she had missed so desperately. "James...I—"

Without letting her finish, James took four fast strides over to Eden, took her face in his hands, and kissed her. The kiss lasted a long time, as they embraced with the emotion of weeks of separation and anxiety and hope mixed together.

Finally, she pulled away.

"I'm sorry, Eden. I meant to wait to hear what you had to say. I hope I didn't..." He trailed off.

"You didn't. James, oh my God, I missed you so much! I have so much to tell you. But first..." Now it was her turn to trail off. She was suddenly too embarrassed to say what she was thinking.

But she didn't have to tell him what she was thinking. James was clearly thinking it too.

He walked past her, locked the door, and took her by the hand, leading her into his office. He laid her on the leather sofa, where they made love before saying another word.

Afterward, with a scratchy tartan wool blanket over them, they finally talked.

Eden started. "I wanted to say...me too," she said with a smile.

James smiled back, looking confused, but amused. "Um, okay. You too what?"

Eden pushed herself up on one elbow and looked down at him. His lock of dirty blond hair had fallen in his eye, as it always did. His mouth had that sexy hint of a smile it always did.

"Me too," she repeated. "The last time I saw you, you said you loved me. And I wanted to say...me too." She smiled mischievously at him, and his breath looked like he couldn't breathe, almost like he might cry.

He lifted enough to kiss her with that intoxicating combination of gentleness and force that made it hard for *her* to breathe.

And then they made love again. Slowly. Passionately. And, for the first time, with true abandon, no longer with a cloud hanging over them of what would happen when Eden finally had to go home. She *was* home. She was more home than she'd ever been.

Later that evening, Eden and James drove over to the Penley-

Smith house and surprised Susan, Peter, and Tommy who had been engaged in a high-emotion game of Snakes and Ladders. As soon as Tommy heard Eden's voice, he came tearing out of the living room and threw himself in her arms.

Eden burst into tears and hugged him to her as tightly as she could until he finally complained. "Ouch you're hurting me!"

They both laughed, and she put him down.

Eden had talked to Tommy on the phone daily while in New York. She'd told him she was having to work there and sort some business things out, which had been true. After those sweet conversations, Susan would come on the phone, each time asking Eden what was going on, what she was deciding, and how much longer they could tell Tommy she was away on business without figuring out what was best for him in the long run.

But now she was back.

Peter got champagne and everyone spilled out of the house onto the terrace in the warm early summer evening. Tommy took off, running around with Wellie, and James, Eden, Peter, and Susan sat at the long wooden cedar table, faded gray from years of sun and rain, and caught up.

"I'm staying," Eden said right off the bat.

Peter let out a cheer, and Susan said, "Oh wonderful! How did you decide what to do? What happened in New York?"

"Well, a lot, I guess. First, I met with Bob." She turned to James and explained, "He's the head of the history department." She turned back to face everyone. "He offered me a full tenured position!"

Susan's mouth fell open. "Oh my gosh. And you turned him down!?"

Eden just looked at her with a level stare. "Yes. I absolutely and definitely turned him down. It wasn't that I didn't think about it. In fact, I spent most of these five weeks doing nothing but thinking. I think I wore through two pairs of sneakers walking around New York...thinking. I'm still exhausted from it." She took a sip of champagne and felt the bliss of cold bubbles in her mouth and the moist, warm evening on her face. Then she went on, "And while I was there, I also met with Robert a few times."

She paused and looked at James, who simply smiled warmly and gave an almost imperceptible nod, seeming to say both that he understood why she would have done that, and that he understood that it was nothing for him to worry about.

"The more I walked around, thinking and thinking, about jobs and Robert and cities and countries, the more I realized, I knew everything already. I knew the answers in my gut with total clarity. I just let my head get in the way and talk me into things that I thought were rational and smart and grown-up decisions. But they weren't what I actually wanted. As soon as I let myself just be me, and listened to my body, I never felt clearer in my life. I called Bob and told him I was incredibly grateful, but I was leaving my job at the university. I told Robert that things were over and had been all along. And I listed my apartment for sale. It was just the most amazing feeling. I realized I'd been living this whole life that I didn't really want. When I listened to my heart—okay, that sounds so corny, ugh. But it's true. When I listened to my heart, I just wanted to come home. Here. The cottage, you all."

She smiled and looked around at the familiar faces smiling back at her, at Tommy running around the garden, at the village in the distance. She thought of Mrs. Welsh and smiled sadly, knowing that she, too, was here, in a way.

"So," she said, "I came home."

This time, everyone let out a cheer, and they all raised their glasses together.

At nine o'clock, James said, "As much as I hate to say it, I should go so poor Mrs. Innskeep can go home. She was so sweet to agree to stay late today with no notice."

"I know, I should get Tommy to bed. It's so late," she said, smiling, as she had been all evening.

"So wonderful to see you both and hear the best news of all that you are back for good!" Peter said, with a big hug for Eden and a strong, friendly slap on James's back.

"Good night, everyone," Susan chimed in, kissing Eden and James on the cheeks.

The couple walked to their cars, got Tommy settled in his seat, and then James took his time kissing Eden, before finally stepping back.

"God, I'm glad you're back."

Eden just smiled.

After Eden had taken Tommy back to the cottage and tucked him into his old familiar bed, completely exhausted, Eden fell asleep and dreamed of Barton Heath. Of Mrs. Welsh, smiling and drinking tea from a jar that swirled and sparkled with herbs.

Her old friend looked very serious, and said, "You should see a doctor, my dear."

Then, she dreamed of Tommy, riding a huge elephant. Of James in the ruins of the church in the woods. And then of Beatrice, who appeared at the church ruins with them, suddenly, in the patch of ancient weeds and herbs that had once been a garden. She looked up at them, touching the dead stalks, which suddenly came to life as she ran her fingers through them, turning from the dried winter stalks Eden had seen that day to ripe succulent herbs and flowers as her hands passed over them.

And then her dream flashed to the row of portraits on the wall at Mrs. Welsh's cottage. The line of healers from the Middle Ages to Mrs. Welsh, to Eden herself, then to a brand-new painting. A familiar face Eden couldn't quite place.

She awoke with a start, back in her room in the quiet cottage, and the dream drifted away.

*

The following morning, Eden called Jennifer at social services and said that she wanted to start the paperwork to formally adopt Tommy. She hadn't thought that this was how she would become a mother, but really, she couldn't have imagined any of this a year ago, and she now wouldn't have it any other way. She knew this was just exactly how she was meant to become a mother.

Now, she knew things with certainty. And one of the things she knew was that she loved Tommy as much as she could love any child she had created herself. And he seemed to love her just as much.

Eden fell easily back into her routine of writing and going daily to the cottage with the blue door, to dispense herbs and teas to ailing villagers, but now without the help of dear Mrs. Welsh.

"Hello, Mrs. Welsh? How are you today?" Eden would call out as she entered each day, completely sure that her friend was there in spirit, watching her and smiling that knowing smile. She would touch the locket that she wore every day now as she talked to her.

While she worked, Eden often spoke to her. "I think some mint tincture today for those high summer fevers" or, "Rhubarb in Mr. Jones's tea, I think. I'm sure his stomachache is constipation."

And she felt Mrs. Welsh's gentle presence agreeing with her and keeping her company.

In the afternoons, she went long walks with Tommy and Wellie, both of whom seemed to have limitless energy. She, on the other hand, was tired all the time. It had been an enormous amount of change in a short period of time, she thought, so she let herself rest often. And there was a huge sense of relief in having made so many big decisions. In having faced Robert and New York and all of it. And to have settled it once and for all.

It didn't help her energy level that she was often up late at night, sneaking in passionate lovemaking with James in one or the other of their houses while the children were sound asleep. But she hoped it wouldn't last long, this fatigue, as summer was arriving, and the outdoors beckoning, and there weren't enough hours in the day to do all the things she loved in her new life these days.

One day, while Tommy was in school for one of the last days before summer break, Eden drove herself to the ruins in the woods. It was a beautiful sunny day, and as she walked the path to the clearing, she remembered the last time she was there, the storms, both real and emotional, that had raged. How far away that seemed now.

She walked to the front of the chapel and found the stubs of her old candles and the cross she had made. Eden brought a new white candle, which she added to the crumbling makeshift altar. And a small bag of seed to offer the birds. She sat in happy, peaceful silence.

And then she felt it. The tingle and buzz she had missed so much, that had become an important part of her life.

And then suddenly there was Mrs. Welsh, right in front of her, as real as if she were alive again. Eden jumped up.

"Mrs. Welsh!" she exclaimed. She fought the urge to run to her and hug her, knowing there was no physical form to this version of her friend.

"Hello, my dear," the apparition replied, calm and soothing as always.

"I've missed you so much," Eden said, tears stinging her eyes.

"Oh, but you mustn't, dear," Mrs. Welsh replied. "I'm always with you. I'm always here, dear. I know you feel that."

"Yes, I do. I feel it at your house," Eden said.

I'm so glad you found your own knowing and came home," Mrs. Welsh said. "I really wasn't sure what you would choose."

"I got very confused after you passed. Actually, I came here, but there was no help, no knowing, just silence. I felt that when I needed help the most, I was alone. Why did that happen?" Eden asked, still relying on her old friend's wisdom.

"Some decisions are not fully written, my dear. We knew why you were here, but you needed to make some decisions yourself, not because we told you to. Otherwise, you would eventually have doubted them. But when the knowing comes from within, it can never be doubted."

There was a silence as the two friends smiled at one another, smiles of love but with a touch of loss.

"I must go for now, dear," Mrs. Welsh continued. "I am always with you. And, dear, do go see a doctor about that fatigue." She smiled, then walked towards the woods and disappeared into mist.

Eden's brow furrowed. How did Mrs. Welsh know she was tired? She laughed it off and rose to head back to the village, fully at home with having just had a conversation with her friend who had died.

Eden had lunch with Peter and Susan that day, sitting in the sunshine at the tables the pub had put out for summer. Peter and Susan gave her an update about the cottages on Mere Lane.

"Two have already sold, if you can believe it!" Peter said enthusiastically. "And one is rented out for a full month later in the summer. Family reunion nearby, or something of that sort. One cottage was bought, as we anticipated, by a London couple with a young child, looking for somewhere to have a patch of grass and a bit of country living on the weekends. They seemed very nice and couldn't wait to have their things moved in. The other buyer was more surprising," Peter continued. "The second cottage sold to Mrs. Pershing. I don't know if you know her, Eden, but she has lived in the village most of her life. She had a nice three-bedroom home in the village, where she had lived with her husband and raised three children. Her children are all grown now, moved away years ago, and her husband died almost five years ago now. She was thrilled to be able to stay in Barton Heath, but move into a much smaller home, much less expensive, and much less work to maintain than the large house and garden she had. She's fairly wealthy so didn't qualify for one of the smaller council houses. And she was on the verge of moving to Newmarket, where she could get an apartment, but she said she'd been very sad to have to leave Barton Heath and all her friends."

"That's wonderful!" Eden said. "I never even thought of that market, people wanting to downsize, but stay in the village. That makes me really happy to think that those homes will make that possible. And that will be nice for Bert, too. He and Mrs. Pershing aren't far apart in age, even if they are, well, from different sides of the tracks, so to speak. Well, I think that's very exciting!" she declared. "Soon it will be just as I had imagined it, neighbors waving to one another from their tidy little cottages, dogs and children chasing balls in the cobbled street." She smiled and felt huge satisfaction knowing she'd helped resurrect this tiny bit of English village life. The income wouldn't hurt either, and they all agreed on that.

*

And then it was Sunday. School was out for summer. James arranged for Bea and Tommy to spend the night at a sleepover at his house with Mrs. Innskeep. He took Eden away for an overnight trip to another village, to a charming romantic hotel, in what was once a country home.

They had dinner by a small fire, comfortable in England even in June. They talked and laughed and held hands across the table.

As the waiter brought their coffees and the meal was ending, James dropped his napkin and bent to pick it up. When he lifted his head, Eden noticed he was still on the floor. At least one knee was.

Her heart stopped a split second before he lifted the small velvet box out of his pocket. He opened it to reveal a ring. A simple diamond, surrounded by tiny dark blue sapphires. Her mouth fell open.

The entire small restaurant fell silent as patrons looked on with wide eyes and big smiles, many with hands to their mouths or over their hearts.

"Eden," James said, looking up at her with such love and sincerity that it made her heart hurt, "will you do me the great honor of becoming my wife?" Simple. Classic. Romantic. Exactly like he was.

"Oh my God, James!" she gasped. "Yes, of course, yes!"

He stood up and swept her into his arms in one quick move, kissing her while smiling ear to ear. The restaurant erupted in cheers and applause and the couple kissed. Then James yelled, "Champagne!"

Chapter 23

Two weeks later, they married. Eden dressed in the cottage, her mother and Tara helping her. The wedding was being held at the most sacred site that Eden and James could think of…the old church in the woods. The ruins of the ancient holy site, set amongst trees and stones. It would be a simple wedding, wellington boots required. Just family and a few village friends.

"Beatrice Beck, you look like an angel," Susan said, finishing tying the wide pink satin ribbon behind Bea's back.

The little girl beamed and twirled in her new dress. She clearly felt very grown up and important changing with all the women in the cottage.

"Eden," Susan said, turning to her daughter and only child, feeling radiant in her simple white gown. "You look absolutely beautiful." She carefully wiped a tissue under her eye.

"Mom, don't cry. It took me twenty minutes to get your makeup looking that good!" Eden said with a laugh.

"How do you feel?" her mother asked her.

"I feel so happy it almost scares me. I didn't know I could feel this happy. Exhausted, but happy!"

"I'm so glad," Susan said. "But you should get that exhaustion checked out after the honeymoon. You've mentioned it a lot lately. Your teas are magical, but never hurts to see a doctor too."

"Oh, Mom, okay," Eden said indulgently.

Eden and James had gone to the chapel two days before and strung long rows of white lights between the old stone walls. They placed little candles in what remained of the ancient windows and along the stone walls.

Today, Eden wore a simple, white gown with an overlay of lace embroidered with small flowers, and her knee-high, green Hunter boots. Everyone thought the outfit matched her personality perfectly.

James's mother and uncle came down from London and were seated on chairs that had been brought in, ancient walls beside them, above them nothing but the blue sky. The wedding was sacred. Moving. The vicar had agreed to officiate. Since the ruins had once been sanctified as a church, he had no objection to holding the ceremony there. James and his best friend, Simon, stood at the end of what was once the aisle. On a small table that had been brought in were a prayer book and some flowers and two candles.

Tara and her friend played violin and flute, as Bea appeared at the entrance to the old church, adorable in white dress with a wide pink silk belt. She looked extremely serious as she concentrated on dropping rose petals all along the path as she went.

Behind her walked Tommy in his first real suit, looking equally serious and grown up as he held a small pillow with the two rings on top.

James had been looking down, looking nervous, but at just the right moment, he looked up and saw Eden as she entered what was once the door of the old church. She was flanked by Susan on one side and Peter on the other.

In her fitted gown and thin veil, her long hair flowing down her back, she felt radiant. James beamed at her, unable to suppress the joy of seeing her walk toward him, to become his wife.

Vows were exchanged. And rings. And in just half an hour, the pair turned, arm in arm, and walked out to cheers and clapping and showers of birdseed used as confetti in the quiet, sacred woods.

The honeymoon was delicious. James and Eden went to Mallorca and swam in sensually warm water, ate fresh fish and dripping ripe fruit, and spent long, languorous days naked and hot, lying in bed, making love, with the white linen curtains waving, as an ocean breeze blew over their bodies.

They rented a room that turned out to be more like a cabin,

which was on stilts over the impossibly clear ocean water. They walked from the main hotel, along the beach, and then over a long wooden walkway to reach their private cabana. They could lie naked on the deck in the sun, dive into the ocean, and feel the blissfully warm water on their skin, then fall into bed and make love, all with no one but the tropical fish to see them.

After a week of this, they arrived back in the village, feeling transformed, satiated, and blissfully happy.

Just when Eden was thinking life couldn't get any better, she went through her emails and found one from one of the publishing houses in New York to whom she had sent her manuscript.

"They want it!" Eden screamed from the kitchen where she was reading email and drinking tea. "Someone wants it!"

Eden sat back down and looked again at her screen. She had to reread the email three times to make sure she wasn't misunderstanding. She had had rejections from two publishers already, things moved much more quickly in the age of email. She had become resigned to the fact that this may be her great unpublished novel, but she resolved not to give up. She would keep writing. So, when the email came saying the publisher loved the book and wanted to meet in person, Eden couldn't believe her eyes.

After slowly rereading it a third time, she yelled for James to come in the room. He raced in, probably thinking something bad had happened by the almost hysterical tone of Eden's voice.

"Oh my gosh, someone wants to publish my book!" she yelled as James appeared in the doorway, looking worried, wondering what all the screaming was about.

"Eden, that's incredible," he said with a huge smile. He grabbed her and twirled her around. "I knew they would!"

"Wait, here, you read it," she said, still sure she was misunderstanding the email. Surely this was too good to be true.

James bent to the computer screen and read. Then he stood up and declared, "Yep. They love it. Of course, they do. And they are flying you back to New York for a meeting. This calls for a celebration!" He went off to get a bottle of champagne out of the fridge. There seemed to be lots of champagne lately.

As she heard the cork pop in the living room, she wondered how this had all happened. It was like coming to England had put her finally on a smooth, paved road, where before she had been toiling up a jagged hill all the time. She was almost afraid it was all too good to be true.

James went with Eden to New York, where she met the

publisher. He hadn't been in years, and it was like a second honeymoon, the opposite of the sensual, lazy beach trip. This time they took in museums, shows, ate tandoori in Little India, moo shoo in Chinatown, and sushi at Asia. Eden introduced James to Bob, and to her other friends in the city, and several of her girlfriends said, with mischievous smiles, that now they understood why she was staying in England.

And they were right. But it wasn't just James. As she and her new husband strolled around New York, the greatest city on earth, she thought she would always love it. But it would never be her home. It never was. She thought how fun it would be to come back with Tommy and Bea one day, take them to see a Broadway show, or to Rockefeller Center. Maybe one Christmas...but, really, she longed to return to Barton Heath. To the quiet, rich life she had at home.

Eden dressed for her meeting with the publisher in clothes she hadn't had on in over a year. A form-fitting, but professional, dress, stockings, and high heels. The publishing house offices were gorgeous, sleek, with lots of glass and metal. The opposite of the earthy, thatched cottage and ancient village. She liked the change.

She met with a female editor, who loved the book, and they talked about practical matters for an hour. Eden had hired an agent before leaving England, and the brass tacks would be worked out between her agent and the publisher over the next few weeks. Eden felt professional and confident, and she walked out with a sort of quizzical grin on her face. Surprised that she hadn't felt like a fraud, as she somehow always had when teaching at the university. She wasn't a fraud. She was a very intelligent, accomplished historian. But it had never really felt like it was her.

James was waiting anxiously at the door of the building, and when she came out with a girlish grin and gave him a thumbs up, he laughed and grabbed her by the waist and kissed her.

"We're going out! What's the nicest restaurant in New York?"

"I actually don't know," Eden said, realizing it was true.

"Okay, then, where do you want to go?"

In the end, they went to a small Italian restaurant right near their midtown hotel. It was romantic and intimate, and they ate soup and pasta and cheese and bread and finally tiramisu, practically rolling back to the hotel room at midnight.

Two days later they flew home to England.

*

The day after they got home, Eden got a call. She was in the kitchen of the cottage, which was now their family home. James was slowly moving his and Bea's things in, and they were deciding whether he would rent out his house or sell. They planned to eventually add onto the cottage. Meanwhile, they had painted the third bedroom yellow, at Beatrice's request, and she and Eden were having a great time decorating it with little lights, and a canopy over her bed. She had a bookshelf full of her favorite books and another full of her favorite toys. It was cozy and sweet, and Beatrice clearly loved it.

It turned out that Mrs. Welsh, in a final act of generosity, had left her cottage to Eden. Eden knew she would keep it as is and use it as an herbal dispensary and herbal pharmacy. The herb garden in the back was as sacred to her as a church, and it contained lifetimes of labor and love, growing hundreds of herbs, flowers, and weeds to heal the sick. She thought she might rent it out for a little extra income if someone was a keen gardener. But she didn't need to decide that now.

James was upstairs with the children when the call from Eden's doctor came. She had gone in the day before to finally have this persistent and, at this point, slightly worrying, fatigue looked at and have some blood tests run. Thyroid maybe. Or, God forbid, something worse.

She got the news as she watched her handsome family descend the stairs, ready for a new day. She replaced the receiver as

Beatrice walked over to the table, where Eden had been busy grinding some herbs with a mortar and pestle before the phone rang.

After hanging up, she looked at James. He smiled over the heads of Tommy, now with his hand in the cookie jar, and Bea now at work grinding the herbs herself. He cocked his head and smiled at her in the way that made her heart skip. She smiled back. Then she walked over and whispered in his ear.

His eyes flew open, and he swooped her up in his arms.

Then he put her down very carefully, looking suddenly worried. "Oh my God, did I hurt you? Is it okay to do that?"

"Yes," she answered, in almost a whisper. Her face hurt from smiling so big. "I'm not sick. I'm pregnant."

They looked over at the two children with love in their eyes, then turned to each other and kissed a soft, sweet kiss. "I'm far enough along that they can tell if it's a boy or a girl. Do you want to know?"

James didn't hesitate. "Yes!"

"A boy," she said, and tears filled her eyes. "It's a boy."

James gently took her face in his strong hands and kissed her with such tenderness that, when they pulled apart, they both had tears in their eyes.

The spell was broken when Bea spoke.

"What's that? Ooh...that feels so funny," she said in her sweet high voice.

"What does, sweetheart?" Eden asked, smiling as they turned to look at her, James's arm protectively around Eden's shoulder.

"When I do this, when I mash up these leaves, my hands and arms go all tingly. Like sparkles or fairy dust feeling. Like pins and needles, but a good kind," she explained.

And as she said it, Eden got goosebumps over her whole body. She realized in an instant that the familiar face she had seen in her dream, the face in the next portrait hanging on Mrs. Welsh's wall, which had come to her in her sleep, was looking back at her right now.

Beatrice was the next herbalist.

Eden snuggled into the crook of James's arm and smiled.

The End

About The Author

Heather Morrison-Tapley is a nationally licensed acupuncturist and Chinese herbalist. She also has a master's degree from the University of Chicago in Social Science and an undergraduate degree in Anthropology. Heather was born in New York City and grew up just outside the city. She is a dual US/UK citizen and spent her summers in England with her family, part of the time in London and part of the time in seventeenth-century thatched cottage in a small village. She lives with her husband, children, dogs, cat, and chickens in coastal southern Maine.

Made in United States
Troutdale, OR
05/29/2023